I0646465

New York
Theater Review 2008

Also in this Series

New York Theater Review
ISBN 13: 978-1-4116-6483-8
ISBN 10: 1-4116-6483-3

New York Theater Review 2007
ISBN: 978-0-6151-4307-1
Black Wave Press
www.nytr.org

New York Theater Review 2008

Brook Stowe, Editor

Black Wave Press
New York

BLACK WAVE PRESS
P.O. Box 250898
Columbia University Station
New York, NY 10025
www.nytr.org

Copyright © 2008 by Black Wave Press

All rights reserved. No part of this publication may be reproduced, stored in a retrieval system, or transmitted in any form or by any means, electronic, mechanical, photocopying, recording or otherwise, without the prior written permission of the publisher.

Cover Photography by Erica Parise
Cover Design by Sheila Callaghan

ISBN: 978-0-6152-0056-9

First published in March, 2008

Body Text set in Garamond 11pt.
Auxiliary Text set in Palatino Linotype
Printed in the United States of America

<u>On the Cover</u>: *NYTR's Jody Christopherson previews the 2008 edition. Recording the moment are, back row (l to r): Feliciano Martinez, Annie Scott, Kimberly Stowell; front row (l to r): Monica Risi, Cristin Whitley, Ana Valle*

*This edition is dedicated
to the legend and the memory of the*

Caffe Cino

founded fifty years ago this year

*31 Cornelia St.
West Village
New York City*

Contents

Illustrations

Acknowledgments

To thank everyone whose efforts have gone into producing this edition would require a book-length list of its own, with production of these tomes having now pretty much become a year-round endeavor. I want to give special thanks to the 2008 Blogsters **Johnna Adams, T. Nikki Cesare, Garrett Eisler, Nick Fracaro, Jason Grote** & **Steve Luber** for tolerating my incessant pestering with grace and aplomb. I want to especially thank *everyone* on Jody's crew who helped make our fundraiser last October at Performance Space 122 such a success. Special kudos to **Heather Cohn** for once again taking charge of the chaos and calling another excellent show, and a big shout-out to PS122's **Carleigh Welsh, Karl Allen, Derek Lloyd, Eileen Goddard** & **Keith Skretch** for making their upstairs space available and for providing such excellent production support, and to **Andy Horwitz** for getting the ball rolling. Many thanks to **Marya Sea Kaminski** for flying out from Seattle just to be at our party, to **Tommy Smith** & **Reggie Watts**, to playwrights **Adam Szymkowicz** and **Anne Washburn** for stepping up and testifying and to all the folks with Bluebox Productions, Direct Arts, Flux Theatre Ensemble, Hoi Polloi, the New York Neo-Futurists & The Shalimar who, along with **Beth Collins** and The Rising Fallen (aka Banana, Bag & Bodice) helped to make last October 22 truly memorable. Thanks to **Allen Hubby** and the Drama Book Shop for their continued support of this series. And, once again, an extra-spesh thanks to NYTR Event Producer **Jody Christopherson**, who continues to take my half-baked, quasi-sociopathic promotional schemes and spin them ever so effortlessly (well, it *looks* that way) into gold.

Omissions & Oversights
2007

- In a footnote on p. 190 of our 2007 edition, erstwhile Williamstown Theater Festival Artistic Director and all-around *bon vivant* **Roger Rees** was inexplicably identified as "Richard" Rees. (Perhaps now he knows how Leo McGarry felt).
- On p. 268, in the introduction to *Elliot, A Soldier's Fugue*, the descriptive phrase, "under the artistic direction of" should have read, "under the direction of" – as P73 has no artistic director.
- Also on p.268: "Daniel Schiffman" should read, **"Daniel Shiffman."** The production listing also inadvertently omitted sound designers **Walter Trarbach** & **Gabe Woods** and the stage manager, **Jennifer Grutza**.

New York
Theater Review 2008

On Porch Supports and Obscurity:
Or the Past into Future
Introduction to the 2008 Edition by Brook Stowe

2008 is a year of anniversaries. Ten years ago this June I stood in the sagging dampness of the 130+-year-old Avery Hall on the campus of Vassar College before an array of framed photographs hanging outside the musty old proscenium theater now abandoned and empty and slated for demolition. My ears still ringing from the cross-country road trip that had ended in a parking lot off Raymond Avenue the day before, encased in the cocoon of early-summer Hudson Valley humidity I found oddly more sensual than oppressive, I pondered the series of photos before me: The Vassar Experimental Theatre. 1928. Seventy years back. In this same room.

They were very intense, the young women in these photos – dark, austere, posed against sets both abstractly minimal and casually naturalistic. Seventy years back. Back to the 1920s, at the end of the rail line in Poughkeepsie, NY. In the same theater now decaying all around me, poses of the *avant-garde* from these starkly serious students, locked in a singular moment of performance forged from nothing but optimism and desire in an old dirt-based horse stable/gymnasium and a little woman from Iowa with a huge talent named Hallie Flanagan to guide them.

I had no way of knowing, as I gazed at the photos on that dark, ripely fragrant morning in early June, 1998 that I was on the beginning of a journey that would lead me directly to this moment right here, right now – in a musty, decaying old building in Morningside Heights where I sit, gazing out the window at the frozen street, concurrently exhausted and exhilarated by the intensity and the scope of the trip thus far and by my own highly unlikely place in a theater community that, likewise, continuously both exhausts and exhilarates, often concurrently.

That morning hadn't been about the photos. It hadn't started out to be a field trip to study a moldy old wall. The morning had been about something else, something I've since long forgotten. An appointment of some sort, probably – a techie, a writer, maybe a production office I'd been searching for ... a wrong turn and there I was before this grimy, shadowed wall of stark old photos. Ten years later, it is the photos I remember, photos both completely foreign for one fresh from the languid shores of the SoCal Pacific and entirely familiar: a stage. A pose. A moment. As though I was observing the past merging with the future – a time long gone yet one seemingly filled with new possibilities, possibilities I had yet to discover and make my own. Make it new.

Today – six years in NYC – it seems to me more and more that theater – my theater, anyway – the theater that fills the pages of this book – is poised for something new. Ready (almost) to embrace a future fashioned from our past. Ready to claim theater defined by the moment we are in and make it ours, define an identity seasoned with the past yet focused on the future. Our future. This moment. Millennial theater. Getting close(r), but … not quite. Yet. But close. With a healthy mixture of defiance, fearlessness and invention inherited from our scrappy, street-savvy forbearers who forged the original Off-Off Broadway movement fifty years ago, our theater at this point in time strikes me as a brilliant, brooding adolescent locked in her room, teeming with potential and promise and bent upon rebelling against Mom & Dad whilst still so desperately seeking their approval. Our adolescent is funnysadsexyhot. She is beautiful and strong and smart and I really think it's time she left home and made her own way in this world.

It's a scary world, make no mistake about it. Immediate. Rough. Fast. And morphing constantly, furiously (and did I say fast?). How to make sense of it all? To help define and explain this brave and baffling new millennial blur we live in, I went to six of my favorite NYC bloggers – Johnna Adams of *blindsquirrel*, T. Nikki Cesare & Steve Luber of *Obscene Jester*, Garrett Eisler of *Playgoer*, Nick Fracaro of *Rat Sass* and Jason Grote of *Jason Grote*. In a wide-ranging discussion in the "Interview" section, we dive into a number of topics facing those making theater of substance in NYC today: how does the continuing rise in alt-theater self-production compare in quality to the more traditional top-down production models of Off-Broadway? Is it a classic "paradigm shift" or merely a passing phase? In this era of instant-everything we've now come to expect in the wired and wi-fi world of the internet and instant communication, what rules, if any, apply to criticism in the blogosphere? How does the ubiquity of digital media impact modern theater? More fundamentally, what's it like coming to NYC these days and slugging it out as a playwright, anyway and – perhaps most essential – is theater in NYC really any better than theater in other parts of the country, or is there just more of it here?

On that last point, two very talented theatermakers formally of NYC, now residing in points West hit that mark and hold forth in our "Essays" section with a pair of fresh takes on theater that is of NYC … but it's … elsewhere. It's theater with the sass and the spunk and the downtown pedigree gone … somewhere else. Writer-performer Marya Sea Kaminski, formerly with PS122 and various East Village crash pads, now with Seattle's Washington Ensemble Theatre, offers a "love letter" from Seattle to New York on the future of the American theater. Zachary R. Mannheimer, formerly of Brooklyn, now of Des Moines, Iowa, contributes a follow-up piece to his 2006 *NYTR* essay on planting roots for a new American theater. Zachary writes about taking NYC theater not just to the streets, but to the cornfields. Inspired in no small way by the work and vision of Hallie Flanagan's (yes, *that* Hallie Flanagan's) Federal Theatre Project of the 1930s, Zachary relates the upshot of his 22-city, 16,000+ mile cross-country odyssey in the Summer of 2007 in search of the beginnings of a modern-day national theater and why Des Moines is the new Brooklyn.

Like I said, 2008 is a year of anniversaries. Fifty years ago, in a rank little hovel on Cornelia Street in the West Village known as the Caffe Cino, the Off-Off Broadway theater movement was born, quite unplanned and entirely illegitimate. I've been in awe of those hardy Cino pioneers for some time now. I've also been more than a little captivated by East Village writer / actor / performer / director Victoria Linchong since she first revealed to me that, at age fourteen, she lived in a cage in the basement of Theater for the New City and knew some of the surviving original members of the Caffe clan. I implored her to contribute an essay on the movement's beginnings from the people who were there when it began. Victoria contributes a detailed, incisive portrait of those haphazard, hardscrabble early days of downtown NYC theater that includes new interviews with Cino *habitués* Robert Heide, Robert Dahdah and Mari-Claire Charba about the little hole-in-the-wall place that helped launch the careers of such major 20th-century playwrights as Lanford Wilson, Tom Eyen and Sam Shepard.

Plays are always tough. And while this works well as a kind of overview observation on everything about and connected with plays and playwriting, I speak specifically here of choosing the plays for the *Review*. Space limitations decree that there will be room for three only, and the sheer volume of new work produced annually in NYC makes it literally impossible for me to see everything, or to even come close. Consequently, I rely heavily on recommendations from those whose taste and opinions I value, theaters that consistently produce *NYTR*-esque work, and, sometimes, happy happenstance. There is just no way I can include all the new plays I like; I don't even try for "the best" (whatever that might mean). But I do try for three plays from the previous year that I think go best together.

This year is no exception. The three full-length plays included in this edition capture both the vibe and the pulse of NYC alt-theater in 2007 and, hopefully, appear of a piece in theme and content. After the hardest part, deciding which three plays we'll go with, is done, I do the smart thing and turn each play's introduction over to someone who knows much more about them than I.

This year, like the two prior, I was very fortunate to get three very talented and thoughtful individuals to introduce the plays in this edition. Performer and dramaturg Nina Mankin writes on Taylor Mac's achingly funny/sad *The Young Ladies Of*; Craig Lucas introduces Tommy Smith's searing *White Hot*, and Sara Michelle Zatz, who co-wrote *Undesirable Elements* with Ping Chong, writes of both the process of developing this play specifically, and of the larger, ongoing series that examines various manifestations of The Other.

Speaking at our 2008 edition fundraiser last October at Performance Space 122, playwright Anne Washburn spun a transporting tale that captured both the essence of the impetus behind this series and my hope for its ultimate contribution to the larger body of contemporary NYC alt-theater – a body that remains, sadly, largely ephemeral.

Anne's tale imagined the journey of a single volume of the *New York Theater Review*, from its debut here in the City, through its passing from hand to hand, reader to reader, to its inevitable slip into complete obscurity, to its ultimate rediscovery by an aspiring young playwright eighty years hence – as part of a porch support in rural Idaho.

Alone and isolated, the young dramatist extracts this ancient tome from the stack of debris supporting her sagging porch and takes it back to her room where, turning through its warped and crumbling pages, she discovers a time long ago where theater was made and lived by people now long gone. And she is, this lonely, talented young playwright, inspired by them. She feels, from this glimpse of the long-ago theater of 2008, a sense of community, of belonging, of common bond and purpose. She takes, perhaps, this chance encounter with the past and from it, shapes her own future. She goes out into the world.

Past into future. A year of anniversaries. It will be eighty years this summer since Hallie Flanagan and her Vassar Experimental Theatre struck those poses I gazed upon that heavy Hudson Valley morning ten summers ago. When I think of my own journey since, I am often drawn back to that morning, standing alone in a warped and crumbling theater, surrounded by the past while thinking of what might be, ahead.

It's what we have, these moments. One into the other into another's. It's what we all share. Ultimately, it's who we are.

– *Brook Stowe*
New York City
March, 2008

Essays

Magic Time
Caffe Cino and the Origins of Off-Off Broadway
by Victoria Linchong

I wasn't around in the 1960s and I've never idealized that decade's hedonism or radicalism. Yet the 1980s, the decade when I came of age and first began working Off-Off Broadway, was in many ways the last gasp of the anti-establishment, non-commercial impetus that began with the Beats in the late 1950s and continued with the hippies in the 1960s. Caffe Cino, which opened in December of 1958, fifty years ago this year, was a remarkable example of that impetus. With minimal publicity and without charging admission, it managed to stay open for ten years, during which time it became the genesis for the Off-Off Broadway movement.

The force behind the Caffe Cino was a gay Sicilian-American dancer, Joe Cino, who never imagined that he would give birth to a movement when he opened a coffeehouse on Cornelia Street, just around the corner from the dozens of poetry cafés that catered to wannabe Beats on MacDougal Street. Cino just envisioned a space where he could gather with his friends. "My idea," he said in a 1965 article by Michael Smith in the *Village Voice*, "was always to start with a beautiful, intimate, warm, non-commercial, friendly atmosphere where people could come and not feel pressured or harassed. I also thought anything could happen. I knew a lot of painters, so my thought immediately was, I'll hang their work. I was thinking of a café with poetry readings, with lectures, maybe with dance concerts. The one thing I never thought of was fully staged productions of plays ..."[1] Cino decorated the L-shaped storefront with old photos, magazine clippings, tinsel and glitter. Jean Harlow vied with religious icons and Kate Smith in an inviting disarray. Robert Patrick lovingly described the café as a "robber's cave. Long and dark. Pleasantly cool. Wind-chimes and Christmas tree lights. Bentwood chairs around tiny tables. A jukebox glow and walls fluttering with magazine pages."[2]

In less than a year, poetry readings turned into fully-staged theater productions. By 1960, Caffe Cino had become the first coffeehouse to offer a regular, weekly schedule of plays. That year, the *Village Voice* first coined the term "Off-Off Broadway." Joe Davies recalls in *Playing Underground*, one of a recent spate of books on the origins of the Off-Off Broadway movement, "Tuesday was poetry night and then there was a music night and then there was

[1] Smith, Michael "Joe Cino's World Goes Up In Flames" *The Village Voice* March 11, 1965
[2] Crespy, David A. *Off-Off Broadway Explosion: How Provocative Playwrights of the 1960s Ignited a New American Theater*, Back Stage Books, 2003, 35

a dance night, and finally someone said, well, let's have a play reading!"[3] It was direct-action theater – actors, writers and directors who took production into their own hands. Davies was an actor who worked Off-Broadway often and according to him, "Slowly, through networking, [the Cino] became a kind of green room. The first place people would come after summer stock would be the Cino. Or people from a Broadway show, when they'd finished the run." [4]A makeshift 8x8 stage was created in a corner of the room next to the counter. Before each show, Cino would ring a set of wind chimes and announce, "Magic time!" Then he'd randomly dedicate the show to Maria Callas or Ruby Keeler or some other iconic artist. [5]

All this came about in an unconscious, organic way. Cino famously never read any scripts, though later, he sometimes found writers by attending performances elsewhere.[6] A writer or director would be given a time slot and trusted to come up with something good. Actor Neil Flanagan recalls, "No judgment was made on these scripts, often a play produced was done because Joe liked the person's face."[7] Michael Smith wrote that Cino preferred to "choose the people not the plays."[8] Dahdah recalled that upon their first meeting, "He asked me when I was born and I said, March 8th and he said, 'Oh, a Pisces, good! You can do shows here.'"[9] High school students were as likely to be granted a production, as were trained playwrights and directors.[10] "I'd like to feel that we're open to everything ..." Cino was quoted as saying in 1966. "Sometimes I've let people do things here for no particular reason and their work has turned out to be very special."[11]

Cino's instinctual approach to curating led to wide fluctuations in both quality and content. In a 1962 article about a production of *Alice in Wonderland*, he admitted, "We've had bad shows ... but there is always next week. If, for example, you do not like *Alice* ... you may like Jean Genet's *The Maids*, starting Sunday. If you do not like Genet, there is always coffee."[12]

Idiosyncratic, but with a method to his madness, Cino's main criteria was a certain honesty and passion – he despised anything phony or pretentious.

[3] Bottoms, Stephen J. *Playing Underground, A Critical History of the 1960s Off-Off Broadway Movement*, University of Michigan 2004, 42-43
[4] Ibid., 43
[5] Robert Dahdah, interview with the author, November 19, 2007
[6] Robert Heide, interview with the author, November 29, 2007
[7] Stone, Wendell C. *Caffe Cino: The Birthplace of Off-Off Broadway*, Southern Illinois University, 2005, 45
[8] Ibid., 45
[9] Dahdah interview
[10] A play by a high school student, variously listed as Kelly Smith and Kelly Davis, was presented at the Cino on October 7, 1963
[11] Bottoms, *Playing Underground*, 280
[12] Stone, *Caffe Cino*, 5

But as Albert Poland and Bruce Mailman observed, "He saw value in seeming opposite things; he considered *Looney Tunes* and *Thaïs* equally important and comparable artistic achievements. The highest compliment Joe Cino could pay a performer was to call him a Rockette; he thought the Rockettes were sheer genius. Joe Cino was like his room: complex, dirty and brilliant."[13]

With his freewheeling inclusiveness, Cino gave a platform to a new crop of brilliant young writers – many from small working-class towns – among them Doric Wilson, Sam Shepard, Robert Patrick, Tom Eyen and most notably, Lanford Wilson and H.M. Koutoukas, who each had nine plays produced at the Cino between 1963 and 1966. Lanford Wilson had his first notable success at the Cino with *The Madness of Lady Bright*, which shocked 1963 audiences with its poignant depiction of a "screaming, preening [drag] queen."[14] Koutoukas, who can arguably be credited with creating camp theater, was one of the most important writers of early Off-Off Broadway, famous for lyrically absurd romps like *Medea or The Stars May Understand* (1965), which featured Medea dashing bleach into Jason's face and killing their (one) child by throwing him into a washing machine (not forgetting to add the proper amount of detergent).

Camp theater, screaming queens – Caffe Cino did much to encourage acceptance of homosexuality. Like Cino himself, many of the regulars were gay, though there were notable exceptions such as Sam Shepard. The Cino became known for plays that "affirm[ed] in a positive fashion the existence of gays"[15] in pre-Stonewall days when homosexuality was all but unmentionable. Again, this came about in an unconscious, organic way. Though playwright Jean-Claude van Itallie criticized its "general loud swishiness,"[16] he acknowledges that the Cino was "a clique, a family, an atmosphere in a small, dark place, special: fellow gay men, mostly gallantly trying to express their individuality at least ten years before gay consciousness became an active movement."[17] Robert Heide recalls, "People could write about gay characters without thinking, 'Oh, I'm writing a *gay play*.'"[18]

Caffe Cino also became known for actor-writer collaborations: Lanford Wilson and Neil Flanagan; Tom Eyen and Helen Hanft; Doric Wilson and Jane Lowry. Actress Mari-Claire Charba remembers, "You were working directly with the writers. It would change every night. Tom [Eyen] would bring new

---

[13] Poland, Albert and Bruce Mailman, *The Off Off Broadway Book*, The Bobbs-Merrill Company, xvii
[14] Wilson, Lanford, *21 Short Plays*, Smith and Kraus 1993, 23
[15] Stone, *Caffe Cino*, 92
[16] Ibid., 178
[17] Ibid., 59
[18] Heide interview

lines and say, 'Try this here'."[19]

This embrace of text can perhaps explain why so few people know about the Cino today. As the 1960s progressed and other Off-Off Broadway companies opened, ritualistic performances inspired by Artaud's Theatre of Cruelty began to dominate. Text became secondary and Off-Off Broadway now carries a connotation of a rather abstruse, physical theater that is hard to reconcile with Tennessee Williams productions at the Cino or the highly literate absurdity of a Koutuoukas play.

From 1961 to 1967, however, the Cino was the leading Off-Off Broadway theater. Its homespun small scale and inventive flights of prose inspired Robert Nichols to found Judson Poets Theatre in 1961, Ellen Stewart to found Café La MaMa in 1962, and Charles Marowitz and Roland Rees to found London's Fringe in the early 1970s. La MaMa, in particular, is indebted to the Cino. Its first production was Andy Milligan's adaptation of Tennessee Williams' *One Arm*, which had been at the Cino just two weeks previously, and its first seasons were peopled with Cino regulars.

On Ash Wednesday 1965, just after Jean Claude van Itallie's *War* opened, a fire destroyed the Cino. Though officially ascribed to a gas leak, many suspected Cino's lover, Jonathan Torrey, a brilliant electrician who was notorious for his violent temper. Off-Off Broadway acknowledged its debt by rallying in support. Ellen Stewart gave Cino the use of La MaMa on Sunday and Monday nights, while benefits were held at Judson Poets Theatre, Sullivan Street Playhouse and the Village Gate. The solidarity of Off-Off Broadway allowed Cino to reopen just two months later in May 1965, with all its motley assortment of photographs, newspaper clippings and Christmas lights lovingly placed back on the walls.

The Cino went on to a wildly successful year, beginning with H.M. Koutoukas' *With Creatures Make My Way*, and continuing with Robert Heide's existential hit, *The Bed*, Sam Shepard's *Icarus's Mother* and Tom Eyen's *Why Hanna's Skirt Won't Stay Down*. With the critical acclaim of these productions, it was undeniable that a new theater movement had begun downtown and the *New York Times* finally acknowledged this with a spread in the *New York Times Magazine* in December 1965 titled, "The Pass-the-Hat Circuit," which featured photographs of Cino, Sam Shepard and Robert Patrick, along with mentions of Caffe Cino plays by David Starkweather, Lanford Wilson and Robert Heide. The article exposed a great deal of rancor underneath the camaraderie of the Cino. "Much jealousy was roused by [the] two silly pictures [of Shepard and me] in a milieu that had until then seemed disinterested in approval or acclaim from

---

[19] Mari-Claire Charba, interview with the author, November 29, 2007

the boring uptown world," recalls Robert Patrick.[20] "Everyone looked miserable," Bob Heide said, "as if the worst had finally happened."[21]

Similarly, the runaway success of *Dames at Sea* in May of 1966 was a mixed blessing. An ode to 1930s Busby Berkley musicals, *Dames at Sea* starred an 18-year old Bernadette Peters and was "the apotheosis of the Caffe's magic-from-trash ethos" as Stephen J. Bottoms says in *Playing Underground*.[22] Robert Dahdah had literally pulled the script out of Cino's garbage and transformed it with additional dialogue and music, as well as the ingenious use of mirrors and discarded black, white and silver opera costumes to achieve a makeshift silver screen glamour. Cino extended the play again and again until it became the longest running show at the Caffe, clocking in 148 performances over a 13-week period.

Though the show was a hit, it created a rift between Cino and Dahdah. "I was angry with Joe," Dahdah remembers, "because whenever there was trouble between the writer and director, he would close the show. But this show was making so much money. He was getting out of debt and he even took an apartment on East Broadway, when he always slept on a mattress at the Cino…so he wouldn't close it and he kept it running…but he knew that [co-writers George Haimsohn and Jim Wise] were trying to do something bad …"[23] Two years later, justifying Dahdah's worst fears, Haimsohn and Wise took the show Off-Broadway complete with the additional material Dahdah had provided and the leads from the Cino production. Dahdah never benefited from the Off-Broadway run or from subsequent productions. He left and never did another show at the Cino.

The success of *Dames at Sea* was not the only sign that the underground was going mainstream. 1966 was also the year of Andy Warhol's *Chelsea Girls* and the "superstardom" of Edie Sedgwick. Warhol himself had, around that time, begun to frequent the Caffe Cino and Ondine, the star of *Chelsea Girls*, became a Cino regular, first appearing in a Cino production, *Thanksgiving (Jury Duty) Horror Show*, in 1966. Many blame Warhol and his Factory crowd for the escalating drug use at the Caffe Cino. Paul Foster is particularly vitriolic, famously writing, "Then, into Camelot came the serpents, the Pop Art golems, spawned in a silver factory. When these slimy rug slaves entered the door they infected the place and made it unclean. These angels [of] death came with their Campbell soup cans filled with drugs and destroyed the Caffe Cino …"[24]

[20] Patrick, Robert, "51 Caffe Cino Pages - Fame and the Fire", .http://hometown.aol.com/rbrtptrck/ROBERT_PATRICK_PLAYWRIGHT_TIMES.html
[21] Bottoms, *Playing Underground*, 261
[22] Ibid., 281
[23] Dahdah interview
[24] Stone, *Caffe Cino*, 128

Caffe Cino, NYC, July 1965.
Sign advertising "This Is the Rill Speaking," by Lanford Wilson,
directed by Marshall W. Mason, Building decoration by Ken Burgess.
Photo by James D. Gossage. Robert Patrick collection

"Incidents" by Larry Loonin and Yvonne Rainer
Caffe Cino, June 1964
Left, Yvonne Rainer moving the entire audience to the other side of the room.
Center, Robert Dahdah, an audience member, assists her.
Photo by Peter Moore, collection of Larry Loonin, shared by Robert Patrick

"Incidents" by Larry Loonin and Yvonne Rainer
Caffe Cino, June 1964
Standing, right, Yvonne Rainer. Seated smiling man in white is Neil Flanagan,
pre-eminent Cino actor. To his right, the face of Lanford Wilson.
Photo by Peter Moore, collection of Larry Loonin, shared by Robert Patrick

"The Street of Good Friends" by Owen G. Arno,
Caffe Cino 1960.
Joe Cino, Mary Boylan, Margaret Miller.
Photo by Conrad Ward. Robert Dahdah collection

Cino and Torrey became heavily addicted to amphetamines and it began to take a toll on their relationship and on the running of the Caffe. Both men left New York to shake their addiction. Cino came back, still addicted, after a brief visit to his family upstate, but Torrey elected to stay in New Hampshire. In January 1967, Caffe Cino was rocked with the news that he had died in a freak electrical accident.

Torrey's sudden death sent Cino into a spiral of depression and drug-use. Dahdah remembers, "I made up with him, and he came [to my apartment] one night ... and he said that the police were following him on the subway, and I said I didn't think that they were – he had delusions – and finally he went to sleep in the room and I made a big mistake. I put a recording on of music and I remember the song says ... 'Where are you? Where have you gone without me? I thought you cared about me' ... and I heard him sobbing, I heard him cry ... and that next morning, I was working on a movie as an extra and I had to be there at eight in the morning so I had to leave about seven ... I didn't realize that Joe woke up right after me and that's when he went to see Kenny Burgess – he wasn't home – he went to see Neil Flanagan – he wasn't home – and that's when he killed himself."[25]

In the early morning, *Village Voice* theater editor Michael Smith received a distraught call from Cino for his roommate, lighting technician Johnny Dodd. Alarmed, Smith rushed to the Caffe with Dodd's spare set of keys. "There I found Joe, on the floor, in a mess of blood," Smith recalled, "He had been hacking at both his arms with a kitchen knife."[26] Cino was rushed to St. Vincent's Hospital, where he died of peritonitis two days later on April 2. Coincidentally, it was Torrey's birthday.

Caffe Cino survived one year after Joe Cino's death. Management passed to dancer Charles Stanley, who attempted to maintain Cino's programming, but found himself exhausted by the punishing schedule, the deleterious drug use at the Cino and by the city's crackdown on coffeehouses, which sharply escalated just after Cino's death.

The "coffeehouse war" as it was called, had begun in the late 1950s when spontaneous readings in coffeehouses by Beat poets led to the proliferation of poetry cafés on MacDougal Street that attracted hordes of young people inspired by *Howl* and *On the Road*. Residents complained about the subsequent noise and traffic, and city officials began to a crack down on coffeehouses for zoning, fire and health violations.

---

[25] Dahdah interview
[26] Bottoms, *Playing Underground*, 287

There was also the question of whether café theaters should be subject to cabaret laws, which entailed greater licensing fees as well as greater surveillance, since all employees and entertainers would have to submit fingerprints to the police department and purchase a $2 identification card. Just obtaining a coffeehouse license was a struggle, as many coffeehouses, including the Caffe Cino, found their application to the Department of Licenses ignored for months or rejected even if there were no residential complaints.

In 1964, coffeehouse licensing became a key issue when Edward I. Koch, then the District Leader of Greenwich Village and later the mayor who contributed greatly to the gentrification of New York City in the 1980s, founded the MacDougal Area Neighborhood Association (MANA). Despite the opinion shared by many people, including Howard Moody, then Senior Minister of Judson Memorial Church, that licensed coffeehouses "turn over many more people in an evening than the unlicensed ones,"[27] MANA began to pressure city officials to close unlicensed coffeehouses on MacDougal Street.

While Joe Cino was alive, the Caffe somehow managed to dodge all the salvos from the coffeehouse wars. It may have escaped the brunt of the city's crackdown since it was located on the quieter Cornelia Street. It has also been alleged that Cino had Mafia connections because of his Sicilian background. Lighting designer Johnny Dodd recalls, however, that, "we got fines for not paying fines. There was once or twice when we received a deluge of summonses, but Joe, and most of the others, were not around during the day or not up early enough to go down to the department to take care of them."[28] Dodd suggests a tactic by evasion, but Robert Patrick recalls, "I used to see Joe slip bills to neighborhood cops. Others he'd take … in the back and they'd come out red-eyed and sniffling, or zipping up their flies. The cops never bothered us while Joe was alive."[29]

Neither Charles Stanley, nor Michael Smith, who took over the Cino in January 1968, were as adept at handling the continual harassment by the city, which intensified when a marine was murdered in the Village a month after Cino died. MANA served a writ against Mayor John V. Lindsay and his administration for dereliction of duty, particularly in regard to licensing coffeehouses, thus causing "an increase in acts of assault, murder, robbery, rape, purveying of narcotics and use of hallucinogenic drugs, prostitution and pandering and contributing to the impairment of morals of minors and general

[27] Kent, Leticia, "Caffe Cino Summonsed in Crackdown by Police," *Village Voice*, April 2, 1967, 29
[28] Stone, *Caffe Cino*, 49
[29] Ibid, 169

deterioration of public morals and public peace."[30]   The City responded by aggressively enforcing licensing regulations to cafés, whether or not they were on MacDougal Street. Caffe Cino was slapped with seven trials for various summonses and faced fines of up to $1,750. A flurry of personal and public appeals to Edward Koch fell on deaf ears. On March 10, 1968, Michael Smith bowed to the inevitable and quietly closed the Cino.

The end of the Caffe Cino seemed to mirror the death of the original spirit of the Off-Off Broadway movement. Robert J. Schroeder lamented in *The Rise/Fall of Off-Off Broadway* (1969), "Off-Off Broadway once meant Joe Cino stepping out from behind an ancient coffee machine into the glow of the thousand miniature Christmas lights that shone every night of the year to announce that it was 'magic time'. Off-Off Broadway now means a brisk and business-like personage signaling the stage manager, stowing away the cash box and counting the house …"[31]

By then, the Actors Equity Association had finally recognized Off-Off Broadway with the creation of the Showcase Code, which permitted union members to work without pay for short-run productions, but allowed for no more than ten shows over a three-week period. Though union actors were relieved that they would no longer be penalized for practicing their craft, the Code had devastating consequences for Off-Off Broadway as a whole. By limiting the number of performances, Equity made it difficult for a production to find its feet in front of an audience. There was no longer the option to run a show for longer, as Cino had done with *The Madness of Lady Bright* and *Dames at Sea*. Equity also forbade passing the hat, thus ironically depriving actors of the little sum that they made. Doric Wilson believes, "Equity helped kill Off-Off Broadway; there's no question about that … [i]f they were trying to keep actors from being exploited, all they had to do was limit the size of the audience and the amount of money charged at the door, and they could have controlled it. But if you limit the number of performances, you're killing it, because the longer something runs, the more chance it has to move! If someone sees that a play can have a run of eighty performances at the Cino, they're going to put it on at the Theatre de Lys and then everybody can get a union card. But the bottom line was that Equity didn't want us to exist."[32]

Whether or not this is true, the greater legitimacy provided by the union did encourage an influx of actors and producers who saw Off-Off Broadway as a stepping-stone towards commercial success instead of a community of likeminded artists. Legitimacy also paved the way for recognition

---

[30] Ibid, 159
[31] Bottoms, *Playing Underground*, 279
[32] Ibid., 269

from foundations and Off-Off Broadway theaters began to receive their first grants in 1966. Stephen Bottoms in *Playing Underground* writes, "The push was on, across lower Manhattan, to escape the rough-and-ready, amateur spirit of Off-Off Broadway's earlier years. A whole new culture of patronage began to emerge, in which grants began to be seen as a starting point for new theaters, rather than as a reward for work achieved."[33]

Though Cino toyed with the idea of charging admission and finally settled on requiring a $1 minimum at each table, he chafed at the idea of having to pander to foundations. "Grants were offered him," his friend Charles Loubier wrote in 1979, "but he refused them every time. He said grants would kill it. Even when we were half-starving, he refused."[34] Actress Mari-Claire Charba remembers, "There was never a budget at the Cino. There was never a stage at the Cino. There was never *oversight* at the Cino. It was never institutionalized."[35]

Fifty years later, Off-Off Broadway still retains some of the anarchic, marginal, small-scale, rebelliousness of the Caffe Cino, but the economic reality of today makes it impossible to be so thoroughly anti-commercial. The Off-Off Broadway movement was directly related to the economics of the time that allowed a young, literate, working class to search for an alternative to the materialism of the 1950s. "Everyone's rent was under a hundred dollars," Bob Heide remembers. "You could do your own thing and I think that phrase started with Joe Cino, 'Do your own thing. Do what you have to do.'"[36]

The self-reliance reflected in that famous phrase was a hallmark of early Off-Off Broadway. Cino single-handedly kept the Caffe running by working a day job at the American Laundry Machinery Company and for six years slept on a mattress at the Caffe. He never found the need to employ anyone – the actors, directors and playwrights at the Caffe Cino all pitched in to run the place. Actress Magie Dominic remembers, "One night you were making the salads and the next night you were shining on stage."[37] Robert Patrick jokingly referred to himself and other Cino regulars as "temple slaves."[38] "Everyone worked for their craft," Mari-Claire Charba recalls, "Everybody had day jobs.

---

[33] Ibid., 270
[34] Ibid., 280
[35] Charba interview
[36] Heide interview
[37] Crespy, *Off-Off Broadway Explosion*, 43
[38] Robert Patrick later wrote a novel called *Temple Slaves*, allegedly based on Caffe Cino, that was highly controversial for its portrayal of extreme drug use and questionable sexual activity at the "Espresso Buono," a coffeehouse in Greenwich Village run by Joe Buono

We didn't wait for grants. We paid for [Off-Off Broadway] ourselves. We owned it."[39]

When Mari-Claire said that, we both gasped in recognition of some essential truth. "Yes, we owned it," she repeated and nodded her head emphatically. It's hard for theater artists today to believe that there was a time when they weren't saddled with burdensome rents and the need to gratify patrons and organizational institutions. Actors Equity Association and legitimization may have certainly contributed to the demise of the early Off-Off Broadway spirit, but vacancy decontrol in the 1970s and the contiguous population surge in New York City as people moved back from suburbs, is as much to blame. The ingenuous Mickey Rooney "Hey kids, let's put on a show!" attitude that characterized early Off-Off Broadway is no longer viable, now that putting on a show now means $2,000 a week for theater rental - just for starters. "Gentrification eliminated the cheap rent of Greenwich Village," observed Russell Jacoby in *The Last Intellectuals*, "squeezing out marginal intellectuals and artists…even the isolated bookshop or coffeehouse has in recent decades closed, to reopen as a fitness center … cheap and pleasant urban space that might nourish a bohemian intelligentsia belongs to the past."[40]

"Magic time!" was what Joe Cino used to say before each show. And it was.

Joe Cino
Photo courtesy Robert Dahdah

---

[39] Charba interview
[40] Jacoby, Russell *The Last Intellectuals: American Culture in the Age of Academe*, Basic Books, 2000, 21

From Seattle to New York City
A Love Letter to the Future of American Theater
by Marya Sea Kaminski[1]

On September 15, 2001, I pulled my station wagon up to a small artist-run gallery called Secluded Alley Works, just in time to attend an open mic hosted by some old friends from college. It was my first stop in Seattle. My car was dirty from the road and packed with clothes and books. I hadn't showered in two days.

The room was crowded. I couldn't know then how many of those people would become crucial, beloved players in my life. I had no plans to dig my heels in here. My heart was in New York – my heart my people my career. I had just started building my own solo shows, was freshly returned from a terrific run in Scotland, and had spent the last year planting roots at PS122. I was building momentum. And somehow that wind landed me on the West Coast. At an open mic in the middle of a murderous September.

I performed my *White Girls Blues* that night and felt embraced. By my old friends. By Seattle. I could almost taste my own promise, adrenaline on the tongue. I had arrived.

In Seattle, a good place for things to grow –
families communities software giants
rainforests resentments ferns
wet and infinite shades of green.
I crashed in a house harboring a half dozen
artistswritersmusicians determined
to create an art collective.
I enjoyed the energy.
The quality of life
was high and slow.
The coffee was dark.
The beer was local.
The weed was, well, dank.
I sank into a routine immediately. Wooed by comforts.
Wowed by everything I was learning at school.
Warmed by the strange possibilities of this new place.

---

[1] The author appreciates the editorial assistance of Leah Baltus in preparation of this essay

Only a year before this, I was first finding my place in New York City.

***

I get a job waiting tables right away. I am 23
and the Luckiest Girl in Manhattan to be serving falafel
above the Comedy Cellar. Three burn scars later (not funny)
I walk out and spend a week playing guitar and chess.
An old black man named Shep takes me under
his Washington Square wing. And I fly
by the seat of my pants until I get another waitressing gig
and then two more and then a temp post
across from Carnegie Hall. I sneak onto the roof
to smoke to look at the cityscape to wish
I was somewhere else. Rehearsing.
I turn down a permanent post. I turn down
an opportunity to be Charlie Rose's assistant. I wait
tables and for my big break. I yearn for time and space.
Performance Space
122 is my next stop.

In the Winter of 2000, a tiny NYC miracle occurs and I get a job as the house manager there. I pass Mark Russell in the hallway everyday. I talk about theater and performance art. I host opening night parties and critics from the *Times*. I am an incredible house manager. We start promptly at eight and somehow both the artists and the audience feel like the event is taking place only for them. I meet and work with live genius. Live.

Karen Finley. John Kelly. Richard Maxwell. Ann Magnuson. John Fleck. The National Theatre of the United States of America. The Universes. I hang out at Surf Reality and Chashama. I work across the hall from Lee Breuer and Mabou Mines. Richard Foreman hires me to hotglue feathers onto rubber chickens. Finally. I arrive.

At a realization: House managing is intrinsically prohibitive to a career in the theater (obviously). I was working during the hours other artists were performing and creating (obviously). I couldn't audition for any projects because they would conflict with my job (obviously).

Theater theater everywhere but nothing for me to sink
my teeth into. I develop a chip on my shoulder
and a mental block the size of Lincoln Center. This great city
filled with mesmerizing art and performance

paralyzes me.

The world is not waiting for me.
This city barely has room for me.
To make mistakes. Only take tickets and talk sweetly.
Make sure I don't rub the artists the wrong way. After all,
it's my job to take care of the talent.

The city is a sexy conspiracy to keep me from sleeping. There is always something incredible happening somewhere. No matter how late I stay I am always leaving too early. It is exciting enough just to survive in this town. I barely make it to work on time let alone to rehearsal for a play. Why make a play? Another drop into the heavy bucket of under-funded deeply hopeful work already flooding the City. Instead I spend my time soaking in all the sweet strong art. I get drunk on it. I wake up too hungover to try.

I am not brave. I am beaten. My cheekbones droop. Exhaustion gets me out of bed in the morning. My frustration grows guns and I start making solo work. I give a middle finger to the auditions for small roles I'mnotquiterightfor. I write. For my own joy. Perform. On subway platforms across Lower Manhattan.

I write my first full length show, *More Money Less Work*. It includes a tap dance, a bra made of handdrawn bullseyes, and several speeches by Emma Goldman. I travel. To the sidewalks of Edinburgh. Hostels Guinness artistboys haggis lunabars. I make more money on a Scotland sidewalk day than I make in a New York nonprofit week. I make double my plane fare and dirty absinthe love in a graveyard. I heat up. Hit my stride. Assimilate all the genius tricks I took notes on at PS122. I am starting. Finally. I cannot wait to return to New York.

And then I get into graduate school.
Off the waitlist.

I stay up through the night at an internet café. Consult all my friends. Call my mom across the pond. Have hushed hostel bed conversations with my Italian lover. I decide to go. To Seattle. I leave on September ninth.

***

The first thing I learn in graduate school is how much I don't know. And that I don't like to be told what to do. Then I learn how hungry I am. That I have been starving for a vocabulary to talk about all the things I wantneed theater to do. I practice Suzuki with Steve Pearson and Robyn Hunt and stop acting with my fucking face for once in my life. Mark Jenkins teaches me subtlety and Stanislavsky. And Jon Jory blows my world wide open.

> I take meticulous notes with inside jokes
> squeezed into the margins. I am smarter and fuller
> everytime I leave the room. Jory shows me once
> and for always that actors are not doomed
> to be or not to be
> Gordon Craig's *über*-marionettes.
> Actors are autonomous.
> We are blessed with the pursuit of action.

In our second year, Jon assigns us The Ensemble Project. As a class, we have to found an ensemble theater company. We must find a space and funding. We must create a budget and a functioning artistic structure. We must choose a city to pitch our tent in and a full first season to pitch to our city. After six grueling months we present our company. The Washington Ensemble Theatre. We will be an ensemble of actors, designers, writers, and directors who act as full co-artistic directors. We will produce new and original works. And we will stay in Seattle, where our resources are – of course.

Months later, Mark Jenkins calls our class together to tell us a tiny theater space has been donated to the university, and the school has no use for it.

We sign the lease in June 2004. We are twelve strong, four from the original Ensemble Project, and we have three months to restore an empty little space and throw open its doors. Before we find an audience, we have to find seats for them to sit in. Which leads us to an old horse stadium about an hour away by ferry, where we load two trucks full of heavy, unwieldy, straw-covered theater seats. As we drag them into the theater, all of us trying to lift with our legs and avoid mouthfuls of dust, I know this is what I've always wanted. To be a part of something big. Bigger than me and greater than the sum of its parts.

***

I was six when I first got off a Greyhound and made my way through Manhattan in a pink ruffled party dress. My mom had started enrolling me in beauty contests. Young Li'l Miss Greater Orleans County led to Young Li'l Miss New York State, where I won fourth place. My mother framed the photo of my Shirley Temple haircut and pink gloss lips passed out and drooling against my trophy on the trip home. I put my mental picture of New York City in a locket and held it tightly with both hands. I'd never seen anything so important as those buildings with elevators or felt more beautiful than my hyperspeed reflection in those dark subway windows. My calves never felt that heavy before, fatigued from absorbing the energy and heat floating up from the sidewalk. My clothes smelled like garbage and expensive perfume.

Later my mom and I would travel by car – six hours between our driveway and the George Washington Bridge. I missed 78 days of school in the fifth grade for commercial auditions. Barbie. Cabbage Patch. Cutter's Insect Repellent.

My mother was hoping I'd make it big
enough to earn a living so we could all finally leave
my father and his quick blurry temper. Any small nibble
and we would climb into the car with our fingers crossed.
I was hoping to make it big
enough that the city would sink its dirty teeth
into my bobby-soxed ankle and never let me leave.

The only thing I knew for sure is that I wanted to make theater. I'd go see *Charlotte's Web* or *Raisin in the Sun* with my school and I'd point and say, "I'm going to do that." And I knew I wanted to do it in New York City. I don't know what other little girls wanted, but I wanted to make trouble and live fast. Get discovered be forgotten resurface arrive over and over again. I wanted to belong there.

I still do.

***

The desire runs so deep. I still want to make theater and live where it's happening. And after living in New York and so many other cities, I know that theater is happening everywhere.

In an increasingly monopolized economy with a rapidly decreasing middle class, where we wrestle daily with the complicated nightmarealities of war, disaster relief, global warming and fascist legislature – theater cannot be contained on Broadway or in our regional theater system or even in New York. No, the future of the American theater exists in dark corners and on small stages across the county. The future of American theater is not paying anybody's rent.

Regional theaters are dying, weighed down by the wet denim of the 501(c)3 model and union restrictions. Regional theater cannot afford to take a risk.

But for theater to survive in this dizzinglyfastandeasy technological age, we must be ready to burn it down at any moment and start again. That is the beating heart of live art – the possibility and destruction of the moment, the tension between balancing and falling, inhale and exhale, authenticity and expectation. The potential energy between the heft of success and the air of failure.

If we can't take chances in our artistic choices and leadership, how can we take chances in a rehearsal room? How can we do something new? How can we nurture young playwrights to dream?

As humans, we don't learn by doing things the right way repeatedly. We learn by doing them wrong and then trying again. And again. If, as theater-makers, we can't fall toward the impossible and let our communities (our audiences, collaborators, rivals, families, neighbors, check-out people in the grocery store) catch and lift us and let us learn something from our mistakes – then we are doomed. To formula without tension. Success without innovation. We are doomed to grow old and archaic.

In Seattle I am witnessing a revolution. I am on its frontline, of collaboration and ensemble-generated work. When I lived in the East Village, I was twenty years too late for the revolution of Charles Ludlum or the innovations of Karen Finley. When I was in school, I missed the Beats by thirty years and didn't get into the Dead in time to tour. But now, I have found myself smack-dab in the middle of something big. In Seattle.

And in small corners of neighborhoods in NYC. And in cities up and down the coasts and speckled through the red states. It's happening in places where the standard of living is forgiving enough that a part-time serving gig can actually pay your bills while you schedule, run, and dive into your own rehearsals every night. Where there are young people who are talented, trained, and not interested in waiting around to be hired. Where there is space to breathe and to hide, to go away and to come back with a new idea.

***

So we had the idea to throw a party. To wreck-decorate the set for Adam Rapp's *Finer Noble Gases*, the second show of Washington Ensemble Theatre's first season. We had closed our first show, Jane Martin's *Laura's Bush*, to sold-out houses and had been rehearsing for two weeks. The actors were learning to play instruments so they could perform as a rock band in the show. None of us were getting paid or sleeping much, but we were working. Together. It was like our parents were away and left us keys to the car and a credit card for pizza.

Jennifer Zeyl had designed a perfect run-down East Village apartment, which, we all agreed, was too perfect and needed to be fucked-up. Jessica Trundy was designing a projection effect that would require extensive filming of the band's history in this apartment.

So we did order some pizza. And bought some beer. Set up a video camera. Invited thirty of our closest friends into our little theater. As the director, I sat in the audience chain-smoking cigarettes and pounding PBR while shouting directions to the cast and party-goers. The apartment got wrecked (apparently someone even pissed on the carpet), we captured some great footage, and we felt like we were making our own rules.

Since that party in 2004, I've created more than fifteen shows with those folks. They are my community and my collaborators and the people who push me to be better. And they are here, in Seattle, so that's where I'll be staying for a while.

Every few months, though, I hear a small whisper, "… or you can always move back to New York." But the possibilities continue to roll forward on this coast – *The Time of Your Life* with Tina Landau, *Crave* with Roger Benington, my solo show, *In DisDress*; the title role in *My Name is Rachel Corrie* at the Seattle Repertory Theatre.

In many ways, *Rachel Corrie* was the perfect marriage of fringe energy meets regional financing. At the time, Seattle was the only city willing to fund a production of the script and the Seattle Rep assembled an artistic team of young, hungry, local artists. The collaboration proved both a creative and critical success, and an exhilaration to be a part of.

Creating that role and conjuring Rachel's courage, wit, and enormous heart drew out all of my daring and demanded all of my skill. I have never been so excited to get out of bed in the morning as I was to attend those rehearsals. To get to be twenty-three years old again. To return to a world full of journals and cigarettes and firsts all the time.

When I was twenty-three, I was living in a New York City dream of performance art and sidewalk revolutions. Staying out all night before falling down
asleep on a crashcouch on the Lower East Side.

Barely eating. Not hungry.
The Luckiest Girl in Manhattan starring in my own movie –
maybe Woody Allen or *Reality Bites*.
I am Bob Dylan fresh to the Village. Diane di Prima in better shoes.
I am here. I am next. I am Madonna, fair and fearless. Mary Poppins
fucking up a chalk drawing. I am Holly Golightly on the fire escape
with my own hardwood floors and month-to-month.
Wave to me. I'm on the sure.
Scratching at the talent under my skin and ready
for something really, really big to begin.

The Idiot From Iowa
One New Yorker's Journey into Flyover Country
by Zachary R. Mannheimer

In 1955, Robert Gard published a book called *Grassroots Theater*. In that book, Gard wrote about 1948, when he first arrived in Madison, Wisconsin to teach at the university and found the Wisconsin Idea Theater. In that year, Gard put out a call to all the housewives, mechanics, farmers, librarians and everyone else in the state of Wisconsin for new plays to be written by them. The only guidelines given were that the plays be written by a resident of the state of Wisconsin, and the theme of the play must be about Wisconsin in some manner – either historical, folklore, or simply taking place in the state. In less than three months, Gard had collected over five hundred scripts. 1948. Wisconsin.

Des Moines, 2008. The true beating heart of America. The diversity may not be here. The population may not be here. But people co-exist, amongst each other, devoid of competition, at least as devoid as they can be. This is where I've always belonged. It has taken me thirty years to find it.

How I Got Here

Sentence: 7-Years
Location: New York City
Mostly Brooklyn. Thank God.

Goal: Open a Not-for-profit restaurant where the profits go immediately to supporting the theater. Both operations under one roof. And no, not dinner theater, you cheeky bastard.

After several months of bizarrely-mundane research, I had planned my route to decide which city would best, best me.

Qualifications:
- Population under 500,000
- Leans politically right
- Inexpensive real estate
- No Theater like mine
- No Restaurant like mine

Route:
- Pittsburgh

- Indianapolis
- Des Moines
- Omaha
- Lincoln
- Sioux Falls
- Butte
- Missoula
- Boise
- Salt Lake City
- Denver
- Colorado Springs
- Lawrence
- Wichita
- Tulsa
- Little Rock
- Nashville
- Raleigh

Cities Missed:

- Lincoln

Cities Added:

- Reno
- Albuquerque
- Amarillo
- Topeka
- Jefferson City

Timeline: June 1 – August 1, 2007
Miles Driven: 16,471
Theaters Interviewed: 22
Alcohol Consumed: Wine. More. And then beer.
Tires Slashed by Jehovah's Witnesses: 1

See, I have this crazy idea. I don't want to sell my art. I don't want to place a dollar value on it. I want you to place value on it. But this is Capitalism. I gotta sell something. So I'll sell food and wine. Drop out of applying to grad school and learn how to run a restaurant. Become a Sommelier. Learn to enjoy grappa (it's not working). Realize that all of us have a skill that we can sell. Each of us has two jobs. We have to. Sell that other than your art. Sell that to support your art. If we have to sell, sell that.

The Problem: NYC is oversaturated. The only thing NYC needs less of than restaurants are theaters. We are not able to sustain ourselves. Our art will not alter someone's life. Our art will further the lives of those who agree with us.

Our responsibility as artists is to be the catalyst. Throughout the history of time art has done this. And art has been so subdued, so subtle, so abhorrently ironic for the last 30 years. We've had moments of throwing our weight around. But there must be a reason why we have completed our nomadic voyage to come to live only amongst each other. We are merely catalysts of our own demise.

I wasn't afraid in NYC. I had no reason to worry. What drove me was the desire to achieve more by name than by work. I was content. I made theater. I worked two other jobs to do it. I slaved away for the romanticism just as much as the reality. I drank with other artists. Some really great ones. Some who will twist your stomach with a head movement. I made theater. I served wine. I made theater. I served wine. I had a show. Lots of people came. They all agreed with me. I did an anti-war play, they all nodded in appreciation. They did an anti-war play. I nodded in appreciation. Getting high on the art but not the action. Getting high on creatively making our friends question our logic. Never coming in contact with the outside world. Loving it right there. This is wonderful, you think, wonderful. I have all my friends here. I make theater. I'll always have two jobs. I'll always make my friends' heads nod.

At some point between 1970 and now we forgot the middle ground. We forgot that the entire point, on both sides, was to converse, to decide together what the outcome of such and such an event should be. But instead we shout at each other in our own ways. The protesters shout, mount performance art calling it theater, and create great gangs of like-minded shouters to shout down an enemy who is not listening. The leaders hide in their buildings, knowing that the protesters don't matter, and continue on with their day's events.

We hear all this talk from politicians of how the country is divided. And in many ways – some secret, some not so secret – we are pleased with this result. You stay over there, I'll stay over here, and we'll all get along. We are the gated communities of America. Why are we content with a country that sees us as nothing more than a novelty? Theater artists are vinyl records.

Theater is dead in America. That reality must be faced. We are not almost dead. We are dead. It is time to reinvent the wheel.

Burning Coal Theater
Raleigh, NC

Darkhorse Theater
Nashville, TN

Nightingale Theater
Tulsa, OK

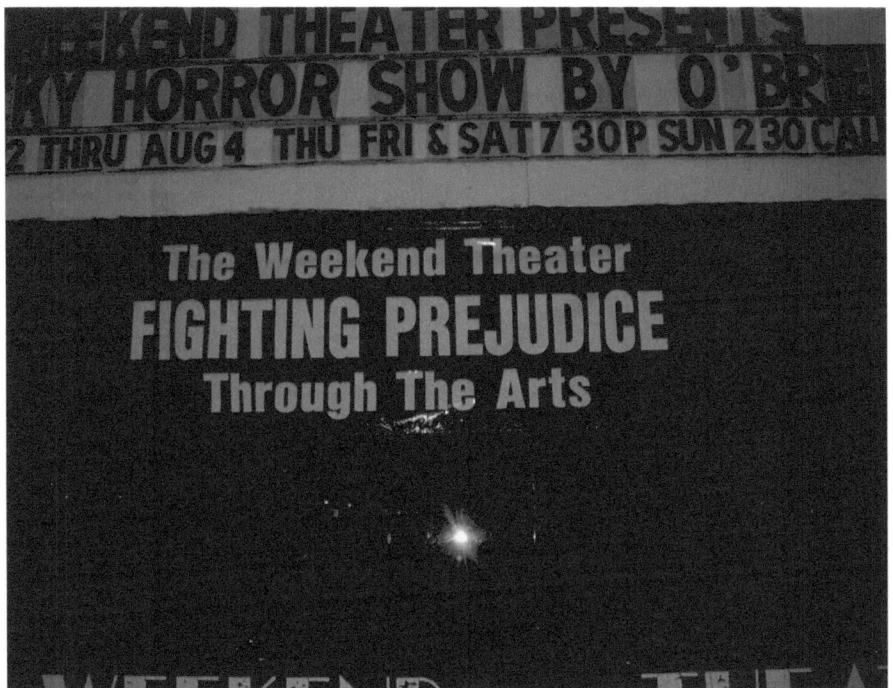

The Weekend Theater
Little Rock, AR

The New Protest

The new protest has to come from out of our comfort zones. We do not have the advantage of the other arts – we cannot travel at a rapid pace *a la* music or film; you can't Xerox us or e-mail. We can't even be reproduced properly. So why should the rest of the country where we're not give a damn about us? They feel the exact same way about us as we do about them. And neither is particularly flattering. And this will continue as long as we stay where we are, worsening the strength of the skin. And we will become relics, a cool thing that our parents used to do, our ancestors.

The new protest is not fist waving and shouting. It is not clogging the streets with signs and painted faces. It is not civil disobedience toward the higher powers that be.

The new protest is in your face discourse. Complete dialogue. Open debate. Action that has a meaning and a consequence. We protest as we always should have done, and once upon a time used to do – we protest through our art.

The new art protest is not anti-war plays. It is not obstructionist painting, tagging or rapping. It is not films about conspiracies.

The new art protest is art taking place in the unlikeliest of places. Until now that would have meant spray-painting a sewer grate, or rants on YouTube. But those are no longer the unlikeliest of places. Des Moines is one. So is Tulsa. Sioux Falls. Not walls – entire cities. And it is not showing up in those cities and performing our masturbation from NYC. It is showing up in those cities and performing alongside the locals.

I chose Des Moines because it fits into all of my categories, as well as the fact that no one here produces the type of theater I produce, or operates a restaurant similar to the restaurant I will operate. (Or, as I jokingly tell people here who inevitably, everyday, ask me what I'm doing here, "I ran out of gas.") Additionally, there is an almost perfect blending of the red and blue here, not to mention how incredibly informed everyone is (this is especially true right now, as I write this two days before the Iowa Caucuses.)

One other distinction stands out, however. As I meet those in the Slow Food movement and those involved in lobbying for organic food, local food and country of origin labeling (as these are all very important issues for me) in order to create partnerships with local farmers for my restaurant, I have noticed the one major similarity between NYC and DSM. Just as the independent theater artist is being pushed further and further into the fringes of NYC culture, so too is the independent farmer in Des Moines, or Iowa as a whole.

What's most attractive about this is the fight that is not being fought in cutthroat NYC: The older farmers' major lobby to the government is to ease regulations and create more financial aid so that younger farmers can continue on with their work. They're not writing angry letters and marching on Capitol Hill for their own benefit. They understand that their art is dying and stands only a few years away from being replaced entirely by corporate farming.

What Robert Gard realized in Madison in 1948 was how the people there wanted to express themselves no differently than anyone else on the planet, and all he had to do was tap into that, offer them an outlet, and by doing so, receive one himself. Des Moines in 2008 is no different.

You could get fed up with this country. Move to Europe, Canada, as most do. Say, "Fuck it." to your home country. The sad part is, this is seen as admirable these days. I see this as giving up.

Stay. Fix the problem. But don't do it in NYC. Don't do it in LA. Don't do it in Chicago, Boston, DC, Seattle. Do it in Des Moines. Do it where Presidents are made. Do it where you will have the most impact.

We have the capacity at this moment in time to transcend what Gard, and many others of our predecessors have pioneered for us. We have not forgotten them. We have not forgotten the outbreak of Fringe Festivals around the country. We have not forgotten Gard's predecessors – Hallie Flanagan and the heroes of the Federal Theatre Project. We have not forgotten their predecessors – the Provincetown Players and the visionaries of the Little Theatre Movement.

Almost 100 years ago, plans were being laid to send theater folk from NYC, Boston and Philadelphia out into the great wide open of America. Let's make it a centennial and follow their lead.

Des Moines, Iowa (Not Idaho)

Des Moines – I am surrounded by people more foreign to me than a Parisian. Their ways are not terribly different, just distinctly wacky in too many small situations. I move faster than they do. I want a meeting set to discuss renting a space; I want it tomorrow, they take a week or two. I want a slice of pizza. Not happening after 10pm. I want to go see a show – I'm at the movies. I want a kick-ass bar … there are plenty. But they do close at 2am.

I'm the outsider here. I am viewed at all angles as someone who may be here just to rip them off or set them free. I'm either the most genuine or the most fake depending upon who you talk to. I'm alone. I didn't know a soul here. No family. Friends. Not a single anything tying me to this place. Starting from complete and utter scratch. The feeling is unquenchable.

I have accomplished more in three months in Des Moines than in seven years in NYC. I showed up. I made phone calls, e-mails. I went to bars and got drunk with the other drunks. I attended political rallies and community meetings. And through this I have made virtually every connection I need in order to open my space.

Strangely – the only thing I really miss about New York is going out my front door, walking about ten feet in any direction, and being able to get whatever it was I wanted. But I'm dealing.

I miss my friends. But I don't miss the people.

People out here don't see Global Warming as a reality. That's because it's goddam freezing and snowing when it's supposed to be. Global Warming is hitting the coasts first. That's why many people out here believe that the earth is simply going through a cycle *a la* the ice age. This is where that idea comes from. I can understand it now and have a real debate. They don't come in contact with many people who believe that Global Warming is real. Back in NYC, I didn't come in contact with many people who believed it wasn't. If we are to solve a problem, we have to debate. Not via satellite. Not by writing one book that refutes another book. Not by producing theater that tries to make people more "aware" of a subject for an audience that is already entirely aware.

Physical Death

My jaunt this summer was brought on initially through indecision. What it became opened my eyes up to the theater that does exist in America, and needs help. What it became proved to me that I was correct about what lay out here, and the reasons for much of it being barren. I could have written about the forty-odd groups I met with, and how there is hope and much lifeblood in American theater. But I did not see that. I saw glimpses of sheer passion from every artist, but I also saw fear – fear of the wolf at the door on his iPhone.

Apple did launch the most inventive and productive advertising campaign of the last twenty years. A technology company is teaching the world that they too are artists. YouTube, the blogosphere, MySpace – anyone can make anything and put it up for the world to see.

This may all sound wonderful – but what about theater? Well, who cares about theater, it's an art that has evolved into film, television, photography and the internet. It was great but now it needs to go away, it is no longer needed.

What do we lose when we lose theater?

Ben Cameron, former Theatre Communications Group grandwizard, gave a speech not long ago to a group of theaters and educators from the South. In this speech, Cameron said that a theater must ask itself several vital questions if it is to survive – and the one that struck me the most was: "You must ask yourself what would happen to the community we exist in if we were to close our doors?" Would there be any sound in the forest? Would they even notice?

So what would be lost?

The most important thing in the world. The thing that only theater can do. The thing that is not dead, like theater, but barely noticed for breathing. Physical contact. The ability to witness something spectacular on a daily basis next to someone you don't know and then form a relationship due to it. Be it a discussion. An argument. A drink. A marriage. And anywhere between. Theater puts people in a space and makes them interact with the artist. The theaters who stick around will be the ones who keep that interaction well after the play is over.

No other art form puts the artist and the audience head-to-head, live, right in front of each other. We've got them all there – why do we stop once the curtain drops? That is not the end of the play. That is the beginning. What happened on stage was a pre-show. The real show is about to begin, and we can be there for it.

If for no other reason, theater is important because it puts people in places with other live, breathing people.

I see artists as a nationality. We have a grand responsibility. Let's get that fire back in our bellies – the fire that was there when we first started and didn't give a fuck about where we were gonna find the money to do this – just pure, unadulterated passion – motoring out of us at 100 mph. The passion that convinced us this was a good idea in the first place. The passion that is still there.

The question you must ask yourself is: "Do I make theater for me or do I make theater for those around me?" If the answer is the latter, and you live in a large city, it's time to move on. I've lived on the East Coast of America and the West Coast of Europe my entire life. I didn't even know where Des Moines was. I didn't really care, either. But then something happened that cemented my recent Iowaness ...

Last Christmas, at a family party, sitting in the living room drinking wine in Manhattan. A group of middle-aged ladies I had just met across from me chatting about the latest show at Lincoln Center. The conversation suddenly turned to politics and my ears perked up and away from whatever inane story my brother was telling me. One lady: "You know – I really don't know how I feel about those idiots in Iowa making this decision ..." My reaction was swift and immediate. I was incredibly insulted. / "Have you ever met one of those idiots in Iowa?" / "Well, no, of course not." / "Hi – my name's Zack. I'm an idiot from Iowa."

Never in my life have I actually felt that not only my art, but my life, is being embraced by my community. Oh! And here's something you New Yorkers may like. You know what the largest difference between theater artists in NYC and the rest of the country is? Out here, you can actually make a living off your theater. No two jobs, my friends. In NYC, you tell someone you're starting a theater company and they may reply, "Oh yeah? Me too." Here they say, "Thank you."

So come to Des Moines. No! Wait. Don't come to Des Moines. Go to Tulsa. Reno. Little Rock. Butte. Sioux Falls. Amarillo. Salt Lake. Don't come here. And don't stay in New York. Go go go create where creation is most necessary!

For more information about Zachary's summer vacation – visit
www.zacksblog.subjectivetheatre.org.

Last exit to Brooklyn ... Iowa

P^{lays}

Drag Queens, Freaks, Mermaids, Shaman, Humanity, and the Art of Being Uncool[1]

An Introduction to Taylor Mac's *The Young Ladies Of ...*

by Nina Mankin

"I'm just trying to find ways to remind people that they're human."
— Taylor Mac

Preamble

No one recognizes Taylor Mac on the street. The performer who has made a career covering himself with a creative assortment of found materials and giving his insights into the workings of love and politics (while wearing 6 inch stilettos) is, offstage, a soft spoken white guy in a t-shirt and jeans. "I don't reveal myself in life the way I do onstage," he said recently, "My performance is about turning myself inside out and putting my inside on the outside."

Taylor Mac grew up in suburban California in the 1980s. Not the California of organic food and the internet boom, but the lower- and working-class California; "tract houses blending into nothing," he writes, lining endless expanses of malls and auto supply stores. Taylor's mom started an art school for kids out of his childhood home. Taylor traces his own theatrical aesthetic, in which such crafty materials as thumb tacks, rubber gloves, soda cans, envelopes and rubber bands adorn his body in costumes that he calls "drag," back to these days. As he says, "there was always a lot of collage going on."

Taylor Mac is a drag artist who never dresses in what most people think of as drag. There are no fake breasts or traditional make-up or women's clothing. And while his expressionistic costuming is at times extremely sexual, it isn't about the traditional trappings of gender so much as it is about the beauty (and ugliness) of disguise itself. Because, as Taylor is fond of saying, whatever role you play, "it's all drag." It would be a mistake to call Taylor a transvestite While his work pays homage to a history of cross-dressing that, in Taylor's personal history, goes back to drag clubs in San Francisco and Provincetown in the 1990s, Taylor never "cross" dresses. Still, Taylor Mac claims such drag

---

[1] Excerpted from the forthcoming book, *Out of Silence: Censorship & Self-censorship in Theatre and Performance*, edited by Caridad Svich. Manchester University Press, 2008

queen/transvestite icons as Mother Flawless Sabrina and Ethyl Eichelberger as personal heroes and mentors. Along with Sam Shepard and Shakespeare.

In his plays and his solo performance work, (a differentiation that Taylor Mac himself has recently decided to reject, calling all his work "plays"), Taylor never plays the part of men or women so much as he *plays* with his audience's insecurities (and pleasures) – about their own gender identification, sexuality and disguises – by revealing his own (or those of the character that is "Taylor Mac.") It is sometimes discomforting, but "comfort" is one of the things Taylor Mac has made it his life's work to challenge.

Taylor's work often contains graphic descriptions of gay sex, told as personal stories in his solo work. There is usually nudity: in his apocalyptic high-jinx musical about the imminent "revitalization" (real estate euphemism for "obliteration") of Coney Island, *Red Tide Blooming* (or "*RTB*" which premiered at PS122 in 2006) everyone gets naked at one point or another. All of his work challenges conventional norms of gender: Taylor's fantasmagorical characters largely identify both as masculine and feminine (the hero of *R.T.B.* is a hermaphrodite sea creature, Olokun) and even his more "conventional" heroes, like the central character in his yet-to-be-produced play "Blue Grotto," struggle with issues of gender identification. But Taylor's main political *bête noire* is not about sexuality or any particular interest group's particular subjugation. It is, rather, what he refers to as "the homogenization of culture," a process of, again to use Taylor's language "dwindling down to same" that is often represented in his work by the evils of the religious and political right.

Taylor Mac realized he would be an actor about the same time he became a political activist. In high school he sneaked off to the San Francisco AIDS Walk, to the horror of his teachers who asked him to remove his ACT UP! button on his return (he didn't.) And he was very involved in the environmental movement. Taylor left San Francisco State after one year of actor training to walk across the country in protest of nuclear energy. He credits that year of communal living (and dumpster diving) as the basis for much of his artistic ethic. Taylor eventually continued his actor training at the American Academy of Dramatic Arts (AADA) in New York City and worked Off- and Off-Off Broadway, acting in other people's plays, throughout the late '90s and into the '00s.

Even while Taylor was performing in other writers' work, he was developing his own writing and performance in the world of downtown clubs and impromptu performance, spaces where new vaudeville and burlesque flourished from the late '80s. . Five years ago, Taylor Mac was presenting his drag performance and plays almost exclusively at these downtown parties and burlesque/vaudeville clubs. Though this is still very much Taylor Mac's world, he is now also invoked by theater and performance curators as one of the leading lights of a new generation of theater artists. Taylor was named one of ten New York playwrights to watch in 2005 by *Improper* magazine and one of fifteen *nytheatre.com*'s people of the year in 2006. And, as a testament to Taylor's success at blurring the boundaries between performance and playwriting, he was recently elected into the exclusive theater community of New York's New Dramatists.

Getting More Personal

I first met Taylor in 2004 while working on the HERE Arts Center adaptation of the Orpheus myth (directed and co-conceived by Kristin Marting.) I started working with him as a dramaturg, and also as a singer/performer, shortly thereafter. In *Orpheus*, Taylor played the (very straight) pop rock star title role. Halfway into the run, Taylor brought in a publicity postcard for his show *Live Patriot Acts* (2004, PS122). The piece, a cabaret-styled performance of downtown artists responding to the current political climate, was a follow-up to his *The Face of Liberalism* (2004, The Marquee) which was Taylor's solo response to the "War on Terror." Taylor had been doing performance pieces at bars and clubs while also pursuing a career as an actor. It was in *Liberalism* that Taylor first put together the "mish mash" of rants, original songs, stories and wild costuming that would become his signature: theater in which Taylor "brings the party" to his audience, while doing fundamentally political work. *The Face of Liberalism* featured such songs as the raucous, "The Revolution will not be Masculinized" and the beautifully poignant *a cappella*, "Fear Itself" ("We've nothing to fear but fear itself/I'm afraid of fear itself ...") This solo-performance piece ran for six-months, once a week, to sold-out audiences in a basement bar on the Bowery.

The postcard for "Live Patriot Acts" shows Taylor standing, back toward the camera, wearing only a g-string and stilettos, his red, white and blue painted face turned provocatively back toward us. I was stunned: Taylor Mac never hides; he's just completely unassuming. And his salt-of-the-earth, poised and unobtrusive persona hardly suggests the political and aesthetic extremes of his performance credo and idiom.

Taylor embraces his role as societal clown. He has recently taken to referring to himself as a Shakespearean fool – a highbrow shaman. Even his most "naturalistic" writing contains extremes of corporeality and theatricality that make one feel like the drama could blow apart into comedic insanity at any moment. Or go someplace emotionally devastating – both of which are true.

Taylor mostly acts in his own plays and he is always IN the audience. At times he demands audience complicity through direct participation. In the workshop production of *The Young Ladies Of* ... Taylor's epistolary exploration into desire, loss and cultural obsession with fathers, (which premiered at Taylor's artistic home, HERE, in the Fall of 2007) the audience wrote letters that were used in the piece. In *RTB*, he wanted the audience to have flash cameras so that they become creative soul-snatchers. Taylor believes in audience participation (in whatever form it takes.) He sees participation as part of his own duty, both as a theater artist, and as a citizen.

Taylor Mac's clownish corporeality is often confrontational, as when his actors do naked gymnastics down center stage, under the noses of a stunned front row. It is sometimes arresting, like when he talks about the dried semen flaking off his chest following a vacuous sexual encounter. And sometimes it's terrifying, like when he wrenches off the duct tape that has been securing his penis to his butt in *RTB* ("It really doesn't hurt that much," he'll tell anyone who asks afterward. "It depends on how well I shave.") But, once again, Taylor doesn't see this as characteristically "avant-garde" (and he's not interested in shock value) so much as it's his way of giving his audience a good time – bringing them together, finding collective human commonality, in the wildness of the event.

Pastiche

"My dramaturg says ..." Taylor declared to my infinite discomfort at the 2007 NoPassport CUNY conference, "that I am an artist working in the genre of pastiche." The term came up over one of Taylor's and my marathon breakfast meetings when he was struggling with how to label himself. "You embrace discontinuity," I suggested. "You enjoy stylistic collisions; your work is excessive; you don't care if you're cool and, in fact, you would rather be kitsch than cool; you're a *pastiche* artist." Taylor now says that he is a theater artist working "in the genre of pastiche."

I recently turned to that bastion of contemporary culture, Wikipedia, and was delighted to find the advisement that, in architecture, the "mere invocation" of the word pastiche can be enough to condemn a piece as "unworthy of further consideration" and that writers should "use the term with caution"(!) In fact, one of the coolest things about pastiche is just how historically *un*cool it is. The modernist idea of pastiche (Rococo being the most recognized genre) infers that the artist doesn't know what he is doing – he's just arbitrarily taking things (ornament, iconography, historical and structural components) out of context and throwing them together: collision for effect, not for meaning.

But postmodernists know that there is no such thing as content without meaning. Pastiche, to postmodernists, infers a void; before the pastiche, there was a place that desired filling. The interesting question then becomes, not so much what is the pastiche, but rather what is the void that this excess (because "pastiche" implies excess) reveals?

Inviting his audience to experience the variety of being human is Taylor Mac's theatrical mission. Taylor sees himself, and his cohort of "freaks" (an accolade he gives to anyone who consciously lives outside the homogeneous world of "same" – public nudity being a shoo-in for nomination) as emissaries of heterogeneity. And this work takes place wherever they choose to don their drag – whether it's in a theater, on the street, or at a cultural event like the Coney Island Mermaid Parade.

Heterogeneity, Discomfort and Boys on the Boardwalk

Taylor Mac is dressed (or *not*, depending on your point of view) in a hula-skirt of multi-colored hand-painted six-pack plastic rings (that do actually look something like seaweed). His shaved head is half covered by a fraying blond wig. His large sand-covered feet sport six-inch pumps. Sky-blue grease paint covers his entire face. His green-painted cheekbones float like tropical islands in the blue, while the glued-on seashells arcing above his eyebrows create the effect of some kind of weird African mask. Taylor is also sporting a long strand of pretty white seashells that descends down from the blond wig all the way across his bare torso to his gold-emblazoned nipples. He looks like some androgynously lusty Neptune who has been dressed up by a group of nine-year-old girls at a birthday party. We're on the boardwalk at Coney Island just after the Mermaid Parade. This is one of the most important yearly performances for Taylor and his community of freaks; missionaries, as Taylor sees it, of all that is good in the world – missionaries of heterogeneity.

Taylor and his post-parade cohorts (most of whom also work in the club and new vaudeville circuit) are on the boardwalk in a Felliniesque *mélange*. Most of the others are dressed more conventionally "mermaid" than Taylor. James "Tigger" Ferguson has on a long shimmering white fishtail cut so low it exposes his red pubic hair. He drops the tail to reveal a large plastic octopus covering his sex. Taylor's friend Darrell is all pink and pastel blue with a luxurious tetra head-fin and enormous fake eyelashes. His gorgeous airbrushed tail is poised, impossibly, half way down his butt. Dirty Martini, the definition of voluptuous, her gorgeously large bare belly and breasts defying any contemporary notion of "fit," has her mouth stretched wide in a happy guffaw.

It is, as Taylor writes in *Red Tide Blooming*, a "freaky conglomeration…a divine picture."

There is a section in *The Young Ladies Of …* when Taylor writes a letter to his Vietnam War lieutenant dad who died when he was still very young. He asks his father about the nature of bravery and pride and then he tells him about himself: "I have learned that bravery comes in all kinds of forms, as does fear. I like to think I'm a brave person although sometimes I falter." And he continues, "Bravery comes from overcoming fear in the need to make a change." This is the bravery Taylor Mac is celebrating when Olokun stands up to the Collective Conscious (in *RTB*) And it is this bravery that is exhibited as one of the mermaid comrades drops her tail, smiles, and puts her arm around a confused-looking young man who thought he was there just to gawk.

This is the good that freaks do for society; freaks create discomfort, they shake things up. They bring joy and anxiety and sheer "what the fuck!" amazement at what Taylor Mac sees as the best of humanity: our continual variation, our homogeneity; our *humanity*. These moments, these "interventions" (my word) are what Taylor Mac relishes in his work. In a group email Taylor sent out from his recent tour of the UK, he recounted an interaction he had with "a three-toothed old macho man in the audience for one of the shows." "He kept talking back to me all through -- he was either drunk or crazy or a little bit of both. At one point I called him 'darling' and he said, in an offended way, 'You call me darling!' I'm not sure what brought him to the show but by the end of it I had him up on stage dressed up in mylar and posing feminine with me. When I bowed, he came up on stage and shook my hand saying, 'Well done.'" And Taylor concludes, "Some of you do this on a daily basis, and I am in awe." Indeed.

THE YOUNG LADIES OF
by Taylor Mac

THE YOUNG LADIES OF

Copyright © 2007 by Taylor Mac

CAUTION: *The Young Ladies Of* is reprinted by permission of the author. All performance rights in this play are controlled exclusively by Taylor Mac. For rights contact:

Morgan Jenness
c/o Abrams Artists Agency
275 Seventh Avenue, 26th Floor
New York, NY 10001
Morgan.Jenness@bramsart.com
646.486.4600 x223

***

The Young Ladies Of received its premiere at the HERE Arts Center in New York City on September 19, 2007. It was a co-production between The HERE Arts Center and Ethyl Crisp Productions. It was directed by Tracy Trevett; dramaturgy was by Nina Mankin; the set design was by David Evans Morris; the lighting design was by Juliet Chia; the puppet design was by Basil Twist; the sound design was by Matthew Tennie; the costume and makeup design was by Taylor Mac; the movement advisor was Alexandra Beller; and the production stage manager was Ann Breitbach.

The Young Ladies Of was given a commission by the Battersea Arts Center in London where it received a development workshop.

Dixon Place and Performance Space 122, both in New York City, presented early workshops of the play.

The play was made possible by a generous grant from the Peter S. Reed Foundation.

CAST

The Young Ladies Of is a play performed by at least one actor and the audience. Although I wrote this play and performed in it solo in the premiere production (and have first refusal on performing it in future productions), an ensemble could easily perform this play. *The Young Ladies Of* is not a play intended only to be performed by its author. If you want to cast someone (or yourself) who is up for playing the character of me – have at it. A male, female, male to female transsexual, female to male transsexual, or anyone who has embraced living as the third sex can play any of the role(s). An important thing to consider is not to get too bent out of shape about making the characters believable. Balance is the key. Investing in the characters, while at the same time allowing the audience to see the actor(s) having fun playing on a stage is the delight of this play. *Young Ladies* is not about transporting the audience somewhere away from themselves. I did not set out to let them forget who and where they are. The goal is to remind them of our shared humanity (partially by getting them to take note that they're in a theater having a shared experience). Also, like all my plays, improvisation here and there is encouraged but premeditated rewrites are not. Stick to the text but if something goes awry or comes to the actor(s) in the moment – it should not be ignored.

SETTING

We are in a prom-version of heaven (which is actually limbo). It should look as if a human being created the space: more imagination and skill with thrift than expertise and cash, more love of craft than polished spectacle. The environment seems to say, "One person worked extraordinarily hard at creating something phantasmagorical out of very little." It is a CinemaScope landscape in a blue world with dangling letters hanging from the grid on fishing wire (or Christmas tree lights or whatever suits the designer's fancy). The letters envelop both the audience (they break the fourth wall) and the playing space and would be stars if this where a more traditional representation of heaven. There is Fog. A dangerously tall wooden ladder sits up center. The world shimmers and moves gently. The envelopes throw big and small shadows all over that sway gently (don't be afraid to dangle them in front of lights). When backlit we can see that the envelopes have letters in them. We are in a reimagined, recreation of an opening scene to a favorite movie. It should look as if Taylor created the space as a gift. As if he worked all summer long, saving up to buy a pretty present in hopes to get a little attention. It is an unrequited lover's bargaining tool. The space is desperate, fanciful, extreme, glorious, a delight, strange, inviting, cold, handmade, grand, peaceful, and chaotic all at the same time. Look to the opening scene of *Carousel* the movie for inspiration.

HANGING LETTERS

These are metaphorical unanswered correspondence. They represent curiosity and a lifetime of reaching out. They should look as if made to entice. There should be an eclectic array of envelopes: small ones, large ones, some adult, some childish (with drawings for writing), most have sparkle, most are different colors and sizes. They can be abstract and should be magical but also recognizable as letters. It should look as if someone at various ages of their life (from four to thirty-four) created them. They are laminated to give shine and reverence.

STAGE LETTERS

These envelopes are identical, white, personal sized letters, addressed, sealed, and marked with a suggestion of a mailed stamp in their upper right corners. There are literally 20,000 of them (more if you have the budget – they should fill the entire playing stage, pilling up onto each other like mounds, once they come out). There is a strong distinction between them and the hanging letters.

COSTUME

Taylor is dressed as if all the tough, Texan, macho, military, heterosexual males in his family got together, when he was two, and dressed him up in their idea of drag: didactic blond curls, white church dress, and an overachieving bonnet (think Shirley Temple, Baby Jane, or the daughter from *Carousel*). The idea was that he would wear the dress for an hour and the joke would be done but over thirty years later Taylor, in love with the look, has yet to take the dress off. As a result his look is tore up from the floor up. It is a deconstructed mess. It is beautiful, sad, funny, demented, iconic, camp, hopeful, devastating, sweet, innocent, and heavy with experience all at the same time. Essentially, he looks like a doll that was either loved too much or not enough. Underneath his dress he wears a bra as a thong (an original Taylor Mac creation).

PUPPETS

The lady/dress is a puppet, easily animated by one performer, which can fit into a box much smaller than the puppet (so when she is taken out there is a surprise), made entirely of letters, and capable of being turned into a dress and put on, on stage, with consistent ease. She is elegant, magical, frumpy, majestic, sad, classy, and silly all at the same time.

PHOTOS

If you're doing your own production of *The Young Ladies Of* that I'm not in, the Taylor photos should be recreated with the actor playing me. That means the actor will have to dress up in lots of various drag. Ha cha cha. All the photos can be sent upon request.

SONGS

Sample recordings and charts can be obtained upon request but it should be noted that the songs are primarily patter songs and are performed loosely. They were all originally played on the Ukulele but it could be lovely to have many more instruments (especially if the play were to be performed by more than one person).

Dedicated to Lt. Robert Mac Bowyer, Joy Aldrich, and Robin Bowyer

THE YOUNG LADIES OF
by Taylor Mac

(TAYLOR is heard whistling in the dark the beginning of the Carousel *Waltz. Lights up on TAYLOR sitting up-top a dangerously tall ladder, with his ukulele. Laminated letters hang around him and the space. He is in a community theater version of heaven, that he calls purgatory. TAYLOR takes in all the hanging letters. He speaks the beginnings of a letter to his father.)*

TAYLOR
Dear Dad.
> *(notices the audience and begins to laugh as if to say, "did I start my play as horribly as that.")*
No.
> *(to audience)*
Hi! That's to you not to Dad. Hi! Yes you can say hi back, it's okay. You were worried it was going to be a real show.
> *(regaining his composure, he speaks to Dad)*
Dear Dad, this is my last letter to you. A singing telegram.
> *(NOTE: Sung lines, as in the following, are in ITALICS throughout.)*
My boy Bill
> *(to audience)*
I have been told that my father's favorite movie was the musical *Carousel*. So ... Dear Dad, this is my last letter to you, a singing telegram from the movie musical *Carousel*.
> *(to Dad)*
My boy Bill, I will see that he's named after me
> *(to audience)*
For anyone out there who grew up without a love for the American musical (more power to ya), "My Boy Bill" is a song from the movie musical *Carousel*. The actual song is called "The Soliloquy," which tells you it's going to be a very long song. Buckle up.
> *(to Dad)*
My boy Bill! I will see that he's named after me, I will.

(TAYLOR comes down the ladder slightly.)

(MORE)

TAYLOR (cont.)
> *(to audience)*

Just in case you didn't already know this, my name is not Bill. My name is Taylor Mac. My father's name wasn't Bill either. He's name was Robert Mac ... Bowyer. My full name is Taylor Mac Bowyer. In a way I was named after my father because all the men in my family, our middle names are all Mac. Taylor Mac, Robert Mac, Jim Mac, John Mac, Don Mac and my uncle, well his name actually is Bill ... Mac ... Bowyer but my father was Robert.

> *(He goes back up the ladder.)*

TAYLOR
> *(to Robert)*

Dear Robert, this is my last letter to you. A singing telegram.
My Boy Bill.
> *(to audience)*

I imagine.

> *(TAYLOR descends to the ground.)*

TAYLOR
Assumption!

I imagine my father's favorite character in the movie musical *Carousel* was the central character of the wife beater. No, not the t-shirt but the actual person. Bill, that's his name. And Bill was a tough macho kinda guy, as wife-beaters tend to be.

Assumption!

He was a barker on a carousel. And he would use his barking expertise to pick up chicks. But then he gets married and ends up punching his pregnant wife. Anyway, it all works out in the end because, well, he dies. Falling on his own knife. He was a clever fellow the wife beater, as wife beaters tend to be.

Assumption!

And years later he's hanging out up in limbo or
> *(gesturing to the top of the ladder)*

purgatory, or wherever dead wife-beaters go, and he finds out that he's got the right to go back down to
> *(gesturing to where earth is)*

(MORE)

TAYLOR (cont.)
earth for one day. I quote, "Well everybody's got the right to go back for one day. One day to fix the trouble he helped create. "Trouble?" So he does go down to fix that trouble. "Trouble?" But he finds out his boy Bill was really born a daughter. And he ends up slapping *her* out of frustration. And the daughter –

(TAYLOR runs stage left and poses as the daughter.)

TAYLOR
The daughter, after her magnificent and slightly dysfunctional dream ballet where she dances with an imagined, and much sexier version of her father, only to come home and get smacked upside the head by her real daddy dear, in eidolon form, that's a specter, an eidolon, well, she says to her mother:

DAUGHTER
"But is it possible mother, for someone to hit ya hard, real loud and hard, and it not hurt at all."

TAYLOR
And the mother who'd been beaten her entire relationship with the living eidolon, she says –

MOTHER
"It is possible dear, for someone to hit ya, hit ya hard, and it not hurt at all."

TAYLOR
But before all that happens, before Bill dies, well he's running around on the beach, singing, what I imagine

Assumption!

What I imagine was my father's favorite song.
        (running back to the ladder)
So Dear Dad, Robert, this is my last letter to you. A singing telegram, from the movie musical *Carousel*. Rodgers and Hammerstein. Slightly fucked with for artistic purposes.

BILL
My boy Bill! He'll be tall and tough as a tree, will Bill
like a tree he'll grow with his head held high
and his feet planted firm on the ground
and you won't see nobody dare to try
to boss him or toss him around!

TAYLOR
> *(to audience)*

Like the daughter from movie musical *Carousel*, I never knew my father.
"Trouble?" He also died when I was very young. He was riding his motorcycle,
he'd had a few, as was usual, he crossed the yellow divider line ...whoops. And
my mother doesn't like to talk about him much. And my only memory of him
is from the age of four, riding his motorcycle. Him with one arm around my
waist, while he steered with the other. But other than that, well he's always been
a bit of a mystery to me. And I have always been exceedingly curious about
him. Through some deductive reasoning skills I have pieced together a few
ideas as to the kind of man he was. For example: why I imagine Robert's
favorite character was the central character of the wife beater is, well, he came
from a tough, Texan, conservative, macho, military, farm family who would
brag of their faggot bashing stampedes and who would use the biblical reference
of Rib to refer to their wives: I quote, "Hey Rib, gimme a beer." Not
everybody got that. Don't worry, two o'clock in the morning you're gonna
wake up – "Rib! Ha!" Or maybe not. And because of the whole Rib thing I've
come to assume,

Assumption!

I've come to assume my father, like his father and brothers, was a bit rough
trade. And not in a homoerotic way. And that perhaps we wouldn't have that
much in common. Example, dad's favorite character, the wife beater, he sings:

BILL
And I bet that he'll turn out to be the spittin' image of his Dad.

TAYLOR
Yes my father looked exactly like
> *(referring to himself)*

This.

BILL
But he'll have more common sense than his puddin' headed father ever had.

TAYLOR
I think this last part is true. That I have more common sense. For example, I
live in Blue State Bliss New York City, not Texas. Common Sense. I don't
know if my father was puddin' headed, and nothing against conservative Texans
but, let's face it, common sense is not their forte. Oh! Oh, by the way, for the
two percent of the audience members who grew up with loving, stable, present

(MORE)

TAYLOR (cont.)
fathers, you may be thinking, "Yet another father play that I can't relate to." If
you could just do me a favor and if every time I talk about dad, if you could just
think of another conservative Texan, one in your life, who has functioned in a
sort of absent father role – you're gonna relate just fine. Back to Bill. Bill
awaiting the birth of, what he thinks is going to be his newborn son. And, I
imagine,

Assumption!

I imagine Robert,

> (TAYLOR *sits on the bottom part of the ladder as if in a movie theater seat.*)

TAYLOR
My father, staring up at Bill on the big screen, and awaiting the birth of me, well
he mouths silently along,
while Bill sings:

BILL
I'll teach him to wrestle and dive through a wave
when we go in the mornings for our swim
his mother can teach him the way to behave
but she won't make a sissy out o' him!

TAYLOR
Whoops! So perhaps Dad and I wouldn't have much in common. And perhaps
he wasn't particularly the kind of man I'd enjoy hanging out with. But father is
not assumption alone. And so,
        (climbing the ladder)
In hopes to discover some common ground, and bridge the gap between us, I
have been writing letters to dad my whole life, asking for information about
him, from him. But not once have I ever received a reply. Perhaps because
he's dead but, well still, everybody's got the right to go back for one day. So, I
imagine
        (descending the ladder)
Assumption!

I imagine Robert, well he's seen this movie a few dozen times. He knows the
words. Why by now he and Bill are the best of friends. So he starts singing in
that movie theater in full voice:

ROBERT/BILL
I could see him when he's seventeen or so and startin'
to go with a girl
I can give him pointers
very sound
on the way to get round any girl
I could see him, I could see him, I could see him, I could see him, I could see him ...
Wait a minute!

TAYLOR
And now Robert and Bill they both stop. And they both say:

ROBERT/BILL
"Wait a minute. Could it be? What the ...What if he is a ..."

TAYLOR
"She."

> *(TAYLOR sings, "She" in a high falsetto for a long time. The lights shrink all around him. A small envelope drops down from the sky. A special comes on for the envelope, in the shape of an envelope. The letter that has fallen missed its light. TAYLOR goes over to the letter and drags it to the center of the special. He looks up, as if amazed that the letter hit the center of the light perfectly [acting as if it had never missed its spot]. He puts the letter to his head. He can read the contents without opening it.)*

TAYLOR
"Dear Taylor,"
> *(to audience regarding the nifty way he can read it without opening it up)*
Theater.
> *(back to the letter)*
"Dear Taylor, I've been cleaning out the garage, for the first time in thirty years and I came across a few letters that belonged to your father. I'm sending them to you. Love mom."

> *(A small army bag gets thrown on stage. TAYLOR picks it up and empties the contents. The* Carousel *Waltz begins to play. TAYLOR sees another bag off stage and goes to get it. The following is a comedic dance. TAYLOR returns with a medium-sized army bag. He dumps the contents of the bag. Hundreds of letters fall out. He exits. Comes on stage dragging a giant army green "Bigger-Than-a-Santa-Claus-Bag" full of letters. Dumps it. Exits. Comes in carrying three steamer trunks. Dumps them. Exits. Enters pulling a massive cart full of boxes, full of letters. He begins emptying the boxes all over the stage. As he does this and the*

music gets louder — heaps of letters are thrown on from every orifice of the stage. Suitcases full of letters fall from the sky and hang. Suddenly it begins to pour letters all around him. He is consumed. TAYLOR emerges from the pile of letters.)

TAYLOR
(to audience)
My thong fell off.
(adjusting his thong)
Bra as thong. It's a bra. Used as a thong. Some people invent cures for diseases, I invent bra as thong.

(He empties a couple more boxes with wonder. He throws some letters up in the air and whoops with joy. He picks up a different letter for each line.)

TAYLOR
2nd Lt. Robert Mac Bowyer.
2nd Lt. Robert Mac Bowyer
2nd Lt. Robert Mac Bowyer
(disappointed)
Not letters from Robert to me, but letters to Robert.
2nd Lt. Robert Mac Bowyer
2nd Lt. Robert Mac Bowyer
2nd Lt., I was told my father was a 1st Lt.
(shaming the lie)
2nd Lt.
(taking in the letters)
2nd Lt. Robert Mac Bowyer had a lot of friends. Or one very aggressive stalker.
2nd Lt. Robert Mac Bowyer.
2nd Lt. Robert Mac Bowyer
2nd Lt. Robert Mac Bowyer

(He holds a letter up to his forehead like a magician.)

TAYLOR
Dear 2nd Lt. Robert Mac Bowyer.
Dear Lt,
Dear Lt,
Dear Lt,
Dear Lt,
Dear Robert,
Dear Robert,
Dear Robert,
(noticing a special one)

Dear Bob,
Dear Robert,
Dear Bob,
Dear Bob,
Dear Robert,
Dear Lt., scratch out, Dear Robert, scratch out, Dear Bob.
I am answering,
I am answering,
I decided to write,
I noticed in the paper,
Hi, this is in response to
I am answering your advertisement
>   *(to audience)*
Dad was an advertiser.
>   *(on a letter)*
I am answering your advertisement in the *Daily Telegraph*
>   *(to audience)*
He placed an add in the *Daily Telegraph* – if there are any of the 80% of
Americans without passports that are in the audience, the *Daily Telegraph* is an
Australian paper.   Kinda like the NY *Post*. Not my kind of paper but ... Dad
was an advertiser.
>   *(on the letter)*
I am answering your advertisement in the *Daily Telegraph* dated May 6, 1968
asking Australian girls, between the ages of 19 and 26 to write to you.
>   *(to audience)*
He wasn't an advertiser, he placed a personal. He was a personal placer.
>   *(on the letter)*
For Australian Girls between the ages of ...
Australian girls.
Australian.

EXAGGERATED AUSTRALIAN LADY
>   *(in an overdone Australian accent)*
I am answering your advertisement in the *Daily Telegraph* dated May 6, 1968
asking for Australian, Australian girls to write to you ...

TAYLOR
>   *(to audience)*
No. Australian light.
>   *(in a primarily American accent with a few Australian elements and back to the
>   letter)*
I am answering your

>   *(MORE)*

TAYLOR (cont.)
> *(pronouncing it the Australian way)*

Advertisement.
> *(to audience)*

Advertisement. We'll do it light.
> *(back to letter)*

Your advertisement in the *Daily Telegraph* dated May 6, 1968 asking for
Australian girls between the ages of 19 and 26 to write to you with, dot dot dot,
R and R in mind.
> *(to audience)*

Dad was the kind of man who wanted to pick up chicks while on leave.
> *(moving on to different letters)*

At this point I presume
You've probably gotten
I bet you have
I'm probably one in
I suppose by now
By now
By now
By now you've probably received enough replies to last you with the company
of an Australian girl every day of your R&R even if it lasted for twelve months
but I thought I'd write anyway
I wanted to write anyway
I'm writing anyway
I'm crossing my fingers
I'm trying my luck
I hope I'm not too late
I hope you'll consider me
I hope you'll like me best
I hope you'll find me more
I hope
I hope
I hope
Perhaps after due consideration you could pass on my letter to someone else
who might like to correspond with me.
Forgive me, I have not introduced myself yet.
My name is
My name is
I should tell you my name
My name is Kathy
Janice
Judy
Jennifer

> *(MORE)*

TAYLOR (cont.)
Carol
Francise
Marcy
Robin
Pamela
Ginger
Sofie
Nora
Sandy

(Seeing an astonishingly special letter.)

TAYLOR
Peter.

(He puts Peter's letter in his dress – safe keeping for later. He picks up a letter hoping it will be another male name.)

TAYLOR
Sofie. Jennifer. Candy. Mary.
(noticing Mary's forthcoming "parenthesis" Taylor decides to read her letter)
Mary writes. Miss, in parenthesis,

(A light comes up on TAYLOR as MARY.)

MARY
Mary Divine,
I am 19, practically 20.

(Light out on MARY.)

TAYLOR
(a comment on MARY's age)
19.
Laura's 19
Janice is 20
19
21
22
23
24

(MORE)

TAYLOR (cont.)
25
Stacy 26.

STACY
Not too old to be writing.

TAYLOR
Ooo Carol writes.

CAROL
      (in a gruff old lady smoker's voice)
30, perhaps too old but I thought I'd write anyway.

TAYLOR
And she's got Blonde, Sonya's a blonde, Tonya,
Blonde
Blonde
Blonde
Strawberry Blonde
Blonde
      (behaving as if all the ladies are stupid)
Blonde
Blonde
Blonde

Assumption!

Mary writes.

      (Light on MARY.)

MARY
Today my hair is ... best not to describe.

TAYLOR
Work!

MARY
I have blue eyes and my statistics are 36-24-36. I love nights, dot, dot, dot, lots
and dancing too,

TAYLOR
> *(to audience)*

Too. Dancing too.

> *(MARY's light goes out.)*

TAYLOR

Dad liked dancing. Dad liked dancing. Gretchen likes dancing, Pam likes dancing.

VARIOUS LADIES

I love dancing
I love dancing
Dancing
Dancing
Dancing
Dancing
Dancing

> *(TAYLOR continues the dancing line as he dances around with the letters.)*

TAYLOR

And Carol wants Dad to know what her favorite drink is.

CAROL

My favorite drink is beer!

VARIOUS LADIES

My favorite drink is beer
My favorite drink is beer
Beer
Beer
Beer
Beer

TAYLOR

Mary writes.

> *(MARY's light comes on.)*

MARY

My favorite drink is Scotch, ice and dry followed closely by "gin double vodka

> *(MORE)*

MARY (cont.)

and squash," which is my own invention and is great as long as you don't have
too many. Bob. Funny story about liquor. Last weekend the local country club
held a Roman night and sent an invite. Everyone went of course, dressed in
Roman gear. The setup was fabulous, no chairs or tables, only felt on the floor,
which was covered with cushions to sit on. The night progressed everyone was
getting tipsy, then the liquor ran out, time 10:30pm: PANIC. Exclamation
point. But not to worry, then came the flagons of wine. Parenthesis, flagons,
sp, question mark. The night ended about 1:30 a.m., at the club then we all
went for coffee. It really was a worthwhile evening for $2. But Bob. Working
in a hotel tends to turn you off drinking. When you watch what it does to some
of your customers it starts to make you wonder what you yourself are like after
a few. I work at a hotel coffee shop on Friday and Saturday nights, a money
grabber of the worst kind I am. A woman. Double underline.

TAYLOR

So a lot about Mary but not that much about Dad.

> *(MARY's light goes out. Looking for something interesting, TAYLOR find's
> Sandy's letter.)*

TAYLOR

Sandy writes: I am writing as we have been hearing and seeing news broadcasts
on the extensive fighting in Vietnam. Vietnam, 1968, Lt., R and R, Sydney.

> *(SANDY's light comes on.)*

SANDY

I think that here in Australia most of us are apprehensive on hearing any news
of Vietnam – even if we don't have family or friends there. I could hardly begin
to comprehend the difficulty in being there, the loneliness, the poor conditions
etc., etc., etc.

TAYLOR

Dad was in Vietnam.

SANDY

Well, the weather here ...

> *(SANDY's light out. TAYLOR looks for more information about Vietnam.)*

TAYLOR
> *(on the letters)*

> *(MORE)*

TAYLOR (cont.)
The weather
The weather
The weather
The weather
The weather
The weather
The weather
The weather

(He throws a bunch of letters up in the air.)

TAYLOR
It's the small talk blizzard of 1968.

VARIOUS LADIES
It's cold
It's cold
I hate the winter
I hate the winter
Winter
Winter
Winter
Cold

TAYLOR
(to audience)
It's Sydney.
(back to letters but making fun of them)
I hate the winter.
I hate the winter.
I hate the winter
Mary writes:

(MARY's light comes on.)

MARY
Winter is my favorite season as fashions show themselves truthfully in winter.

TAYLOR
Work!

(MARY's light out.)

TAYLOR
(seeing Robin's letter)
Robin writes: "Since you asked, I better tell you what I like and don't like."

(ROBIN's light comes on.)

ROBIN
Since you asked, I better tell you what I like and don't like. I like making things. I'm knitting at the moment, making my son Peter a jumper. My son Peter ...

(TAYLOR pulls out the letter from Peter, puts it to his head.)

TAYLOR
Peter.

(He puts the letter with Robin's.)

ROBIN
My son Peter is 4 years old and is a little tiger as he is always around your legs but he is a lovely child. I also love the water but I am afraid it doesn't love me very much, I can swim, that is enough to save myself, and I attempted water skiing once and ended uh, with a rather tender, quote, never mind, end quote, for about a month but I've never been brave enough to try surfing like you. Will.

TAYLOR
Will. Well spelled W.I.L.L.

ROBIN
Will, comes the times when little girls must sleep so.

(TAYLOR freaks out at how gross that is and doesn't want to be Robin anymore. ROBIN's light out.)

TAYLOR
Dian writes: "Must say good night to you, Robert". Stephanie writes, "Bob" Robert
Mary writes: "Hoping to hear from you"
I hope to see you
I hope to make your acquaintance
I hope you'll write back
Sandy's writes: "I hope this letter finds you"

(MORE)

84

TAYLOR (cont.)
I hope
I hope
I hope
I hope
I hope
I hope
I hope
I hope
Smiley Face
Smiley Face
Smiley Face
>   *(scared of the all the smiley faces he climbs a box but realizes the box is full of smiley faces)*

Smiley Face
Smiley Face
Smiley Face
Smiley Face
Smiley Face
>   *(relieved)*

Sincerely
Sincerely
Sincerely
Sincerely
Sincerely
>   *(scared again)*

Smiley Face
>   *(relieved)*

Sincerely
Sincerely
>   *(with growing desperation)*

Yours,
Yours
Yours
Yours
Yours
Yours
Yours
Kathy
Janice
Judy
Jennifer

(MORE)

TAYLOR (cont.)
Carol
Francise
Marcy
Robin
Jennifer,
Pamela-Ginger
Sofie
Nora
Sandy
Peter
P.S.
P.S
P.S.
P.S.
P.S.
P.S.
Girls, they love the P.S.

Assumption!

Mary Writes:

(MARY's light up.)

MARY
PS: Bob, by the way, like you, I am definitely not fond of "Gutless" men either. When you write, please tell me all about Texas. We hear it is quite a large and un-gutless part of the United States. Write soon

(MARY's light out.)

TAYLOR
So what do we got? Lt. Vietnam. 1968. The thick of it. Personal placer. Likes girls 19-26. Blondes. Assumption. Likes beer. Assumption. Loves dancing or just tells women that so that more women will write him. Player. Assumption. Likes beer. Assumption. Asks women about themselves. Assumption. Loves the water. Surfer. But does not like gutless men. Which I translate to mean ... Exna on the utlessgay.

(TAYLOR gets his uke and pulls down a projection screen.)

TAYLOR
In my family of
Texan soldiers
broad shouldered
men on the range
skirt and booze chasers
with red meat heart pace makers
they have a family male tradition
when a new baby boy is born
fulfilling the name sake
the Mac men all gather
and dress the baby boy up
in girly dresses
It started off with Christening dresses – you know many families do that, they
dress the baby boys up in little Christening gowns – so for example:
This is a photo of my grandfather
> *(a projection of Taylor's grandfather at sixty, looking rather rough around the soul,*
> *is projected)*
Looks like the kind of man who was raised at the Motel 6.
This is a photo of Grandpa as a baby
> *(a projection of Taylor's grandfather as a baby dressed up in a Christening gown)*
But then Grandpa, he decided to take this tradition one step further so:
This is a photo of my father as a soldier
> *(projection of Dad in the army)*
And this is a photo of Dad as a baby
> *(projection of Dad as baby dressed in a ridiculously girly outfit)*
And then I, of course, have taken it one-step further than that.
This is a photo of myself.
As a soldier.
> *(projection of Taylor dressed up in drag on the streets of New York)*
My attempt to bridge the gap.
And for some reason, even though every man in my family for the last three
generations – all the macho Texan cousins, uncles, brothers, and dads – they've
all been dressed up in drag as babies, for some reason, search though I may, I
cannot find a photo of myself dressed up in drag as a baby. Go figure.
But this is a photo of Dad at the prom
> *(projection of Robert at the prom with his date)*
And this is a photo of me and female female
impersonator The World Famous Bob.
> *(projection of Taylor in drag and Bob, a woman who looks like a man dressed up in*
> *drag)*
This is a photo of Robert in a school play

(MORE)

TAYLOR (cont.)
>   *(projection of Dad dressed up as Lincoln in a school play)*
> *This is a photo of me, in a political vaudeville*
>   *(projection of Taylor in drag in performance)*
> *This is a photo of Robert in the Army*
>   *(projection of Robert in a group of army men)*
> *This is a photo of me at a party*
>   *(projection of Taylor at a naked party shot by Spencer Tunic)*
Mary writes:

> *(A different light comes up for MARY – the same one is used for all the ladies who speak in the photo song).*

MARY
Bob, thank you for your letters (underline the plural), and the photo. I was rather surprised to receive two letters from you in little under a week but I enjoyed them both. I don't think you could have remembered writing the first because your second letter is almost a copy.
Glad to hear that you had a good response to your ad in the paper. It must have been rather great to receive so much mail. Per your request, I have enclosed a photo. In case you are wondering, the photo was taken in a club with two girl friends whom I didn't think you would be interested in, so I cut them off.

> *(MARY's light out.)*

TAYLOR
Just to get us back on track, this is a photo of my uncle Jim.
>   *(Uncle Jim as a soldier)*
And this is a photo of uncle Jim as a baby.
>   *(Uncle Jim as a baby in drag)*
Now the Mac men
they photograph the boys
dolled up and precious
fraternity viciousness
acts of humility
male juvenility
the point to feminize
so years later
when baby boys are grown
with broads and shoulders of their own
the dad can pull out
the photo of his son
a dainty girl knockout

(MORE)

TAYLOR (cont.)
feminized
And then you get:
Jeering fathers
knee slapping codgers
you are baptized in laughter
from being feminized
So this is a photo of Uncle Bill
       (Uncle Bill as soldier)
And this is a photo of Uncle Bill as a baby
       (Uncle Bill as a baby in drag)
But try as I might, I cannot find a single photo of me dressed up in drag as a
baby.
       (gesturing to his current outfit)
But I'm making up for it
And this is a photo of Dad at work
       (a photo of Dad with his co-workers in business casual attire)
This is a photo of me at work
       (a photo of Taylor with his co-workers all dressed up like ducks)
This is a photo of Dad exercising in the Army.
       (a photo of Dad exercising in the army)
This is a photo of me doing laundry.
       (a photo of Taylor doing laundry in alien dominatrix drag)
This is a photo of Dad's camouflage.
       (a photo of Dad's camouflage)
This is a photo of me in camouflage.
       (a photo of Taylor sans drag, in a suit)
Robin writes!

    (ROBIN's light comes on.)

ROBIN
Dear Bob, Thank you for the photos. I'm sending two pictures over as will.

TAYLOR
Will. Well spelled W.I.L.L.

ROBIN
The first is a drawing Peter made of you and I dancing. And the second is a
photo of me. That way you well know who you are writing to and what I look
like. You might change your mind about writing me when you see my photo.

    (ROBIN's light out.)

TAYLOR
This is the drawing that Peter drew of Robin and Dad dancing:
> *(the drawing is projected. TAYLOR goes to the drawing and points to what appears to be a giant silver schlong.)*

I'm very curious about this right here.
Also my family
has a tradition
where the Mac men
they give the boys presents
birthday presents
of ribbon laces
dolls in strollers
unicorn figurines
for the boy children

The Mac boys they scowl
throw tantrums, they howl
sulk in corners
become professional mourners
due to the presents
best for their sisters
And then you get
Jeering father
knee slapping codgers
the boys are baptized in laughter
from being feminized

But then the father
pulls out the real gift
monster trucks and
military airplane
model construction
to re-masculinize

Robin writes:

> *(ROBIN's light.)*

ROBIN
P.S.: Bob, Peter and I loved the photo of you with your rifle.

> *(ROBIN's light out.)*

TAYLOR
This is a photo of Dad with a boy's toy.
        (projection of Robert smiling with a handgun)
This is a photo of me with a boy's toy.
        (a photo of Taylor crying with a truck)
And this is a photo of me with ...
        (to young male audience member)
Darling, could you come down here for a second. Yes you. Come down here
and stand right next to me. Act like you know me.
        (a flash like a photograph is seen)
This is a photo of me, with a boy toy.
Thanks babe.
        (the Boy Toy is sent back to the audience)
In the theater there is no such thing as observation that lacks participation.
You're all next.
On my fourth birthday
my grandfather
bought me a pink dog
stuffed animal
canonizing
cuddle sensation
Mac man castration
the point to feminize
I was supposed to scowl
throw a tantrum, howl
sulk in a corner
do the mourning thing
because of the pink dog
best for my sister
Then my Grandpa would bring me the real gift
a rifle for my fourth birthday
The thing is I didn't scowl, howl, or sulk. Instead, I ran to my pink dog and I
gave it a hug
This is a photo of me and my pink dog
        (projection of Taylor and his pink dog)
And there is no photo of me with a rifle
Sandy writes.

        (SANDY's light.)

SANDY
In response to your request for a photo, I stopped writing this to see if I had any on hand but I didn't. I suppose you'll just have to continue to use your imagination and hope for the best.

> *(SANDY's light out.)*

TAYLOR
This is a photo of Dad playing bondage in the Army.
> *(projection of Robert posing in a fake guillotine)*
This a photo of me getting whipped in a children's
theater production of Jesus Christ Superstar.

> *(A projection of Taylor getting whipped by five-year old children in a production of* Jesus Christ Superstar.*)*

TAYLOR
The little girl right there is singing:
Crucify him
crucify him
And this is a photo of Dad in New York.
> *(projection of Robert at the Empire State Building)*
This is a photo of me in New York
> *(projection of Taylor dressed up in drag on 42nd street – a butt shot)*
Turning the other cheek.
This is a photo of Dad in Europe
> *(projection of Robert in Rome)*
This is a photo of me bowling in Bulgaria
> *(projection of Taylor dressed in drag bowling in Bulgaria)*
This is a photo of Dad and his family
> *(projection of Robert with his brothers and dad)*
That's Uncle Bill Mac – the kid with the rifle, that's Dad, that's uncle Jim Mac, uncle John Mac, grandpa Don Mac.
And this is a photo of me and my family
> *(projection of the same naked party)*
I thought it was worth showing again. So the man with his head on the woman's vagina – that's Steven Menendez, the guy in the back on the chair – that's Boylesque star Tigger, There's Machine Dazzle, and the woman with the gorgeous butt, that's Dirty Martini.

> *(A series of photos are shown juxtaposing Taylor's life with his father's.)*

TAYLOR
This is a photo
This is a photo
This is a photo
This is a photo
This is a photo
This is a photo
a photo
a photo
photo
photo
photo
>   *(the last photo is of one of the ladies who wrote Robert)*
Mary writes:

>   *(MARY's light.)*

MARY
Pardon my asking. But who did you cut off the first photo you sent me?

TAYLOR
>   *(getting rid of the projection screen)*
So what do we have now? He is a staunch Red State military exna on the utlessgay conservative who poses with rifles while trying to seduce unsuspecting barely legal ladies. He asks for photos from them and sends photos to them, in which he has, most likely, cut out of the photos other women who have fallen into his evil-doing swinging ways. He sends one response *en masse* to the 1,000 of ladies who wrote, and is unable to keep track of who he's sent letters to so the women get repeat letters, and have become aware of their competition, and are left with no option but to pit themselves against one another.

>   *(TAYLOR gets in the ladder and uses it as a puppet theater. He takes two letters, bending them and puppeteers them like sock puppets. He introduces them. On the left: ROBIN. On the right: SANDY.)*

TAYLOR
Robin. Sandy.

SANDY
Dear Bob,
Today is Sunday, my day of relaxation, a day of listening to records,

(The letter puppet of SANDY puts on an imaginary record – a smooth instrumental jazz version of "If I Loved You" plays.)

SANDY
Sometimes going to church, visiting friends, but mostly replying letters to friends whom I don't see so often and here I am again writing to a stranger.

ROBIN
Dear Bob, Hi, exclamation point. I just received your letter and it made me very happy.

SANDY
I have been allocated my duty ward at the hospital for next week, and I got, dot, dot, dot gynecology. Exclamation point. I am not at all keen about working in a female ward. I am afraid females are far too fussy and so on, no matter.
(directed to Robin in a nasty competitive way)
I shouldn't say such things about my own sex should I?

ROBIN
(in response to Sandy)
I don't have much to say as it's been that cold I've stayed inside sorry.

SANDY
We have a dance at the nurses' home tomorrow evening. I am duly going. I have a long blond wig to wear. It looks great. And even if I say so myself.

(The letter puppet disappears and reappears in a blond wig.)

SANDY
I can go incognito.

ROBIN
(jealous of Sandy's wig)
You won't know what to do with all the letters coming in.

SANDY
So you don't like gutless men and religious women.

ROBIN
(anxiously)
Ohhhh.

SANDY
Well I don't care for such men myself, but even more so religious cranks –
> *(directed to Robin)*

Hypocrites really. I do go to church on occasion, as I said, but it is just an excuse to listen to music. I am a fan of music.

ROBIN
I was pleased to learn your favorite movie is the musical *Carousel*.
> *(directed to Sandy as if to say, "I got one up on you")*

I was in a production of *Carousel* in school.
> *(back to Bob)*

Just in the chorus but I did get to sing my favorite song with all the other ladies ... "What's the Use of Wonderin."

SANDY
Shame on you for flunking out in Latin 1. Believe it or not I studied Latin and French at school.

> *(SANDY disappears and returns in a beret.)*

SANDY
"Plus de buts, plus de jeu!" – translated, "The more goals – the more fun!"

ROBIN
I like your smiley faces, they're great. You seem to have quite a sense of humor. I am afraid I can't draw, not even such a simple thing as a smiley face.

SANDY
Well.

ROBIN
Will,

SANDY
Well, it's getting rather late.

ROBIN
Will, I better close now as I want to go up the street to post your letter and I have to get dressed ...

> *(ROBIN's puppet disappears and reappears wearing lingerie.)*

ROBIN
As I was still in bed when I read your letter. Bob when well you be coming?

SANDY
I will be looking forward to see you.

ROBIN
I well be looking forward to see you.

SANDY
I hope you find a little of this letter interesting.

ROBIN
 And I hope my letters well make you a happy soldier.

SANDY
Take great care.

ROBIN
Love from

SANDY
Kind thoughts.

ROBIN
Robin

SANDY
Sandy

ROBIN
And Peter

SANDY
Perfect smiley face.

ROBIN
Warped smiley face.

SANDY
XX

ROBIN
P.S.: Bob, have you a mate that would like to write to a woman who is 30 and
has 3 boys and would like to write to someone. She lives upstairs of me. As she
was with me when I said I was going to answer your ad. Bob she has no
husband now.

(ROBIN exits.)

SANDY
P.S.: I forgot to mention I just had a letter from a girlfriend who has just had a
baby daughter and she wrote and told me the child's name "Kimberly Susan".
How's that for a beautiful name. My goddaughter in fact. Still one more
godchild to be born yet. It's a long story of three very good friends who met at
the commencement of nursing training. We became fast friends; we all became
engaged to be married on the same day. Wendy and Ethel were married the
same day, and their babies due to be born the same day. To complete the
picture my fiancé was killed in action in Vietnam fifteen months ago.

(TAYLOR drops the puppet routine and simply speaks Sandy.)

SANDY
I feel a little sad this evening, memories do come back. Time takes care of
many hurts and well I gave up nursing for a while, but I am back now.

(SANDY moves out from behind the puppet theater/box.)

SANDY
Life keeps on keeping on. Next weekend will mean no work day, means going
to the park day, cleaning the room a bit means jeans and t-shirts, means sandals,
means listening to records, means hope for a letter, means probably not getting
one, means more letter writing, means more expectation, means paralysis means
I would rather put my attention into something more useful but sometimes it
seems all I have is pen and paper and the occasional recognition of beauty.
Pink blossoms that come and go so quickly. Bob, I will not wait for reply from
you. I'm afraid this letter of mine has been a bit too much, too fast, too soon.
Perhaps you will pass on my letters to your fellow combatants and laugh at the
lunacy. My lunacy. That would not bother me. I imagine you need to laugh.
Still, if you did wish to write, please know that I do believe that all we people
collectively are doing is collaborating on how to go about loving, like there's this
great pot and everybody throws in their two cents, and well, I like being brave
enough to throw in mine, so up yours if you can't take a theory, an adventure.
And also, if you did wish to write, please understand that I am not disillusioned
(MORE)

SANDY (cont.)

by the possibility of our loving each other as my letter may suggests. I fully understand that you are not the one for me, just the one right now. This I find comforting and purely dignified. I am going out with fellows and living a normal life, as one should. I have surely gotten off the track again. I didn't wish to write anything, dot dot dot, no matter. Pardon me for being boring.

(SANDY goes back to performing the puppet in front of the ladder this time.)

SANDY

I did have an interesting experience on the train. I had a pleasantly drunk gentleman sitting next to me, trying to roll his own cigarette. Somehow he couldn't quite do it. Must have taken him fifteen minutes to do so. I did offer him one of my cigs but somehow he didn't care for my brand. Well it is time for me to get some sleep. Again take care, I hope you get some nice mail from the young ladies of Sydney.

Sincerely,
Sandy

(The SANDY puppet looks down towards Robin. ROBIN puppet comes back.)

ROBIN

P.S...S. , parenthesis P.P.S. question mark. Write soon.

(TAYLOR looks at the puppets, puts them down and picks up his uke.)

TAYLOR

On August 24, 1973
Lt. Robert Bowyer,
attended the sixteenth birthday party of his younger brother
Bill.

In accordance with the family male tradition on a
Bowyer's sixteenth birthday the men in the family come
together to bring the Bowyer boy to manhood by
purchasing him a prostitute.

The Bowyer boy, fulfilling family lore had gone into
the room with the slightly older but legal woman
who would have to take him through the motions
as it were
that's it, no that's it, no that's, no, no, no, no, no, no ...

(MORE)

TAYLOR (cont.)
yeah okay

*The sixteen-year-old Bowyer boy did not want his first
attempt to last only thirty seconds
and so in order to not climax too soon, he thought
of bloody puppies.*

*But try as he might to keep manhood at bay, the
manhood came, anyway, all the same.
Unclimactically.
For her.
Always unclimactically for her.
But still she patted him on the head and told the new
appointed man what a tremendous job he had
done, perpetuating an entire lifetime of his
misunderstanding on how to please a woman.*

*He asked her if she would not mind pretending as if it
had taken him a longer time
and so they lay in bed, staring up at the ceiling
wondering what to say.*

*And the young ladies sing
"What's the Use of Wondering"*

*After an appropriately heroic amount of time, he
returned to the living room where all the other
Bowyer men were waiting to congratulate him and to
get
their sloppy seconds.*

*First up
after was the
second
youngest
and so Lt. Robert Bowyer, we don't know for sure,
because all the other Bowyer men present are now
deceased, having died from liver failure or too
drunk at the party to tell us what exactly
transpired, so perhaps Lt. Robert Bowyer did as his
younger brother and entered the prostitute's slippery*

(MORE)

TAYLOR (cont.)
slope of magnitude.

Or perhaps he took her in his arms; he told her how
she did not have to do a thing. They sat and talked.
She rolled her eyes at his sincerity but secretly
appreciated being treated as if somewhat human.

Or perhaps he entered her.
And while he did, he thought about his pregnant wife
or of the other women from his life, Kathy, Janice,
Judy, Jennifer, Carol, Francise, Marcy, Robin, Pamela,
Ginger, Sandy or Mary.

And perhaps climax came
unclimactically
for her
or perhaps climactically
for her
or with her
or on her
well, if he'd gone ahead and had his family's way with
her
then perhaps he lay on her.
While all his unexplainable sadness, slowly dried,
creating an adhesive between their bellies.

Or perhaps still perhaps it did not bother him, the moral
conundrums, perhaps they laughed and had a good
time, cajoled and all was fine, he paid her and she
thanked him
all are possible scenarios including her saying, "Oh"
maybe her made her say, "Oh"

At this point perhaps a knock came at the door
wondering if Robert had finished and was it now
someone else's turn.
Perhaps he put his clothes back on or perhaps he had
never taken them off to begin with
perhaps he walked backwards awkwardly
exiting the bedroom with the some slight post-copulation
shame or maybe he bounced with an extra step of
happiness as his older brother stormed on past zipping

(MORE)

TAYLOR (cont.)
down his fly, anxious to get his try.

*We simply do not know the facts but what I do know is
that in the other room a note was passed to Robert
from his father, or perhaps his father just remembered,
or perhaps a phone call came and Robert answered, at
any rate the message came that coincidence of
coincidences on this birthday of his brother, while
Robert was at the party, his pregnant wife had gone
into premature labor with their soon to be name son
Taylor
Mac
Bowyer
that's me*

*Or perhaps the note had come before. Before Robert
had entered the prostitute's sacred chamber stopping
him from being able to enter it.*

*Or perhaps he never would have entered whether the
message of Taylor's birth had come or not*
.

*Or perhaps he got the message and stormed away with
great excitement.*

*Or perhaps he was relieved that now he did not have
to follow through, like his brothers with the family
male tradition and perhaps he looked at all his
brothers and his father, waiting for their turns and
wondered, wondered how he'd raise his child
separate from them. How he'd escape all the weight
of male obligation.*

*At any rate he left the party. Begrudgingly or with
excitement or relief or maybe even feeling bits and
pieces of it all.*

*And perhaps as he drove to the hospital and his new
family, perhaps he thought of how things would be
different. That he would stop drinking and that the
lineage of masculine dysfunction would end. The he*

(MORE)

TAYLOR (cont.)
would paint his new born son's room in gender
neutral colors,

Or perhaps he sang a song from his favorite musical
"My boy Bill will be strong and as tough as a tree
will" he.
Or perhaps, upon entering the hospital room, he
kissed his wife, while he scratched the dried flakes of
his brother's sixteenth birthday off his belly, and
held his new born baby like sculpted pudding.

And the young ladies sing:
"What's the use of wondering? What's the use of
wondering? What's the use of wondering?"
It's a sing-a-long.
What's the use of wondering?
Just the ladies.
What's the use of wondering?
Now add the girly men.
What's the use of wondering?
Now add the dykes.
What's the use of wondering?
Now the hetero men.
What's the use of wondering?
Everybody's a drag queen at a drag show.
What's the use of wondering?
Now you keep going but this side sings:
      (in harmony)
What's the use of wondering?
Now this side
      (in more harmony)
Now everybody quiet
What's the use of wondering?

      (TAYLOR goes to the ladder. He climbs it while the audience sings.)

TAYLOR
Keep going.
Dear Robert,
No.
Dear Dad,

                                                        (MORE)

TAYLOR (cont.)
This is my last letter to you. A singing telegram.
What's the use of wondering?
No.

(*TAYLOR stops the audience.*)

TAYLOR
Dear Bob,

I am writing in response to your advertisement, which was in the *Daily Telegraph* dated May 6, 1968 asking Australian girls to write you. I am not an Australian but I am called "girl" by many people who know me. I'm thirty-four years old. The same age you were, when you crossed the yellow divider line and smashed head-on into the oncoming traffic. I'm 5'11" in my stocking feet. In my stilettos I'm anywhere between 6'2" and 6'5". I'm considered attractive and a happy type, especially at parties. I have blue eyes, like my mom, and if it is not glued on I have no hair, like you. Today however my hair is: Best not to describe.

I also love the water and was pleased to learn it's something you enjoy too. I try to swim three days a week now, in an Olympic size swimming pool in Harlem. There's a skylight that lets the sunlight play games in the water. I like to stay under for as long as possible and watch the fat bellied old men swim past. Gliding by submerged like that they're just about as graceful as a human being can be.

I can't say I'm that fond of "Gutless Men" either but I have learned that bravery comes in all kinds of forms, as does fear. I like to think I'm a brave a person although sometimes I falter.

Religious people aren't my bag of tricks either and it's really nice to know we have that in common. They say 40% of the country considers themselves Evangelical Christians and that they interpret the bible literally. Seems to me they do so because they're not sophisticated enough to understand metaphor. But perhaps that's just judgmental. My mother is a religious person and I do love her – I guess we make exceptions with our dislikes; we must have that in common as well.

My favorite drink is, well anything that's available … no really, alcohol humor, well if it's not passé, it should be. Apparently you were an alcoholic. You spent

(MORE)

TAYLOR (cont.)

some time in Vietnam; perhaps that's why you drank. Did you own a necklace of ears? You did win the bronze star, which is supposed to be for an act of bravery. Although I heard they gave awards out like candy back then so … well I must admit I find it difficult to be proud of someone who wins an award from the army and even harder to reconcile my extreme liberal politics with the desire to have an award-winning soldier superman for a father. I wonder if you were proud.

A lot has changed since 1968.

We have this thing called spell-check now, which makes writing intelligent letters much easier, although people don't write letters anymore. They email. I'd explain but …

They want to start cloning humans, all these sad people who miss their dead loved ones.
          (picking up the letters as if skin samples)
So they saved skin samples to clone them. I found an old book of yours. Cracker crumbs fell out of the pages, from you eating and reading in bed over thirty years ago. I thought I could have you cloned.

          (TAYLOR drops the letters as if creating a magic potion.)

TAYLOR

But you would probably come back as a Keebler Elf. I'd be fine with that.

There's a war on terror. I'd explain but …

I blame John Wayne. He's buried next to you. John Wayne is buried directly next to you. The man who gave me the map to your cemetery, showing me where your plot was, he was impressed. "I'm sorry for your loss, but wow look who he's buried next to." John's stone has a metal carving of him riding a horse. Yours has a typo. Well a mistake. Well a lie. It says you were a First Lt. But we all know you only made it to 2nd. One of your brothers wanted you to mean more than you did. Wanted your legacy to make them okay. You were in competition with Mr. Wayne after all.

John Wayne! Exclamation point. I don't mean to disparage … well maybe he was a role model. A dead role model.

I have dead role models: Claude Cahun, Nina Simone, Judy Garland. Who are the living ones. Who are the men? Who are the father figures?

                                                                    (MORE)

TAYLOR (cont.)

Long time ago. On the highway with mom. Hell's Angels would ride by on their motorcycles. And I'd wave. Mom tells me not to wave. She says they like to kidnap people. So I do it even more. I wave. Hoping they'll take notice. Pull me from the passenger seat of suburbia, hold onto me with one hand and steer with the other.

Long time ago I got a letter from my estranged uncle Bill, your brother, with inheritance of $1,000 telling me of my estranged grandfather's, your father's, death. In the letter he wrote, "Taylor, your grandpa always said if he had an extra $1,000 he'd spend $999 of it on pussy. And just blow the rest. Have fun. Uncle Bill." These were my father figures. They taught me about the kind of man I did not want to be. And so they are estranged. And I did not lose my virginity to a prostitute, at sixteen. I was not dressed in drag as a baby to teach me that femininity was something to be made fun of. And I do feel more fabulous for it.

But still I have to pull myself away from this desire to know and be known: be loved by you ... by people like you. I have to pull myself away from what? Greedy, warmongering, closed-minded, empty of empathy, numbnut, saturated fat induced, champions of idiocy and reality TV. I have to pull myself away from that. From a country, a belief system, a heritage that I don't even want. And yes I make assumptions. You and your history your heritage your pride you are nothing but assumptions. You offer nothing but what I am left to assume you are. You risk nothing but homophobic, sexist, middle-brow, stubborn, ideological, knee-jerk, reactionary, ignorant ...

Assumptions.
     (picking up the letters on the ground and throwing them in one of the boxes)
But the minute and made up details I've collected about you are not enough to bridge the mammoth gap between us ... Drag Queen and soldier, glitter and guns, father and son. Between you and I there is an entire polarized country. I have been writing letters my whole life, hoping my curiosity and effort will shrink the distance.
     (referring to the letters that hang)
What is your favorite ice cream? How'd you lose your virginity? Have you ever kissed a boy? What was growing up in Texas like? What was surfing like, for you? What does your voice sound like, what does your skin smell like? I can't remember. Are you messy like me? Did you want to have children? When were you happy? When were you not? How many times have you fallen in love? Have you fallen in love? Why did you like the sea? How do you shave? I already know how but I want to learn it from you. Is your favorite movie

                                                                              (MORE)

TAYLOR (cont.)
really the musical *Carousel*?

Would you be proud of me? Would you like my job? Are you even someone worth wanting?

How long do you hold on for a love that will never come. How long do you come so much more than half-way before it is time to stop. So, this is my last ...

I just want us to be better. I have created this, for you, so that we could hate each other a little less. So that we could be better. So that you can have your one chance to come down and fix this. But what are you going to do with that chance? Hit me so hard I can't feel it at all? Write me a letter to make up for the life time of letters I've sent you, the 20,000 letters from lonely ladies ... No. Scratch out. Courageous, open, giving women who, despite the insurmountable odds at ever getting any real response back, wrote to you.
I'm writing anyway.
I'm writing anyway.
I'm taking a chance.
I'm crossing my fingers.
I hope I'm not too late.
I hope you'll consider me.
I hope.
Robin writes: I'm hoping to see you. Mary writes: I'm hope to make your acquaintance. Sandy writes: I hope this letter finds you. I hope.

> (*TAYLOR goes to the box he dropped the letters in. He drops more letters in as he says each line. This time using it as a great big pot – the women throwing in their two cents – a cauldron.*)

VARIOUS LADIES
I hope.
I hope.
I hope.
I hope.
I hope.
I hope.

TAYLOR
I hope.

> (*TAYLOR signals for the MUSIC to play. Chimes and sparkles fill the air. TAYLOR gestures as if creating magic. The chime music becomes The* Carousel *Waltz. He pulls out a clump of letters that is actually a life-size lady made of*

letters. He has his Lady of Letters acknowledge the crowd, animating her. Then the lady sees him. He takes his wig and dress off. They dance together with great joy. The lady of letters becomes a dress, which TAYLOR puts on. He dances in the dress. It is a heroic, sad, enchanting, stupid, learned, beautiful, silly, masculine, and feminine action – all at the same time. It is abashedly hopeful. Hope despite the knowledge that there is little. The Carousel Waltz ends. TAYLOR stands in the dress made of letters.)

TAYLOR
Love,
me.
P.S.:

(TAYLOR smiles as we fade to black.)

END OF PLAY

***

(The following is a letter audience members can take with them as they leave.)

Dear Reader:

Thanks for coming to the "The Young Ladies Of."

As part of an ongoing project, I'm asking members of the audience to write a response to Dad's advertisement. Don't worry if you're not the appropriate gender, age, nationality, or sensibility Robert requested in 1968. The world is so much more complex now; who knows what he would prefer today.

You may say as much or as little as you like. You are encouraged to be brutally honest or fictitiously phantasmagorical. I hope you will take this opportunity to share with Dad something of yourself (perhaps the one thing you've never told anyone) but if you would prefer – talk about the weather. Bob has been deceased for thirty years and since the letters are addressed to him – they will remain sealed and will not be read. You can send the letters to:

Lt. Robert Mac Bowyer
c/o (theater's address here)

Thank you for your participation.
Sincerely,
Taylor Mac

PS: The letters will accompany me and will be added to the set and accumulate over the years as I continue to perform this play. Eventually it will get Beckett like.

Lt. Robert Mac Bowyer's Advertisement

American Soldier, serving in Vietnam, seeks correspondence with an Australian young lady, 19-26, with R and R in mind (I'll be coming to Sydney for leave soon). I'm a Texan farm boy who is not fond of gutless men and religious women but who enjoys the ocean, surfing, and beer. If interested, write to: Lt. Robert Mac Bowyer. Hope to hear from you soon.

***

Taylor Mac in the HERE Arts Center production

Taylor Mac in the HERE Arts Center production

The White Space
An Introduction to Tommy Smith's *White Hot*
by Craig Lucas

"LIL: I am telling you my thoughts as they come to me.
BRI: I'm getting sick of that."

hite Hot is a black, cold play. It takes place in an upside down, dyslexic world where right is wrong and what is left out is the real play. What cannot be said is what must be said and is never said, so dangerous in fact that it must be snuffed out. The only fulfillment in this life is death, the only feeling one can yearn for is pain.

The story is linear, but there is little or no causality. *(Caution: the following contains spoilers!)* A pregnant wife is visited by her sister who has come in pursuit of drugs; in exchange the sister gives the wife the phone number of a thug she recently had sex with. The wife and her husband then sit in a park and bicker; the husband discovers the thug's phone number in his wife's purse and is told it belongs to a chiropractor recommended by the sister. The husband visits the sister, learns the truth and has sex with her. Meanwhile, the wife visits the thug and he beats her up and gives her a gun. The sister, the wife and husband all take a vacation at the beach. The sister is also now pregnant; the play ends in gruesome violence.

This is bleak terrain, a buried cesspool of self-loathing and unseemly, sadistic yearnings in love. The play can be read as a critique of the deadening fallout of our reactionary, materialistic, exploitative and soulless era. It can be read as a bad dream or a soap opera about the banality of evil. However you read it, it doesn't go down easy.

The pregnant Lil who knits pink caps in the shape of bunnies knows that something is awry in her relentless pursuit of the "nice." Her debauched sister warns: "knitting paves the pathway to madness." Like all addicts, Lil lies without even trying – it's how she's wired.

Her husband repeatedly lacerates her for a history of drug-taking, but then insists she take new drugs to contend with her depression. (I suspect the meaning of our national reliance upon mood-altering drugs has never been so vividly dramatized as the brilliant political sedative it represents.)

In this mirror world of a play, Lil has broken every mirror in her home so that the blinding reflection of herself cannot be found. Oedipus blinds himself after learning who he is, Greek-style; but Lil's optimism is the American way: denial. Bri mishears every kind word she says as sarcasm and bitter disappointment. "I know who she is even when she doesn't say it."

According to Sis, the only love to be found in this life is crushingly brutal; her thug with the huge cock and slippery Slavic accent, as unreliable as the meaning of familiar words in this world, has recently raped Sis's throat and ass and then honored her requests to do "some other fucked up shit." By way of explanation: "I'm shitting blood but it's nice, you know. Tender. These bright red swirls of blood clouding the bowl 'cause that's like, that's love, you know?"

Throughout, Bri has his theories about the kinds of stories people want to hear. "Stories have to show people something. And there has to be hope. Every great work of literature has hope [...] Shakespeare. The Greeks. Even the Greeks had hope."

Humorously enough, it is the hopeless Bri who demands art with *Hope*. But if there is any hope in this play, it is in the white space between the black cold lines. And like all things that live in the white space, they are invisible, which means they may not be there at all. This play we are watching could well be Bri's worst nightmare, the one play he would never want to see: the inverted reflections in those shattered mirrors.

White Hot is a photographic negative and a "flipped" version of Shakespeare's black play, *Othello*. Black is now white. The "right" side of the image is now on the left, the wrong side – easy enough to do when you are making a movie – one switch and the picture reverses, not to mention that there no longer is such a thing as a "negative" in the current technology of film; everything is digital – it's binary – zeros and ones – yet still somehow this story we are watching is a *very* negative one, in which none of the characters are aware of that negativity: normality is now defined entirely by the abnormal.

In this *Othello*, Desdemona is counseled by her Emilia to cuckold her husband; she carries the handkerchief with her and can barely be bothered to lie about it; Othello's suspicions need no prodding from without for he carries Iago inside him at all times; most impressively, he needn't even bother murdering his bride, she does the deed for him. He has already moved on to Emilia who is pregnant with someone's child – maybe his, maybe the thug's, who knows or cares.

"The past isn't important," Bri proclaims, as he sets about recreating it. A college professor gives him a cold black accurate assessment of his character; as he tells it: "she lets me have it. Saying things like I only processed information and didn't understand it and I didn't actually read books I just consumed them and lacked the ability to think critically about abstract concepts and finally I'm like, that's it. I am better than everybody in this room. So I went into the entertainment industry."

Sis is the truthteller in this universe: "The wedding vow nullifies honesty." When Bri says he wants to grow old with his children, she says, "On what planet? Your children are going to be living underground eating dirt." An even colder, blacker place than the one of *White Hot*. Sis interrogates Bri, threatening to bring out the "black interrogation mask. I'll slip it over your head. I'll shut off the lights. I'll tie your hands to a chair and push your face in a bucket of water. You'll talk."

The only way Lil can acknowledge much less contend with the pain inside her (a kiss to her forehead causes her to say, "Ow") is to extinguish the body that contains it. But even in death, in the play's final image when she fires a gun into her own skull, the splattering of brains and blood on the wall are in the shape of a heart. Even in death she's a sunny-side-up kinda gal.

That shot is meant to be an end to Lil's doubt, the stark images of hopeless futures she carries with her, and to need, to love. All hurt goes away. And the past that Bri doesn't believe in.

But what about us? What about our doubt, our stark images, our need for love, our hurt and our past? This is the big blank white page *White Hot* leaves us with: how to fill, what to do.

If there is any light in this play beyond the white light of Lil's death, I would say it is in the photographic negative we've been denied by our new binary technology: theater as antidote to global dominance from above. And if I were to direct *White Hot*, I would direct my colleagues' attention to the idea of hope as it is contained in fear; all things contain their opposites in their definition; things are what they are because of what they are not. In other words, hope is not an aspect of love so much as it is the universal, Platonic balancing out, the *negation*, of fear. It is darkness that defines light.

I fear and hope for Tommy Smith. He's writing in the shadow of our most daring and politically incendiary of martyred playwright saints, Sarah Kane and Edward Bond (the latter martyred in the sense that his plays cannot get significant productions here or in his home of England.)

No, there is no easy optimism in this play. It is a devastated, cracked, lifeless terrain. The only hope is in those cracks, those hot interstices out of which some kind of new unthinkably white hot lava could flow, covering over the hideous mess we have made and create a new landscape.

Perhaps we will catch up to such a vision. Perhaps we are even there, ready to hear it. I fear not but I do hope so.

WHITE HOT

by Tommy Smith

WHITE HOT

Copyright © 2007 by Tommy Smith

Derek Zasky and Elsa Neuwald
William Morris Agency, LLC
1325 Avenue of the Americas
New York, NY 10019
dsz@wma.com; emn@wma.com
212.903.1396; 212.903.1552

Professionals and amateurs are hereby warned that the following play, *White Hot*, being fully protected under the Copyright Laws of the United States of America, and of all countries covered by the International Copyright Union, and of all countries covered by the Pan-American Copyright Convention and the Berne and International Copyright Conventions, and of all countries with which the United States has reciprocal copyright relations, is subject to royalty payments for its use.

All rights, including, but not limited to, professional and amateur stage performing, video or sound taping, motion picture, recitation, lecturing, public reading, radio and television broadcasting, and the rights of translation into foreign languages are expressly reserved, permission for which must be secured in writing from the playwright or the playwright's designated representative.

***

White Hot was originally developed at the 2007 Soho Rep Writer/Director Lab, Sarah Benson, Artistic Director. Lab Facilitators were Maria Goyanes and Jason Grote.

White Hot received a First Workshop Production at HERE Arts Center in New York City in June 2007; Leigh Goldenberg, Producer. May Adrales directed the following cast:

LIL ....Patricia Nelson
SIS...Mary Jane Gibson
BRI...Ben Beckley
GRIG...Joel Israel

Costumes were by Kate Cusack, lights by Cat Tate, set design by Rumiko Ishii, sound design by Greg Hennigan, fight direction by Lisa Kopitsky. The Stage Manager was Michael Caban.

CAST OF CHARACTERS

LIL, early thirties, pregnant

SIS, mid-thirties, Lil's sister

BRI, mid-thirties, Lil's husband

GRIG, thirties

Note for actor playing Lil: She has no ability to defend herself.
Note for actor playing Bri: He is not mean; it is just how he communicates.
Note for actor playing Sis: She never takes a breath.
Note for actor playing Grig: He is extraordinarily kind.

For Biss

WHITE HOT

by Tommy Smith

1.

(An apartment.)

SIS
So then he came over.

LIL
No.

SIS
I called him like that and he came over.

LIL
No.

SIS
I've only seen him in a hoodie. I only met him at clubs. This thug. This thug
with the Eastern European accent.

LIL
He's from where?

SIS
The Ukraine. And I said is that an independent country or a province of
Russia? I didn't remember. Last I looked Ukraine was a province and he said
he didn't know either. Which makes me doubt he's from the Ukraine or Russia,
which makes me think he's lying and if he's lying that's more exciting. Someone
lying to me. I love when people lie to me. I love the moment when I figure it
out. I'm like, there, I got white hot justice on my side.

LIL
So this guy.

SIS

So this guy, like, the first thing he does. Caresses my cheek. Real sweet. And I'm like, fuck, I haven't had tender in years. Tender flew out the window. There's been a lot of kisses, sure, a lot of fucking and kissing. But something tender? I didn't even know I missed it. I mean, how long can you go without, you know, someone being nice, like really nice to your body? It was a real panty soaker. All from three fingers tracing two inches on my cheek. And by now his accent's slipping. I'm also really drunk and very stoned and I've taken a few pills and I haven't slept in like three days at this point, so I don't call him out on the slipping accent, I don't even have the words for it. You reach a certain point you can't find words. You're standing in front of someone with the words in your mind but you're so powerfully beyond by that point that your lips refuse to open. So you smile. So I smiled.

LIL

And then?

SIS

I won't bore you. I mean, you can sum it up in your head. No need to pore over the gory details.

LIL

Come on.

SIS

I don't have much dignity but I have some. His dick is fucking huge though. Thick like a baby arm. And he shoves it down my throat and I spit up some acidy Caesar barf but it's kind of warm so it lubricates his cock. He flips me over and pushes it up my ass and later I'm shitting blood but it's nice, you know? Tender. These bright red swirls of blood clouding the bowl cause that's like, that's love, you know?

LIL

He's from where?

SIS

They have these places you go on the computer where you can find people like him.

LIL

What's he like?

SIS
Hard to say. But he'll do anything, you know, I asked him to do some pretty fucked up shit and he went ahead and did it.

LIL
Can you call him?

SIS
Sure, yeah, I can call.

LIL
Can you call for me?

SIS
You got one already. You got your man. Snared him like a bird. He's your nest now.

LIL
I need something else.

SIS
That's not what you said at the veil thing, you know, you were veiled and there was Jesus all-muscular on the cross and you said I do. I was there.

LIL
Bri's a sweet man.

SIS
Better call him shit than sweet.

LIL
I love Bri.

SIS
But Bri's a problem, right? You've settled into him and you settle into guys and they lose their status. Commitment sours a man. Soon as he starts flossing your undies it's over. Soon as he listens to your stories, actually listens, like, not looking off in the distance or checking out a girl on the side, soon as he actually knows the names of the people you work with, that's it, you've turned him, he's a turtle belly up in the sun.

LIL
I'm just alone so much.

SIS

This guy, this Ukraine hoodie guy, he won't solve that. He's temporary like rain. I can get by on that because, well, there's nothing inside me, there's an echo and that's it and you can fill an echo but you can't hold it or keep it or get it to visit your parents.

LIL

I'm not in control. I'd rather be in control.

SIS

But we're not the same, Lil, we're built different with different parts. What works for me doesn't work for you. Our sicknesses are separate so I feel bad prescribing the wrong medicine cause it could kill you.

LIL

I'm a grown woman.

SIS

No you're not cause if you were you wouldn't need to say it. As soon as you proclaim something it becomes false, believe me, I know, I say all sorts of shit to all sorts of people and they know, they know I'm lying about being sober and compassionate because if I need to convince someone I'm sober and compassionate I'd do it, not say it. You're a good girl.

LIL

No.

SIS

You're wearing a university sweater. You shop organic and buy baby magazines.

LIL

I'm like everyone else.

SIS

Yeah, and that's fucking sad and depressing. Another stroller mom ornamenting the street. You're so calm, why are you always so calm?

LIL

Am I calm?

SIS

Dead. You get married and suddenly you're someone else.

LIL
I live a domestic lifestyle.

SIS
Naw, it's something else, you don't want to say it but it's there. It's something bad, right? I can tell by that face, you make that distant face. You're afraid.

LIL
No.

SIS
You're afraid, Lil.

LIL
You don't know what's in my head, Sis.

SIS
I know it enough. We came from the same hole. I just turned out yang. See, that's the separation between us. You think bad things but you don't do anything about it. You want to be a nasty person because it feels good, for a time, it feels great to cut yourself open and play with the wound. But you know if you open up that cut you won't be able to close it so you revolve the thought in your head and in the mean time you're getting a great deal with your cellular provider. You're really happy about your voting choices. You're saving up to vacation in the Caribbean because you heard about this great place that's only sixty dollars a night and ignore the locals who look at you sideways because in your heart you're a decent person. Jesus, I must look like shit, do I look like shit?

LIL
No.

SIS
I feel like I look like shit. You got a mirror or something?

LIL
I broke all the mirrors.

SIS
Dramatic.

LIL
I was sitting around and I broke them.

SIS
Why?

LIL
Bri left for work. I made myself some eggs. The sun was very bright.

LIL
There were all these mirrors we bought. They kept blinding me. The reflection of the sun. I thought it was getting in my eyes. The light. Like my eyes were storing up this painful light. I smashed the mirrors. I put sheets over the windows.

SIS
You need a hobby.

LIL
I have one.

SIS
Knitting paves the pathway to madness.

LIL
I made you something.

(LIL *pulls out knitted white hat with pink bunny ears.*)

SIS
My point exactly.

LIL
You don't like it?

SIS
It's nice. You're nice.

LIL
Try it for the fit.

SIS
Does it go like this?

LIL
Like this.

SIS
Mmm. Comfy.

LIL
You look great.

SIS
I'll take your word.

LIL
No, you look beautiful.

SIS
Look at my nose.

LIL
Oh, that's funny.

SIS
My little bunny nose.

LIL
That's amazing your nose can do that.

SIS
Hold off the awards.

LIL
I love bunny noses. Bunny noses always sniff. Even when they're sleeping.

SIS
Bunnies are stupid rodents.

LIL
Bunnies are smart.

SIS
Bunnies are stupid then you eat them.

LIL
The bunnies we had were pretty smart. They knew when bad weather was
coming. Remember? Dad kept them out back. He wouldn't let us name them.

(MORE)

LIL (cont.)
When you give something a name you can't kill it. So it was Number Twenty
Three. Sixty-Two. But if you said it right, if you said their names with
sweetness, they'd respond. How are you today, Thirty-Two? Enjoying the
weather? And if it was nice out she'd come up to your finger and nibble. But if
there was a storm, she'd shake. Shiver in the corner of her cage.

SIS
Ah, memories.

LIL
I thought they laid eggs. This was before I knew about, well, how things were
with things that make other things. Nine got sick. Dad said she'd be fine. I
saved food and fed her. I thought she was getting better. Her stomach got so
big. And then one day her stomach was back to normal. But she was frantic.
She ran from one end of the cage to the other, banging her body against the
meshed metal. What's wrong, Nine? It was her children. She birthed her
children and they fell through the spaces between the metal wire. They were in
the feces, down below, this mound of little pellets. These gray things. They
looked like little seals, writhing and gasping and their faces all muddy. I buried
them. I could have saved them. But I shoveled them under the shit.

       (Beat.)

SIS
So it's, what, two months now?

LIL
Three.

SIS
You're not showing any signs.

LIL
No.

SIS
Can you feel it yet?

LIL
No.

SIS
Isn't it supposed to be moving by now?

LIL
Yes.

SIS
But it's there?

LIL
That's what the doctor says.

SIS
Suck.

LIL
I can't get around it. I can't imagine this thing right here. I suppose it will be nice.

SIS
Yeah, man, I don't know, I've seen the videos of it happening, like, gushing blood and the mother dumping feces all over the place.

LIL
Really?

SIS
You birth a turd with the baby. Sort of oddly metaphoric.

LIL
What do you mean?

SIS
Ah, you know, depressing shit I don't really mean but say anyway. How long did this hat take?

LIL
Three months. Do you like it?

SIS
It's fucking gaudy. It's terrible. You wasted your time. I'll never wear it again. I'll smile and say I love it. But next time I puke I'll clean the floors with this hat.

LIL
That's nice.

SIS
I puke a lot. Comes with the territory. Deviants can't stomach much. They can't hold anything inside. Better to be empty and ready.

LIL
You could change.

SIS
Change what?

LIL
Your life.

SIS
Did I say I was unhappy?

LIL
Aren't you?

SIS
I'm here. That will have to do.

LIL
I always had this vision that some day life would straighten itself out. But that never happens, does it?

SIS
No. It wouldn't be any fun. Death straightens us out in the end. Lies us cold and content in the hot ground.

      (SIS hands LIL a scrap of paper.)

LIL
What's this?

SIS
His number. Don't call after ten.

LIL
Why not?

SIS
I don't fucking know, it's just what he told me.

LIL
What do I say?

SIS
What do you feel like saying?

LIL
What did you say?

SIS
I told him about my whiskers. About my hot white fur. I told him I had big ears and my ears loved to be stroked. I told him I'd shit my babies in the ground.

LIL
Bri can't know.

SIS
Bri won't know and if he did he wouldn't say anything. You're safe. You know, the kid. You've got a mortgage. He wouldn't want to fuck that up.

LIL
Thank you.

SIS
Fuck off with your thank you.

LIL
I suppose you want some pills.

SIS
Of course I want some pills, why do you think I'm here? The conversation?

LIL
Bri got me these yesterday.

SIS
So your husband, like, he makes you take drugs?

LIL
They're not drugs. They're good drugs. They fight the depression I developed
as a young woman. Bri's worried about me and the baby but mostly the baby
because it's living off me and I used to take a lot of drugs so I might deform the
baby, I wasn't thinking, I wasn't thinking when I was young about the future
and now I'm feeling the negative mental and physical repercussions.

SIS
That's not your voice. That's someone else.

LIL
I've been reading a book about drug addicts for former or current drug addicts.

SIS
You weren't a drug addict. You were young. That's like the same.

LIL
I love Bri and I'm doing it for him because he loves me.

SIS
Yeah, save it for the Judge. I talk with everyone, like the family and mom and
shit, mom asks how you're doing, you never return calls, not since you got
pregnant, and I get to lie to mom and say you're fine. What's the matter with
you, anyway?

LIL
I need time.

SIS
What does that mean?

LIL
Those were the first words that came into my head.

SIS
Whatev, bro.

LIL
You shouldn't take these all at once.

   (SIS takes them all at once.)

SIS
Well, see you in a couple days.

LIL
Where are you going?

SIS
Stroll around a bit. Wait for these to take over.

LIL
Be careful.

SIS
I won't.

LIL
I love you, Sis.

SIS
What did you really want to say?

LIL
I hate you.

SIS
And?

LIL
You sicken me you fucking piece of shit I want to kill you, I want to fucking stab your neck you bitch fucking bitch fuck you!

SIS
There. You're learning.

2.

(A park.)

BRI
That's not how a story goes. No one will want to listen to that story. But he didn't listen. So I said it again and again. This story won't work. There are a million stories but this isn't one of them. Stories have to show people something. And there has to be hope. Every great work of literature has hope.
(MORE)

BRI (cont.)
And I gave him examples. Shakespeare. The Greeks. Even the Greeks had
hope. And he says, This is a different time. There isn't any hope anymore. We
can't coddle people with stupid optimism anymore. He actually said stupid
optimism.

LIL
Look at that hot dog stand.

BRI
What about it?

LIL
It's nice.

BRI
Do you want one?

LIL
No.

BRI
I'll buy you one.

LIL
I don't want a hot dog.

BRI
Then why are we looking at it?

LIL
I don't know.

BRI
Why would you say look at that if you don't want it?

LIL
I just thought it looked nice.

BRI
You're impossible today.

LIL
I'm sorry.

BRI
Are you feeling all right? Do you want to go back?

LIL
I like walking.

BRI
But you're not feeling good.

LIL
I'm fine with walking.

BRI
It's too cold out. Is it too cold for you?

LIL
I like it like this.

BRI
But you'll get sick.

LIL
Do you want to go back?

BRI
No, I asked you if you did. You always turn things around on me.

LIL
I'm sorry.

BRI
I'm trying to work with you, Lil.

LIL
I appreciate your patience.

BRI
It's hard doing this all by myself.

LIL
I know.

BRI
I thought it would be nice to go away.

LIL
You're going away?

BRI
No, the both of us. Go away somewhere.

LIL
Where?

BRI
Someplace warm.

LIL
Like Jamaica.

BRI
No, not Jamaica. Why would you say Jamaica?

LIL
Jamaica's warm.

BRI
Are you smoking drugs again?

LIL
No.

BRI
Drugs got you here.

LIL
It wasn't that.

BRI
Drugs put holes in your brain. We're not going to Jamaica so you can smoke drugs. Did you take your pills?

LIL
Yes.

BRI
They're good for you.

LIL
I know.

BRI
I was thinking more like the Dominican Republic.

LIL
Sure.

BRI
They have this great festival for the dead. Like Mardi Gras. We can make masks.

LIL
That sounds fun.

BRI
You don't want to go?

LIL
I said it sounds fun.

BRI
But not with that tone. That tone says I don't want to go.

LIL
But I said I did.

BRI
You're always lying to me.

LIL
I wasn't lying.

BRI
It's okay. I can just tell.

LIL
I'm sorry, Bri.

(Beat.)

LIL
I made something for you.

BRI
What is it?

LIL
It'll fit this time.

BRI
What is it?

(*LIL fits a gray knit cougar cap on BRI's head.*)

LIL
It's a cougar.

BRI
I see.

LIL
Is it okay?

BRI
It's fine.

LIL
You look nice.

BRI
I don't look anything, okay? I'm a grown man.

LIL
You're right, Bri.

(*Beat.*)

LIL
Look at that man.

BRI
What man? There's a man?

LIL
That man on that bench.

BRI
That's a garbage bag. No, wait, it moved.

LIL
He's wearing that black garbage bag.

BRI
How do you think he got there?

LIL
To the bench?

BRI
How he got homeless.

LIL
One thing happens after another I suppose.

BRI
Probably drugs. He probably did a lot of drugs. And look at him now. Sitting there under a garbage bag. He probably slept outside last night. He probably hasn't had a hot meal in days. When I get to that place, remind me to kill myself. We're paying for him, you know? He lives off of us. The government pays him to sit there and take drugs. Like it was a job. You hear about guys beating up homeless guys and I can see why they do it. I could probably work myself up and kill a homeless person. I could do that. Show him what life is all about by killing him.

LIL
He's sleeping.

BRI
What?

LIL
I just noticed that he was sleeping.

BRI
Why? Why would you notice that?

LIL
It's something I saw and said out loud.

BRI
Where are you going with this?

LIL
Nowhere, I was just –

BRI
Are you freaking out again?

LIL
No, Bri. I'm very calm.

BRI
You're not acting calm. If you were acting calm you would be like this. You'd be like me. See, this is calm. Not that. Not that thing on your face. Not that face you're making.

LIL
It's very pleasant out.

BRI
Then why aren't you happy?

LIL
I'm fine, Bri. I'm super.

BRI
I just want you to be happy.

LIL
I appreciate that you care for me.

     (Beat.)

LIL
Would you leave me alone for a moment?

BRI
What?

LIL
I need to be by myself for a minute or two.

BRI
I'm not going to leave you by yourself in the park so you can be raped by
strangers.

LIL
I'm going to have to stop speaking soon, Bri.

BRI
I'll sit with you.

LIL
Bri –

BRI
I won't say anything.

>   *(They sit in silence.)*

LIL
Do you hear that music?

BRI
No.

LIL
There's music.

BRI
I don't hear music.

LIL
Listen.

>   *(They listen for a while. There is no music.)*

BRI
I don't hear anything.

>   *(LIL hums tune she thinks she hears. After a few bars:)*

BRI
What are you humming?

LIL
The song I hear.

BRI
There isn't anything there.

LIL
It's gone now.

BRI
It wasn't even there. It wasn't ever there.

LIL
It was like a band. Like a marching band. They were playing the national anthem. Not our national anthem. An anthem from another country. Like a Middle Eastern country. There were all these exotic instruments. And it was like I was there. In the country. For a second I was in another country but I was right here too, I was here and there at the same time. And it was warm there. Like Morocco. I went to there once. Morocco. I took a boat from France. I didn't speak whatever language they were speaking. I smiled a lot. People came up to me and I gave them money like a Queen. And I was in this city, this winding city and the buildings were all tight and tan. It was a national holiday and people were shooting guns in the streets. But it was fun. Not violent. It was violent and fun at the same time. Both things at once. And there were marching bands all over the place. All playing the same national anthem. These red soldiers passed, soldiers in bright red uniforms, marching past, each with their own exotic instrument. I followed them through the streets. I walked behind them and closed my eyes and let sound guide me. And it was like I wasn't there. The only thing left was sound, this beautiful sound carrying me through space. But when I opened up my eyes I was in a deserted part of town. And the band members were breaking for the hills. And I didn't know my way around, I didn't speak the language, and it was getting dark, and there were these men in the shadows and I could see their knives glinting in the dark, reflecting the sunlight but it was dark so it must have been the moon but I remember it being day too, it was day and night at the same time.

BRI
You never went to Morocco.

LIL
I just never told you.

BRI
You've never been out of this country.

LIL
Yes I have.

BRI
You've never been on a plane. You're scared of flying.

LIL
I'm not scared.

BRI
You never go outside. This is the first time in months.

LIL
I go places, Bri.

BRI
Oh yeah? Where do you go?

LIL
Just places. Different places.

   (Beat.)

LIL
What are you thinking about?

BRI
God, Lil, every time I'm lost in thought you have to go ask me that.

LIL
I'm sorry.

BRI
I'm thinking about why you would ask me what I'm thinking.

LIL
You seemed some place else.

BRI
I was thinking about the kid.

LIL
What kid?

BRI
The child, our child in your stomach.

LIL
My uterus?

BRI
Yeah, your *uterus*. I wonder if he's going to be happy.

LIL
She.

BRI
What?

LIL
It's a girl.

BRI
How do you know?

LIL
It feels like a girl.

BRI
But you don't know for sure. You have no way of really knowing.

LIL
No, I just have feelings.

BRI
It's a boy. It should be a boy. I want a boy. A boy is better, don't you think?

LIL
I'm happy that you have expressed your desire.

BRI
But you want a boy, right?

LIL
I'd prefer not to speak at this point.

BRI
Just say it. Say it. Say you want a boy.

LIL
No, Bri.

BRI
You just have to tell me what you want. You want a boy. You want a boy.

LIL
I want a boy.

BRI
See, that wasn't hard.

(BRI *kisses LIL on forehead.*)

LIL
Ow.

BRI
Ow?

LIL
That hurt.

BRI
That didn't, how could that hurt?

LIL
Your beard, you're growing these spiky hairs.

BRI
You love my beard.

LIL
That's right.

BRI
You've changed your mind?

LIL
I was temporarily confused and I am sorry to have included you in the
confusion that was solely generated from me.

BRI
Oh, is that like one of those sentences from your book? One of those
sentences of reparation. "I'm sorry that I hurt you in the past because I love
and value the time you spent with me when I was damaging my mind and spirit
and I apologize for the grief I caused you because I love and value our
friendship?" I can't stand this anymore. Just tell me things plain. I can't have
these conflicted emotions. You tell me one thing then you tell me another. If
you change your feelings I need to know right away. It's like I don't know what
to believe anymore because you're my moral foundation in life and you're
always shifting. My beard doesn't hurt.

        (LIL punches herself in the face, hard.)

BRI
What are you –

        (She punches herself three more times. BRI restrains her.)

BRI
People are watching.

LIL
I'm very dizzy.

BRI
You need to calm down because people can see how you're acting.

LIL
I think my nose broke.

BRI
What if we saw someone we knew? Huh? Beating yourself in the face. What
would they think? Do you think they would think we're happy? Your nose is
bleeding.

LIL
I'm going to sit down and can you get a napkin, I have napkins in my purse.

BRI
I can't do things like that. Rummaging in your purse. Here's your purse, get it yourself.

LIL
Thank you.

BRI
What's this?

(BRI *picks up a scrap of paper that has fallen from her purse.*)

LIL
I don't know.

BRI
It came from your purse, what is it?

LIL
What does it say?

BRI
It's a number. There's a number here, I don't know this number.

LIL
I don't know how it got there.

BRI
But there's a number here. Why is there a number? There's a scrap of paper with a number on it in your purse, why? Why?

LIL
It was Sis.

BRI
What did Sis do? What's she doing putting numbers in your purse?

LIL
A back specialist.

BRI
Like, a specialist for your back?

LIL
My back hurts from the baby and I need a specialist and she knew one and wrote down that number.

BRI
Should I call it? I got my cell right here, I'll call it on my cell and we'll see, right?

LIL
Go ahead, Bri.

BRI
No, I'm not going to do anything you say. You've lost your rights. Your right to privacy. Your privacy is mine now. I'll be there even when I'm not there. I'll follow you. You won't even know I'm following you. It'll just happen. One day I'll creep up on you and grab your shoulder. I'll be right behind you, always. Because I'm more powerful than you. So just sit there and bleed. No one's going to help you. It's all your fault. Why am I still wearing this?

> *(BRI removes the knit cougar cap.)*

BRI
I was telling a story about that guy. Where was I?

LIL
Stupid optimism.

BRI
Yeah, he calls optimism stupid. And I tell him I don't know what business you're in, but I'm in the business of entertainment. People don't go out to feel bad, they go out to have a good time. So here's the bottom line. Your characters are monsters. No one can relate to them. And he goes, that's sad. And I go, well, that's simply how it is. And then he goes off about using characters to express a deeper psychological complexity about human suffering in this modern technological age where the loss of religion and emotional instability have caused too many options and that we no longer have contact with wisdom and blah blah blah. I stop him. Look. We think you're very talented but you'll never go anywhere if you can't have hope.

3.

(Another apartment.)

SIS
I woke up feeling like shit, and I mean, shit, like *shit* shit. Like four in the morning. I poured myself a glass of wine, like a big glass in a mug I got from the Olympic Games. I smoked a couple joints, like three or two and went for a walk. But I got a couple steps outside and I'm like, nope, no, not today, you're staying inside today so I went back and smoked a couple more joints and ate a salad. Somewhere in there I jerked off. And I was crying, you know, and I'm like: odd. I'm crying because it feels so good but simultaneously depressing cause when I come that'll be it. Back to *feeling* again. But I come and it sort of sucks so I wipe up and stare out the window at this pack of blackbirds flying in unison over a skyscraper.

BRI
Flock.

SIS
Flock?

BRI
It's flock of birds.

SIS
Thanks, English Major.

BRI
I'm sorry. Go on.

SIS
I was done. You want a drink?

BRI
It's three.

SIS
Yeah, shouldn't you be at work, *Bri*?

BRI
I took the day off.

(Beat.)

BRI
Nice apartment.

SIS
I don't know why you would even bother to say that, I mean, you can obviously
see that it's obviously not nice so you don't have to patronize me with your
behavior.

BRI
I'm sorry.

SIS
Where's your wife? Where's my *sister?*

BRI
At the doctor's deciding the sex of the baby.

SIS
She didn't want to know.

BRI
She changed her mind.

SIS
Shouldn't you be with her?

BRI
She wanted to go alone.

SIS
Did she say that?

BRI
No, but I'm her husband. I know what she's feeling even when she doesn't say
it.

SIS
Are you sure?

BRI
Where you going with this?

SIS
I'm just interrogating you, Bri. A little harmless interrogation. I'll bring out the
mask in a little bit.

BRI
What mask?

SIS
My black interrogation mask. I'll slip it over your head. I'll shut off the lights.
I'll tie your hands to a chair and push your face in a bucket of water. You'll talk.

BRI
What do you mean?

SIS
I mean, fuck, have a little imagination, huh?

(She downs a glass of wine and lights a joint, all in one breath.)

SIS
There's this philosophy guy I see time to time. Of course I fuck him and he's
not that good but the conversation's always satisfying. He goes off about the
lack of imagination. Like, there's some quantifiable equation he's coming up
with to chart the loss of imagination over the history of humankind. I don't
know how you'd chart something like that, but then again I'm no philosopher, I
just wake up and stare in the distance, you know? Think about my day without
adding any essays to it. Apparently we've got this date next week, this
philosopher and I, and he's going to bring over the chart. People had more
imagination in the past, apparently, like when there were less people and this
theory is that human beings have a fixed amount of imagination that doesn't
grow with the population. So as more assholes have more asshole kids, the
thinner our collective imagination becomes. We dream less. We get stupid.
What do you think about that?

BRI
I don't know.

SIS
See what I mean?

BRI
No.

SIS
Why are you really here, Bri?

BRI
I thought I'd come for a visit.

SIS
You don't do that, Bri, I mean you've never done that, never, so don't play it off like this is every day, Bri.

BRI
The back specialist.

SIS
Why do you say that, back specialist, I mean, what the fuck do those words even mean?

BRI
You gave my wife, your sister, a number for a back specialist.

SIS
I did no such thing.

BRI
I called. It was this Czechoslovakian guy. He didn't know anything about backs.

SIS
He's Ukrainian.

BRI
He sounded like a Czech.

SIS
His accent passes like clouds.

BRI
So?

SIS
So?

BRI
So why did you do that?

SIS
I'm going to let you do a little thinking before I answer that, Bri. There's some dots and you should put them together and see the design in your head.

BRI
He's not a back specialist.

SIS
Ding.

BRI
He's someone else.

SIS
Warmer.

BRI
Who is he?

SIS
He's a friend of mine.

BRI
What does he do?

SIS
You'll have to ask him that yourself.

BRI
He said not to call, men shouldn't call him he said.

SIS
Then you're going to be tortured by the possibilities. Sucks, huh?

(SIS inhales smoke, blows it in Bri's direction. Then:)

SIS
You want some?

BRI
I don't smoke pot because I hate drugs.

SIS
Yes, Officer.

BRI
Drugs destroy everything.

SIS
Yeah, but they're pretty fucking fun. And who wants to be old, right?

BRI
I want to grow old with my children.

SIS
On what planet? Your children are going to be living underground eating dirt.
Nice future.

BRI
You don't have any hope in your heart.

SIS
Fuck no. Hope is the next step to misery because if you think everything's
going to be all right I got a couple pictures of some glaciers to show you.

BRI
You've given up.

SIS
You say that like it's a bad thing.

BRI
So what keeps you alive?

SIS
I'm here. That's about all I can say. I tried to do it once. You know, tried to
off myself but it just wasn't right. I don't think I did it right, well, obviously
yeah because I'm talking to you I didn't do it right.

BRI
How did you do it?

SIS
Gas oven. It was just fucking boring. My knees got all sore and natural gas just
(MORE)

SIS (cont.)
smells awful, like really sharp farts, but kind of narcotic too so instead of killing myself I just got really high. It was like with whippets. Did you ever do whippets?

BRI
What's whippets?

SIS
You crack open a Nitrous Oxide container into a balloon and suck in the gas. The world goes dark for five seconds and you hear bells, these beautiful bells chiming. It doesn't last very long, which is the sad part, because for those few moments you're nowhere and it's very extraordinarily gorgeous.

BRI
That sounds like an actual hell.

SIS
When a girl needs to go away, she does it hard.

BRI
Why did you want to go away?

SIS
A couple of stupid things, just a couple things in my life that were going in circles and I couldn't seem to shake them. There was a man at one point but he exited. I don't really remember why now, I don't remember the reasons, really, just a lot of yelling in stairwells because the past is pretty blurry after all this time. This man.

    (Beat.)

SIS
Nice sweater.

BRI
Do you like it?

SIS
No, man, it's got the name of your college and you're, like, not in college anymore.

BRI
Communications.

SIS
What?

BRI
That was my major.

SIS
Like, Communications?

BRI
Yeah.

SIS
Isn't that, like, everything? Isn't everything you study Communications?

BRI
I never thought about it like that.

SIS
I'm a pretty smart girl. Could have saved yourself some money if you knew me then.

BRI
What do you mean?

SIS
I'm a pretty cheap date. Not even cheap, you know, money doesn't even come into the equation with me and dating. I don't care where. Taxi cab, elevator shaft. It's all the same.

BRI
You dating anyone now?

SIS
I'm dating many people simultaneously. And again, dating. Not a word that accurately describes what I do. More like baseball. I run from bag to bag.

BRI
We're the same.

SIS
I don't know about that, Bri. You're not a batter. You're a golfer. You walk to the hole.

BRI
What do you mean?

SIS
You say that a lot, you ask what I mean when you know already.

BRI
You're right. I understand you. I've been where you're at.

SIS
And where's that?

BRI
Lost. I was lost. But it didn't feel all that bad. And I kept my life going. I maintained healthy relationships while pursuing unhealthy relationships. I had girlfriends. Lots of girlfriends. Girlfriends in all parts of the city. But I didn't have much time. I divided my time between all of them. So no one was really satisfied. Except me. If I didn't like the tits on one girl I'd get good tits on another. This one's ass sags. This one has hairy nipples. And I thought if I could combine them all, it would be perfect. Assemble all the parts of all the women into one great big whore.

SIS
Hey there, Frankenstein.

BRI
I can't say these things to her.

SIS
No. She's your wife. The wedding vow nullifies honesty.

BRI
But you like it, right? You like it when I talk to you.

SIS
I can't say I prefer you one way or the other. You're here. I'm here. That's it.

BRI
I try to flip her over and she starts crying. Do you let people do that? Do you let people flip you over?

SIS
I'm a street, Bri. You can walk on me any way you want.

BRI
Oh yeah?

SIS
Just no loitering.

BRI
You do this with your friend? The guy with the number?

SIS
Sure, of course, but he's not my friend, he's just a guy. I don't do male friends. That never works. You always end up fucking them when you're weak and then you're yelling on some bridge and you have no clue how you got there, but there you are. So yeah, he comes over, this guy comes over.

BRI
What do you do?

SIS
I'm a lady and ladies don't tell you things about their private sexual lives because it's my private sexual life.

BRI
I just want to get some ideas.

SIS
Some ideas?

BRI
For Lil and I.

SIS
What does Lil do?

BRI
Not much.

SIS
That doesn't sound encouraging.

BRI
Now I can't do anything. She rolls over and I'm staring at the ceiling. I want to punch her. Right in the neck. Wake the fuck up. I pay for all this.

SIS
She took up knitting instead.

BRI
Christ, don't talk to me about that. She calls and I'm in conferences with extremely important people and she wants me to fetch some yarn.

SIS
Did you see mine?

BRI
Your what?

> (SIS *fits the knit bunny cap on her head.*)

SIS
Cute, huh?

BRI
She made me one too.

SIS
Oh yeah? Did you bring it?

BRI
I think I may have it somewhere.

SIS
Put it on.

> (BRI *pulls the knit cougar cap from his coat, fits it to his head.*)

SIS
What is that like a cat?

BRI
A cougar.

SIS
Oh, that's very cute.

BRI
Yeah.

SIS
You look very cute. I don't remember telling anyone that before but there it is, my mouth said it.

BRI
Grr.

SIS
That's funny.

BRI
Grrr!

SIS
"Oh please Mister Cougar don't bite me!"

BRI
"I will bite you!"

SIS
"No, please!"

BRI
"I'm biting you!"

SIS
This is weird.

BRI
Yes.

SIS
We should probably, like, stop, we should stop this.

BRI
Yes.

SIS
Out of respect, you know, because I break a lot of things in my life but some things, you know, I can't do, Bri, I can't do some things because some things are still sanctified because once you got religion in you it never goes away, like a
                                                                        (MORE)

SIS (cont.)
cough, religion's like a coughing sickness so even though you'd like to think you
can do some things some things you can't do, I was raised Catholic, we were
raised Catholic, Lil and I, your wife and I, did you know your wife was Catholic?

BRI
Yes.

SIS
I was supposed to be her, I mean, that was the plan and all, our lives were
supposed to be the same. Did you know that? Little variations, sure, we'd have
different houses and different interests and husbands, different husbands
because I was engaged once but he said choose so I chose this, I chose to be
like this instead of be with him. That's how it goes, right?

   (Beat.)

SIS
Do you want to play a game?

BRI
What kind of game?

SIS
A game between you and me. A game two people can play when they have
nothing else to do.

BRI
Sure.

SIS
Good. I mean, if you're up for it. If you're up to play with me.

BRI
Sure.

SIS
Okay. You got a hanky?

BRI
I do, as a matter of fact.

SIS
Classic man. I like that.

(SIS takes the handkerchief from BRI.)

SIS
I don't ever think I've been alone with you in a room.

BRI
No?

SIS
What's it like?

BRI
What's what like?

SIS
Not having an identity.

BRI
I've got an identity.

SIS
Not in this room you don't. You are who you are because the people around you. No one's around you. And I don't know you very well. So who are you now?

BRI
I'm Bri. I've got a wife. She's your sister.

SIS
She's not in this room. She might show up one day and change that. You'll say things you don't mean. You won't even know you're saying them. But there's this force pulling you outside yourself. The more time she's in your space, the more she pulls you from that other self. So you have to be willing accept that. You might never see this you again. This might already be the past.

BRI
I think I could be okay with that.

SIS
I just wanted to warn you in case someone got hurt.

(She pulls out a large kitchen knife.)

SIS
Now. Take this knife from my hand.

BRI
You want me to steal that knife?

SIS
I want you to try.

> (BRI *tries to take the knife. SIS dodges him. At first, this is very playful. But BRI soon becomes angry. He leaps at her, snarling. Finally, he catches her and pins her on the ground. She stabs him in the thigh.*)

BRI
Oh god oh god oh god.

SIS
You win.

BRI
It hurts I mean it really hurts.

SIS
This is the fun part.

> (SIS *slides BRI's pants down. She dabs the wound with the handkerchief.*)

SIS
There's a lot of blood.

BRI
I know.

SIS
Did you want me to suck some of it out?

BRI
Like – ?

SIS
Suck some of it out?

BRI
Like – ?

SIS
Suck some of it out?

(*SIS sucks the wound, during which:*)

BRI
That would be okay. That would be all right with me. If you wanted to do that,
it would be fine. I have no objections to you doing that. That thing you're
doing is very good, I like that thing you're doing and I will not put up any
barriers to you doing that.

(*SIS rolls over. Hikes up her skirt.*)

SIS
All yours, slugger.

BRI
Thank you.

SIS
Thank me later.

(*She pushes her ass back and fucks him.*)

BRI
Oh God.

SIS
There you are.

BRI
Oh my God, oh my God.

SIS
Stay with me now.

BRI	SIS
Baton Rouge, Louisiana then Indianapolis, Indiana and Columbus is the capital of Ohio then there's Montgomery, Alabama south of	There you are.
(MORE)	(MORE)

BRI (cont.)
Helena, Montana then Denver, Colorado under Boise, Idaho and Texas has Austin then we go north to Massachusetts, Boston and Albany, New York then Tallahassee, Florida and Washington, D.C. and Santa Fe, New Mexico and Nashville, Tennessee and Trenton's in New Jersey north of Jefferson, Missouri then Richmond in Virginia, South Dakota has Pierre, Harrisburg's in Pennsylvania and Augusta's up in Maine and here is Providence, Rhode Island next to Dover, Delaware then Concord, New Hampshire, just a quick jaunt to Montpelier which is up in Vermont Hartford's in Connecticut, so pretty in the fall, and Kansas has Topeka, Minnesota has St. Paul, Juneau's in Alaska and there's Lincoln in Nebraska and it's Raleigh out in North Carolina and then there's Madison, Wisconsin and Olympia in Washington then Phoenix, Arizona and Lansing, Michigan and here's Honolulu, Hawaii's a joy, and Jackson, Mississippi and Springfield, Illinois and South Carolina with Columbia down the way and Annapolis in Maryland on the Chesapeake Bay then Salem in Oregon and from there we join Little Rock in Arkansas, Iowa's got Des Moines. Sacramento, California and on to Oklahoma and its city Charleston, West Virginia and Nevada, Carson City and Atlanta's down in Georgia and there's Bismarck, North Dakota and you can live in Frankfort in your old Kentucky home and Cheyenne is in Wyoming and perhaps you make your home in Salt Lake City out in Utah where the buffalo roam.

SIS (cont.)
There's a nice boy.
Stay with me now.

Stay with me here.
That's a nice boy.

There you are.
Stay with me now.

Stay with me here.
That's a nice boy.
There you are.
Stay with me here.
Stay with me now.
There you are.

Stay with me here.

That's a nice boy.
There you are.
There you are.
Stay with me now.

There you are.

Stay with me here.
That's a nice boy.
There you are.
Stay with me here.
Stay with me now.
That's a nice boy.
There you are.
Stay with me now.
Stay with me here.
There you are.
You're there.
You're right there.
You're right here.

4.

(A hotel room. <u>Note</u>: GRIG has no accent.)

LIL
I have the ice. I put the ice in a plastic bag and I'm setting it right here. Is that okay?

GRIG
Yes.

LIL
Do you want anything?

GRIG
No.

LIL
There's a mini-bar. We have soda pop. Cans of soda pop and milk. If you wanted OJ you could have OJ or pineapple juice. There's beer and wine but I suppose it's too early so you could have coffee or tea. We have both things or maybe just water, you want some water?

GRIG
No.

LIL
I'm going to have water. Is it all right if I have water?

GRIG
Yes.

LIL
I can't place your accent. Sis said you have an accent, like some kind of Russian accent but I can't really tell. Do you know where you're from?

GRIG
Yes.

LIL
That's good. That's great. It's a wonderful thing to know where you're from.
(MORE)

LIL (cont.)
I'm from the West. I grew up among trees. But there aren't any trees here.
Everywhere you look there's buildings and more buildings. I went up on the
roof at my own apartment and looked in every direction. Everything I saw was
made by man. Except the sky, but that's full of airplanes all the time, even at
night, you see these blinking UFOs cross the stars. Do you have trees where
you're from?

GRIG
Yes.

LIL
Are they beautiful?

GRIG
No.

LIL
That's sad to hear. It's sad that places don't have beautiful trees because they
make everything nicer, don't you think? I just think of the future and there
were trees in the past but very few in the present. We might be alive to see it.
The last living tree. It might happen in our lifetime. That will be a sad day but
also ennobling because then we'll realize all these grave mistakes we're making.
I'm not very optimistic about the future. But I have a baby now, a baby on the
way so I have to buck up and get happy about everything. Did you see I was
pregnant?

GRIG
Yes.

LIL
We're very happy. Are you married?

GRIG
No.

LIL
Well, you should find yourself a lovely lady one day and settle down. It's
worked wonders for my life. Wonders. You're never complete until you've
sacrificed your life with someone else. It's a lovely institution. What I like is
that we think the same things. Our thoughts are exactly the same, my husband
and I. He's not home right now. He's away right now. He's away on business,
some business conference and he's gone. This ring, did you see this ring?

GRIG
Yes.

LIL
It's a symbol of our love. We protect each other, like the line from that one
poet, that German poet who wrote letters to that beginning poet telling him all
about life. Somewhere in there he says love is protecting each other's solitude.
And that's what Bri does. He protects my solitude. He leaves me alone. He
leaves me at home. He left me home so I thought I'd call you and come here to
this hotel room with you so you could keep me company. It's good to have
company, right? It's very healthy. I'm just protecting my health with including
you in my company. It's harmless, don't you think it's harmless?

GRIG
Yes.

LIL
I'm glad you agree with me. I should thank you for agreeing with me. It's been
so long since someone did that, since someone listened to me and agreed with
what I was saying. You're a good listener. You had a good mother, I bet you
had a good kind mother who taught you how to treat a lady. Was your mother
good?

GRIG
No.

LIL
That's sad to hear. I'm mainly thinking about myself here of course if you
excuse me. Excuse me if I'm a little selfish and think about myself when I
should be thinking about your mother, I'm just worried about this baby, I know
it doesn't look like I'm pregnant but I am. Six months now. I still don't feel
anything and there's not much there but I have hope. Please go on. You were
saying something. Right? Weren't you saying something?

GRIG
No.

LIL
I could have sworn you were speaking just now. I tend to imagine things that
may or may not have happened. It's a problem. Well, to be perfectly honest
I'm perfectly okay with it but some people in my life don't like it so much so I
usually don't say anything or I say something I don't mean like something nice

(MORE)

LIL (cont.)
that I don't mean when really there's this other thing just right on the corner of my mind, like a little gargoyle hanging over my thoughts, at least that's how I think about it, this snarling gargoyle spitting water on my brain. Does that ever happen to you?

GRIG
No.

LIL
It must just be me then. I must be making this all up. Do you ever do that? Imagine things that aren't there but seem like they are?

GRIG
No.

LIL
That's a shame. You're cheating yourself out of one of the greatest gifts human beings have to offer themselves. Imagination. Thought. You have thoughts, right? You think about things when you're over there staring at me, there's things happening in your head right now right as I'm saying this.

GRIG
Yes.

LIL
Oh good. For a minute there I thought, well, I don't know what I thought. Only robots don't think and I'm thinking, This guy's not a robot is he? Is he? Are you? You're not a robot are you?

GRIG
No.

LIL
But that would be funny, right? If you were. That would be really weird. I don't know what I would then. Did you bring anything? Did you bring anything for me to see?

(GRIG places small black case on table.)

LIL
What's in there?

GRIG
Look.

LIL
No, not yet, it doesn't seem right, I sort of jumped the gun. Ha. Jumped the gun. It's funny because ...

GRIG
Yes.

LIL
You know why it's funny. You seem like a smart person even though you don't say much. Do you want to say anything? Did you want to speak some words in my direction? You can say anything. You can tell me how your day was or what you ate earlier today. You can tell me about your parents or your last vacation, that would be nice to hear, or a girlfriend if you have a girlfriend or what you really want to do with your life. You can tell me about your brother or if you have a sister tell me about her or you could have lot of siblings and that could be an interesting story and then we could talk about what religion you are and if you're using a different religion than the one you were born with and what that might mean, you know, in an ontological sense. I'm just throwing out options here. Or did you want to ask me a question? You could ask me about my hair. I dye my hair blonde but I'm a brunette or maybe you don't care to know that. Maybe you want to hear about the apartment, how much the apartment costs and we could have an interesting discussion about the price of apartments because I always learn so much from that conversation. You're looking at my stomach, the baby, you want to know about the baby? We found out the sex the other day because he's that far along, he's got a penis now and he's not a girl and I didn't really want to find out because I like surprises and I wanted a girl. I shouldn't have said that. I take that back, can I take that back? Would you mind? Would you forget everything I just said?

GRIG
Yes.

LIL
Control X.

        (Beat.)

LIL
Do you want to start?

GRIG
Yes.

LIL
Just the back of the head and my back. Just my neck. The back of my neck is where you should –

(GRIG *punches LIL in the back of the neck, hard.*)

LIL
Okay, stars, that's okay, this has happened before, this has –

(GRIG *punches her neck again, harder.*)

LIL
Okay, that hurt a little more but it's fine, I think you may want to do it again but everything's fine, everything's –

(GRIG *punches her neck again, fiercely, knocking her to the floor.*)

LIL
I might, you know, I might need a minute or two can you prop me on something until this stops and maybe you could get me the ice? I could get it if you don't want to but is it all right if I collect myself and you can give me the ice?

(GRIG *presses ice bag to LIL's neck.*)

LIL
Thank you.

GRIG
Shh.

LIL
It's nice of you to hold that for me I don't think my arms really work that well now.

GRIG
Shhh. You will be fine.

LIL
It really, I know I asked you and everything but it really hurts.

GRIG
You will be fine. All you have to do is listen to my voice. Are you listening to my voice? Are you hearing my voice as it is speaking to you now? Nod your head yes if you hear my voice speaking to you, speaking in your ear and nowhere else.

(*LIL nods yes.*)

GRIG
My voice is the only thing. Close your eyes and listen to my voice. Just take a breath in the darkness and listen to my voice as I'm telling you these words. There is a door right in front of you. I don't want you to open it yet. I want you to look at it. I want you to look at the grains of wood running down the door. Now I want you to touch the door. It's cold, it feels cold. It's windy outside, you can hear the wind cutting cold into the door, cutting into the very fabric of the wooden door right in front of you as you listen to my voice, keep listening to my voice. You see a doorknob. Now you put your hand around the doorknob but don't open it yet because it feels smooth and cold in your hand but familiar, like an object you use all the time, a cold metal object you keep in your pocket, keep it in your pocket all the time, this cold metal object you use to solve problems, this other thing, this thing in your pocket which you can take out at any second and bring up to your face and solve all your problems. Open the door. What's the first thing you see?

LIL
I see her. She's waiting right there.

(*LIL opens her eyes.*)

LIL
Thank you. You're so nice. You're so nice to me. I don't have many people in my life this kind. Should I look now? Should I look in case there? I'll take a look.

(*LIL opens case, gazes inside.*)

LIL
That's beautiful. That's just beautiful. Thank you. This solves everything.

5.

(*A beach house. LIL watches the ocean, a scarf around her neck, faced away.*)

BRI
And as you know, I never actually finished college. Not finished finished. I didn't complete my last English requirement. We had to read books. 20th Century French literature. I didn't understand why we had to do that. They weren't talking about anything important. Just the past. The past isn't important. No one has any reason to care about the past because it's happened. It's no longer here. It has no bearing on how we live our lives right now. And now. And now. See what I mean?

LIL
Mmm hmm.

BRI
But the professor didn't agree of course. We were studying some French guy. We were reading one of his plays. I didn't understand it. I mean, I got what happened, technically. Some French people stuck in a room. I just didn't get *why* it was happening. And I told the professor it was total bullshit. I would love to be locked in a room with some French people. I love people period. I love spending time with them. And she quotes some line from Shakespeare, something like there are more things on earth than I can fit in my mind. Pretty much telling me I'm stupid. So I blow up in class. And she lets me have it. Saying things like I only processed information and didn't understand it and I didn't actually read books I just consumed them and lacked the ability to think critically about abstract concepts and finally I'm like, that's it. I am better than everybody in this room. So I went into the entertainment industry.

LIL
That's a nice story.

BRI
It's balmy in here and you're wearing a scarf.

LIL
Yes.

BRI
I can turn the fake fire down.

LIL
No.

BRI
Then take off that scarf. It's creepy, you wearing it in here.

(Beat.)

BRI
Do you like the ocean?

LIL
The ocean's fine.

BRI
Sure like staring at it.

(Beat.)

BRI
I was thinking we should move. The apartment's too small for three.

LIL
Yes.

BRI
We'll move to a bigger place.

LIL
That will be wonderful.

BRI
We could even get a room for your sister.

LIL
Okay, Bri.

BRI
Your sister needs a solid place to live. I can give her something solid. She could watch the baby.

LIL
That will be nice.

BRI
Just the four of us. Together. A rectangle of happiness.

(Beat.)

BRI
I called your back specialist.

LIL
Yes?

BRI
A while back.

LIL
That's nice.

BRI
He's sounds good. He sounds really good.

LIL
That's nice to hear.

BRI
I loved his accent.

LIL
His accent is very nice.

BRI
Are you going to see him again?

LIL
No. I got what I needed.

BRI
So your back doesn't hurt anymore?

LIL
Everything's fine now. I couldn't be happier.

     (Beat.)

LIL
You've developed a limp.

BRI
I hurt myself falling down a flight of stairs.

LIL
That makes sense.

BRI
Where did your sister go?

LIL
I can't see her anymore. She walked out to meet the waves but I lost track of her.

BRI
A bit chilly for swimming.

LIL
She'll be fine.

BRI
I'll go out and look for her.

LIL
She'll be fine.

BRI
I'll just head out and see where she's at.

LIL
Okay, Bri.

BRI
What do you mean by that?

LIL
I don't know, Bri.

BRI
You were jealous. There was a tone of jealousy.

LIL
That was not my intention.

BRI
Nothing's wrong, Lil.

LIL
I didn't say –

BRI
You know you can stop right there, okay? I don't want to start again. I'll stay here if it makes you happy. We'll wait for your sister here. Let's just have a nice vacation. A nice vacation with you and your sister.

LIL
That sounds fine, Bri.

BRI
Why are you talking like that?

LIL
How am I talking, Bri?

BRI
You're not lively, there's no life left in your voice.

LIL
I've always talked like this, Bri.

BRI
Quit saying my name like that. Don't keep saying my name at the end of all your sentences. I didn't do anything. Why do you think I did something? Jesus. Trying to get a little peace with you and your sister here at the ocean and you have to pull this all over again. Nothing's wrong.

LIL
I didn't say that it was.

BRI
You're just contradicting me. I say something and you say the exact opposite.

LIL
I am telling you my thoughts as they come to me.

BRI
I'm getting sick of that. I totally encourage your growth as a human being but I'm growing pretty sick of hearing about it all the time. You could totally talk about something else. I'm just not in the mood for this today. Especially since you're implicating me. There's nothing worse than that. Being innocent and

(MORE)

BRI (cont.)
someone thinking you're guilty. I'm not guilty. I don't understand why you
don't believe me. You're lucky you have an excuse. You're lucky you're
pregnant and this doesn't turn into a regular argument and stop staring at me,
stop looking at me like that.

    (SIS comes in, sopping wet in bathing suit.)

SIS
I found this dead fucking piece of seaweed, anyone want this fucking seaweed?
I plucked this seaweed from the bottom of the ocean, I swam down and
plucked it. We can cook some of it up with some Japanese food and save some
for later or we can eat all of it now, just eat all of it, and why am I holding this
fucking thing in my hand?

BRI
You plucked it from the bottom of the ocean.

SIS
Oh right.

BRI
Do you want a towel?

SIS
I like shivering.

BRI
You must be freezing.

SIS
Yeah, that was pretty cold, man, that water out there is very pretty cold like
icicles stabbing your skin. I need some like hot cocoa or something, yeah, that
would be nice some hot cocoa to warm up the inside areas of myself but I don't
think I should drink anything, I shouldn't drink anything else cause my
stomach's all fucked up and maybe I should drink some antacid or something
but no, no I shouldn't drink anything.

BRI
What did you drink?

SIS
I didn't bring anything to take, I didn't really have any money and I don't have any money, I don't have any money, and instead of buying groceries I bought something to take but then I took it all and we're in this fucking cabin so I had to take something, I couldn't be here like actually be here because it's too much so I went into the bathroom, the cabinet, the bathroom cabinet and drank some old cough syrup.

BRI
I'll call an ambulance.

SIS
No, man, this isn't hysterics like a hysterical situation.

BRI
You've poisoned yourself.

SIS
No, I've done this before, it passes right through you just have to wait a very long time for the world to wear off and back to the real world am I like speaking to you right now? You should probably not look too hard at me right now and Oh God fuck what's wrong with Lil?

BRI
She's fine.

SIS
Lil, my little lily pad.

LIL
Sis?

SIS
She speaks.

LIL
Come here, Sis.

SIS
What is it?

LIL
I made something for you.

(LIL, still faced away, holds out the knit bunny cap.)

SIS
You already gave me that thing before.

LIL
I made you another.

SIS
Two, I don't like need two of them there's only one of me at the house at all times.

LIL
You lost the other one.

SIS
I didn't lose it.

LIL
I thought you lost it.

SIS
This isn't, this is like, this is my old one, this is the same one you gave me.

LIL
I hope you like it.

SIS
Why did you do that? Did you steal this from me? You took it, right, you took it out of my bag, why did you take it out of my bag? That's like a major breach of trust between sisters, we trust each other, we're supposed to trust each other's shit, right?

LIL
I trust you, Sis.

SIS
Why did you take it?

LIL
I don't know.

SIS
I can see what you mean, Bri, she's difficult, I didn't see this before when it was just me and her in a room together but she's different around you and I don't know why that is maybe it's the shift in environment and the displacement, like the mental displacement of being a young woman sitting and watching the ocean what do you see out there that you like so much oh sister of mine?

LIL
Nothing.

SIS
What are you looking at?

LIL
Nothing. I don't see anything.

SIS
You have to be looking at something because even when you're looking at nothing you're still looking at something like the inside of your eyeballs or eyeballs open and darkness.

LIL
The beach.

SIS
But you're staring, you're staring at something.

LIL
No.

SIS
Just admit to it because I can clearly see you looking at something.

LIL
I always thought it would happen like this. With me sitting right here. The clouds were just the same. This pattern over here, this combination of clouds, I dreamed about it, it was just like it is now.

SIS
Okay, I don't understand that, I don't understand a word you're saying so will you stop looking outside? There's nothing for you to see out there, don't make me turn you away, I want to turn you away from the window, I'm going to grab you and turn you away if you don't do it yourself. I'm going nuts. This was the

(MORE)

SIS (cont.)
worst idea, why are we here, why are we here? You're looking out like you've
got thoughts, do you have any thoughts you'd like to think out loud, Lil, it
would really help me if you spoke right now about what you were thinking
about.

LIL
I was thinking about Communion, Sis. Confirmation. Our little white dresses.
I never liked the wafers. Neither did you. They tasted like moldy cardboard,
remember?

SIS
Yeah.

LIL
And remember we never ate it? We knelt in front of the cross and signed the
cross and slipped the sacrament in our pockets. And mom found out, the sock
drawer, we had hidden the body of Christ in the sock closet, just full of these
tasteless wafers. And you giggled, here's mom yelling at you and you're giggling.
I always admired that, Sis. You laughing at something you did wrong. I'm sorry
I never told you before.

      (BRI puts a towel over SIS's shoulders.)

SIS
Get that shit off me, what do you think this is, man? You don't just sneak up
on me and do that I'm talking to your sister your wife and you can't do that, you
can't do it like that, all nonchalant like that.

BRI
You're going to get sick.

SIS
I'm already sick you can't see it? I drank something and now I'm better but not
really better, not like good, I'm not doing good. And why do you care about
that, why are you nice, you're not nice, are you? Not usually nice.

BRI
I'm trying to be a good host.

SIS
What am I like a parasite? I need to lie down, I'm going to lie down a minute.

BRI
I've been thinking we should go home. I'm not sure if I like the ocean. I
haven't spent much time around the ocean, not in any significant way. I don't
think I like it. I think I hate the ocean. I hate the ocean and we're going home
tonight. We've got work to do. There are things to do back in our real lives.
Right, Lil? Don't you have to get back to things?

LIL
There's nothing to get back to.

BRI
Well, I've got things that I need to accomplish. I don't know about you but I've
got a really great life to get back to.

LIL
Can I shower first?

BRI
I'm not your boss, I don't have dominion over you, you can do what you want.

LIL
I want to be clean for the trip.

(LIL goes out.)

SIS
I think she already knows, Bri, there's this silence that says she knows.

BRI
We're fine.

SIS
I can see the other side of the ceiling. I can see the rain on the roof and it's like
there's no separation between the roof and the ceiling, they're the same thing.
In the waves I tried to imagine it, being in water for the rest of my life, living in
the water for the rest of my life like when I was kid, like a baby, when I was that
little thing I don't remember being, I can't even imagine it, being so small and
tiny but I was there once, you could hold me in the palm of your hand at one
point and look at me now in this bag, this bag of a body. Did you think I was
pregnant when I showed up, I mean, did you have a sense of it or am I going to
have to tell you? You probably didn't guess, you have that look like, Oh shit is
it mine and that's a question I can't truly answer, like it's really baffling me too
because I've had so many so quickly just in and out like it would solve

(MORE)

SIS (cont.)
something, like if it happened enough times something would be beaten out of me and I wish someone would just beat it out of me but you didn't, none of them did, you just pumped away and I let you do it and now I've got this shit up my stomach.

BRI
Oh my God.

SIS
Yeah, yeah, I already went through this.

BRI
What are you going to do?

SIS
Blow my nose.

BRI
What?

SIS
Too poetic? Sorry, Bri. I forgot you can't think pictures in your head and relate them to other possible imaginary circumstances.

BRI
You're not going to do that.

SIS
I want you to look at me really quickly, just scan me a second and imagine me going through with it and how fast I will make the circumstance miserable, no, it makes me sick thinking of it, it would be cruel, it would be the cruelest thing I've ever done.

BRI
You'll hate yourself if you do it.

SIS
No, I really don't think that because it would really be love. Nothing needs to enter this world anymore. We're fine with what we've got already but it's always more and more and more, everything's always on the way and that needs to stop so I'm doing something about it. I hate her but I love her already, she's not even a she and I already love her.

BRI

I won't let you.

SIS

And like who the fuck are you, huh? You're nobody, you're not even a person, I don't even know who you are and why am I even telling you this? I already have enough voices going on, okay? I don't need another one, I don't need yours, I don't need your voice in my head. This is not some drama, not one of your dramas, this is just something that's happening not something we need to get upset over just a small surgical procedure like removing a pimple or cancer, it needs to happen but we can't get too upset about it otherwise we won't be able to get up in the morning.

BRI

Life is the only valuable thing. It needs to continue at any cost. Any cost.

SIS

No.

BRI

Our happiness does not matter. We're in service of something larger than ourselves. And we shouldn't question that. We shouldn't stop that from happening. Our creator gives us everything. We cannot question the life He gives in return. So you're going to keep it. Just listen to my voice. I want you to keep it. You will keep it and love it.

SIS

I'm so afraid, Bri, I'm very afraid all the time and I don't think you can do anything about that because I'm just simply afraid of doing anything anymore.

BRI

That's why you're keeping it. All your fear will be gone soon. In a few months, everything will be okay. Everything's going to be okay, Sis. I promise.

SIS

I hate it when people say promise, it sounds false like a lie like something you want to say but don't really mean and what about your sister, I mean, your wife, like this is such a major thing I don't know if I can live like this, no, man, I don't know, I feel sick, I'm getting sick.

BRI

You have to let me try. It can work. I know it. It's possible.

SIS
You don't really mean that, I mean, you really mean that?

BRI
I know I can make this work because nothing can deter human will.

SIS
I don't know what to do.

BRI
Let's go right now.

SIS
Like, leave?

BRI
Yes.

SIS
And leave her here?

BRI
Yes.

SIS
Just leave her here, leave her alone at the end of the fucking land and she's about to, my nephew, she's about to give birth to my nephew. Can you do that? Because I don't know if I can. I've reached my limit, I can't do anything else to anyone or do anything to myself I'm just going to be still, I'm going to be very still and not move anymore, I never want to do anything ever again.

BRI
Get your coat.

SIS
I can't move, Bri.

BRI
Get your coat, Sis.

SIS
I can't move.

(LIL comes in wearing a bathrobe. She holds a small black case. It hangs open.)

LIL
I'm so glad we came here. It's so nice to get away. Breathe some fresh air. I feel like I can think out here. I'm thinking very clearly now. My thoughts are calm and clear. I want to thank you for being my sister. I know we've fought about things but that doesn't matter anymore. None of it matters and I just want to tell you I love you. Tell mom I love her, too. She didn't always approve of me but that's okay. I forgive her and I hope she'll forgive me when she realizes. I want to thank you for our marriage, Bri. It was a wonderful time. The whole thing was wonderful. I remember your cufflinks at the wedding. These shining golden cufflinks. And I thought any man who could wear cufflinks that brilliant deserves my love. I want to thank you for giving me a child. It has fulfilled me in a way I can't possibly begin to tell you. My life has purpose now.

(From the pocket of her robe, she quickly pulls out a handgun. She fires into her mouth. Her brain explodes into the perfect shape of a heart, splattered on the back wall.)

LIL
And I was thinking about a name. I think Lilith is a wonderful name. Don't you?

END OF PLAY

Ben Beckley as Bri and Mary Jane Gibson as Sis in the
HERE Arts Center workshop production

*Joel Israel as Grig and Patricia Nelson as Lil in the
HERE Arts Center workshop production*

Real People, Real Lives, Real Theater

An Introduction to Ping Chong & Sara Michelle Zatz'
Undesirable Elements
by Sara Michelle Zatz

*U*ndesirable *Elements* is an exploration of the Asian-American experience in New York through an interview-based theater piece, part of an ongoing series of community-specific oral history theater works, known as the *Undesirable Elements* series. The production premiered at the Asian Cultural Festival at Queens Theatre in the Park in April 2007, and was presented as part of the first-ever National Asian-American Theater Festival (NAATF), which brought together over twenty-five Asian-American theater companies from around the United States in June 2007 for two weeks of performances and events in New York City.

The cast consists of six Asian-American artists, writers, and activists from diverse geographic backgrounds (South Asia, Pacific Islands, Central Asia, East Asia), each sharing their own real-life experiences. Therefore, *Undesirable Elements* is not a traditional play or documentary-theater project performed by actors. Instead, *Undesirable Elements* is presented as a chamber piece of story-telling, a "seated opera for the spoken word," according to Ping Chong.

By drawing on first-hand experiences of real people across a broad spectrum of Asian-American backgrounds (immigrants, second-generation, adoptees), *Undesirable Elements* challenges mainstream assumptions about what it means to be Asian-American. It also addresses assumptions, stereotypes and internal prejudices that can exist within Asian-American communities. Each participant speaks about his/her personal background and the paths that led to careers in the arts, activism, and education, and the formation of an Asian-American identity. Cast members' individual experiences are woven together in a chronological narrative that touches on both political and personal experiences and shows the historical evolution of the influence of Asian-Americans on the social and cultural identity of America.

This became the 34th *Undesirable Elements* production, in an ongoing series exploring issues of race, culture, and identity in the lives of individuals living in different American communities. In 1992, Ping Chong, theater and visual artist, choreographer, and seminal figure in the Asian-American Arts movement, was working on a visual art installation titled, *A Facility for the Channeling and Containment of Undesirable Elements*, commissioned by Artists Space in New York. A few weeks before the opening, the curator asked him to create an accompanying performance piece. On the spur of the moment, Chong gathered together a group of individuals who shared little in common besides their status as "new" New Yorkers, and their ability to speak multiple languages. A performance piece was quickly put together and the first *Undesirable Elements* was born. Since then, Chong has created nearly three-dozen original works in the series, in communities around the country and the world. Productions have been mounted in cities such as Atlanta, Minneapolis, Tokyo, Cleveland, Seattle, Madison, Rotterdam, Charleston, Washington DC, Chicago, and Berlin. A touring production, created to commemorate the 10th anniversary of the series, has been presented at the Romaeuropa Festival in Italy, the Lille (France) European Capital of Culture Festival, and the Colorado Festival of World Theatre.

The *Undesirable Elements* series is designed to help communities confront and overcome cultural insularity by forging bridges between peoples and cultures. Each new production is location-specific, addressing the unique cultural and ethnic populations of individual US communities. Each original *Undesirable Elements* piece is created in partnership with local host organizations: universities, performing arts centers, and social service agencies. Hosting partners have included YMCAs, Spoleto USA Festival, Big Brother Big/Sister, Dartmouth College, Seattle Repertory Theatre, the Center for Multicultural Human Services, the Illusion Theater, and *VSA arts*, to name a few.

The process includes an extended community residency, development and rehearsal period. During this time, Ping Chong, myself, and other collaborators conduct intensive interviews with potential local participants, seeking a group that will represent a diversity of voices and themes that will speak to the concerns and issues of that particular community. Typically, up to twenty-five individuals will be interviewed for a final group of five to seven participants. These participants provide the source material for the script, and also become the performers. Most have never before spoken publicly about their life experiences; many have never before performed on stage.

Initial interviews last approximately two hours. Secondary interviews of an additional two hours are conducted with individuals who are chosen to be in the production. Every interview begins the same way, with questions about where they were born, the origins of their names, and any special circumstances of the day of their birth. The interviews, adapted and occasionally theatricalized, form the basis of the script in which the text moves chronologically, weaving together the personal and political narratives of the individuals. Ping Chong and I write the script, with participants retaining a final right of review and approval. The resulting production is a chamber piece of personal testimonies by the performers, addressing the recent history of the 20th and 21st centuries and the collisions of peoples and cultures in the modern world.

Like a sonnet, each work in the series retains a standard structure and form, with creative and topical variations from production to production. In the early years of the series, the participants shared nothing in common other than their geographic residency in the specific city of the work. In recent years, Ping Chong & Company has seen a marked increase in requests for productions as communities around the country struggle with complex issues of difference, tolerance, and American identity. As demand for *Undesirable Elements* productions has grown, the thematic range of the series has expanded. In 2002, Ping Chong & Company partnered with the Center for Multicultural Human Services, a mental health services agency in Falls Church, VA, to create a new work in the series exploring the impact of war and trauma on young people. The production, *Children of War*, featured young refugees who shared the experience of having survived war or domestic trauma before arriving as immigrants to Northern Virginia.

Children of War had a broad national impact. It was featured on *Now with Bill Moyers* on PBS, toured in New York and Los Angeles and was presented as part of 2003 World Refugee Day under the auspices of the United Nations High Commissioner for Refugees. Since *Children of War*, Ping Chong & Company has continued to broaden the scope of the series, with recent works exploring other unique connections binding participants together, such as Native American identity or the experience of living with a disability. Of a recent production in Minneapolis, Christy DeSmith wrote in the *Star Tribune*, "In an era when America-bashing seems to be a no-brainer, *Undesirable Elements* digs deeper. It recognizes where the United States goes wrong, but more interesting, it acknowledges where people go right – and it does so in a genuine, illustrative way. It defies cynicism, honoring the magic of resilience and chance."

As an artist who has himself shifted between multiple worlds, identities, and communities, Ping Chong has used the *Undesirable Elements* series to create a methodology that examines the fluidity of identity, fosters cross-cultural exchange, documents and responds to a community's social issues and tensions, and affirms the power of art to transcend the divides of race, ethnicity, class, and age. As the child of immigrant Chinese opera performers growing up in New York's insular Chinatown community, Chong did not see a Western theater production until he was a teenager. Originally trained as a visual artist and filmmaker, Ping Chong created his first independent theater work, *Lazarus*, in 1972, and formed Ping Chong & Company in 1975. Since then, Ping Chong & Company has brought over fifty critically-acclaimed multidisciplinary works to the stage, including: *Nosferatu, Kind Ness, The East-West Quartet (Deshima, Chinoiserie, After Sorrow, Pojagi), Blind Ness* and *Cocktail*, as well as the puppet theater works *Kwaidan, Obon* and *Cathay*. These productions have been recognized with numerous honors and awards, and have toured extensively in the United States and abroad.

Many of Chong's works concern the interaction of Eastern and Western cultures and/or issues of cultural diversity, and as such he regularly collaborates with established artists from across artistic disciplines and cultural backgrounds, as well as mentoring younger artists. The company is best known for its large-scale international collaborations and its ability to effectively cross cultural boundaries in making works on a wide variety of topics, from the hidden genocide in the Belgian Congo to Norse folk sagas to Japanese ghost stories.

For more than thirty years, Ping Chong & Company has produced works addressing the important contemporary cultural and civic issues. The *Undesirable Elements* series has become a significant program of the company, with up to three new productions created in a given year, and would not exist without the accompanying multidisciplinary theater works that have been the foundation of Chong's career and reputation. At the same time, *Undesirable Elements* has become a source of creative inspiration for Chong, leading him to new subjects to explore in his multidisciplinary productions. Recognizing the significance of the *Undesirable Elements* series in his artistic career, he noted recently in *The Washington Post*, "I have had more standing ovations for [the *Undesirable Elements* series] over the years than for anything else."

***

Upcoming works in the Undesirable Elements *series are in development in New York, Philadelphia, and Syracuse. A book dedicated to the series will be published by Theatre Communications Group in 2008. Visit www.undesirableelements.org or www.pingchong.org for more details.*

UNDESIRABLE ELEMENTS

by Ping Chong & Sara Michelle Zatz

UNDESIRABLE ELEMENTS

Copyright © 2007 by Ping Chong and Sara Michelle Zatz

CAUTION: *Undesirable Elements* is reprinted by permission of the authors and Ping Chong & Company, Inc. The English language stock and amateur stage performance rights in this Play are controlled exclusively by Ping Chong & Company, 47 Great Jones Street, 6th Floor, New York, NY 10012. No professional or nonprofessional performance of the Play may be given without obtaining, in advance, the written permission of Ping Chong & Company, and paying the requisite fee. Inquires concerning all other rights should be addressed to:

Bruce Allardice, Managing Director
Ping Chong & Company
47 Great Jones Street, 6th Floor
New York, NY 10012.
info@pingchong.org
212.529.1557
www.pingchong.org

***

Undesirable Elements received its premiere at Queens Theatre in the Park in New York City on April 21, 2007. It was produced by Ping Chong & Company as part of the Asian Cultural Festival at Queens Theatre in the Park. It was written and directed by Ping Chong and Sara Michelle Zatz, in collaboration with the performers; the lighting design was by Darren McCroom, the production stage manager was Kristina Varshavskaya. It was subsequently produced in June 2007 at Pregones Theatre in the Bronx and Asia Society in Manhattan, as part of the first National Asian American Theater Festival, with Courtney Golden as Stage Manager, Brant Murray as Technical/Lighting Director, and Kristina Varshavskaya as Production Coordinator. This production in the *Undesirable Elements* series was made possible in part by grants from the National Endowment for the Arts, New York State Council on the Arts, New York City Department of Cultural Affairs, the Leon Levy Foundation, Fan Fox & Leslie R. Samuels Foundation, and the Nathan Cummings Foundation, among others.

PERFORMERS

Joseph O. Legaspi

Vaimoana Niumeitolu

Pauline Park

Zohra Saed

Raj Thakkar

Kelly Zen-Yie Tsai

NOTE

Undesirable Elements is a powerful exploration of the Asian-American experience in New York through an interview-based theater work. Constructed as chamber piece storytelling, the performance features real people telling their personal experiences of creating cultural identity out of a rich and complex heritage. *Undesirable Elements* is an ongoing series of community-specific oral history theater works examining the lives of people born in one culture but currently living in another, either by choice or by circumstance. Each production is made in a specific host community, with local participants testifying to their real lives and experiences. Since 1992, Ping Chong & Company has made over thirty productions in the series, in communities around the United States and abroad. For more information, please visit: www.undesirableelements.org.

The authors appreciate the assistance of Brian Hirono in the preparation of this manuscript for publication.

UNDESIRABLE ELEMENTS
by Ping Chong & Sara Michelle Zatz

(MUSIC begins. Order of entrance: PAULINE, MOANA, RAJ, KELLY, JOSEPH, ZOHRA.)

PAULINE
Let's get started!

MOANA
'Okusai tau kamata leva!

RAJ
Chalo humay suroo curyay!

KELLY
Wo-men Kai Shi Ba!

JOSEPH
Magumpisa na tayo!

ZOHRA
Beeyayeen Shurroo Koonaym! – let's get started! Please sit.

(Everybody sits.)

PAULINE
My name is Pauline Park. I was born in Miryang, Korea in October 1960. I have an older twin brother. It was *chusok* – the harvest season. Moana?

MOANA
Ko hoku hingoa ko Vai Moana. Litia Makakaufaki Niumeitolu.
Na'e fa'ele'i au'i Nuku'alofa, Tonga 'i he ho'ata 'oe 'aho 17 'o Sune, 1978. 'I he'aho ne mafana mo langi ma'a 'i Palataisi. Raj?

RAJ
Maroo naam Snehal Dayanidhan Thakkar che, purn budha munay Raj turikay janay che.

(MORE)

RAJ (cont.)
Maro janma chodmi February *ognisau punchoter,* Flushing Hospital, New York *ma tuyo huthoo. Ay divas ay buruf noo tofan avyoo huthoo.* Valentine's *nau divas hutho.* Kelly?

KELLY
Wo jiao Tsai Ren-Yie. Wo sheng zai Arlington Heights, Illinois, *mei guo. Wo sheng qi yue san shi, e jiu qi ba. Wo sheng zai xiawu e dian san shi. Yang guang pu zou de xiatian!* Joseph?

JOSEPH
Ang pangalan ko ay Joseph *Josel Orense Legaspi. Pinanganak ako nuong Nobyembre bente-sais, 1971 sa Maynila,* Philippines. *Ako ang unang anak na lalaki sa aking pamilya. Malamig and panahon.* Zohra?

ZOHRA
Issmimaan Zohra Saed ast. Tawaloot shudaam da bist-e-hoot, nuzda sedeh haftad-e-panj, da shahr-e-jalalabad. Wakhti-keh ba dunya aumadam awaleen kalamehkeh shuneedam ismeh khuda bud. Issmimaan Zohra ast maanawish sitareh subh ast.

> *(All clap.)*

MOANA
Tangata.

JOSEPH
Rosa.

PAULINE
Alma.

ZOHRA
Hassan.

RAJ
Akash.

KELLY
Vivian.

MOANA
Fuifuilupe.

JOSEPH
Carlos.

PAULINE
Dietrich.

ZOHRA
Abdusamad.

RAJ
Priya.

KELLY
Michael.

MOANA
Amelia.

JOSEPH
Antonio.

PAULINE
Anneliese.

ZOHRA
Latifa.

RAJ
Binti.

KELLY
Jennifer.

MOANA
'Aho'eitu.

JOSEPH
Ligaya.

PAULINE
Sven.

ZOHRA
Sharif.

RAJ
Dhaval.

KELLY
Paul.

MOANA
Sauliloa.

JOSEPH
Manuel.

PAULINE
Ingeborg.

ZOHRA
Cihan.

RAJ
Aashni.

KELLY
Tina.

MOANA
Alilia.

JOSEPH
Maria.

PAULINE
Knut.

ZOHRA
Fahima.

RAJ
Radha.

KELLY
David.

(All clap ten times.)

KELLY
Kelly Zen-Yie Tsai.

ALL
Kelly Zen-Yie Tsai

KELLY
(slower)
Kelly Zen-Yie Tsai

ALL
Kelly Zen-Yie Tsai

KELLY
When I meet people for the first time, they often say

RAJ
"Am I pronouncing your name properly?"

MOANA
"Please, teach me how to say it correctly."

KELLY
But pronouncing my name "correctly" in Mandarin involves explaining all these different tones that don't really exist in English. So, when people ask, I usually just give them the straight up English version. Do they really think they'll be able to say it "correctly" after a five-minute lesson in Mandarin? Personally, I think they're being a little over ambitious!

(All clap.)

RAJ
According to my family's tradition, all of the males' names are given by our guru and have "nidhan" at the end of it. Your name predicts the type of person you will be. My father is Dayanidhan:

ZOHRA
Someone who is full of compassion and mercy.

RAJ
My brother's name is Aminidhan:

PAULINE
Someone who is full of sweetness and makes everyone feel comfortable.

RAJ
I was supposed to be named Karunidhan:

MOANA
Someone who cares for everyone and takes care of everybody.

RAJ
But since I was born on Valentine's Day in the US, my parents broke with tradition and named me Snehal, meaning:

ALL
LOVE.

(All clap.)

ZOHRA
Afghan names and their meanings: Hassan.

ALL
Handsome.

ZOHRA
Jameela.

ALL
Beautiful one.

ZOHRA
Zohra.

ALL
Morning star.

ZOHRA
Fahima.

ALL
Wise one.

ZOHRA
Sharif.

ALL
The honest one.

ZOHRA
Latifa.

ALL
The gentle one.

ZOHRA
Salih.

ALL
The righteous one.

(All clap.)

JOSEPH
Philippine names and nicknames: Placita.

ALL
Name.

JOSEPH
Bubbles.

ALL
Nickname.

JOSEPH
George.

ALL
Name.

JOSEPH
Joji.

ALL
Nickname.

JOSEPH
Esperanza.

ALL
Name.

JOSEPH
Cookie.

ALL
Nickname.

JOSEPH
Cheryl.

ALL
Name.

JOSEPH
Nog Nog.

ALL
Nickname.

JOSEPH
Marylou.

ALL
Name.

JOSEPH
Pong Pong.

ALL
Nickname.

JOSEPH
Joseph.

ALL
Name.

JOSEPH
Joel.

ALL
Nickname.

(*All clap.*)

ZOHRA
Throughout history, Asian societies have revered various trans-gendered figures:

MOANA
The Fakaleiti in Tonga.

RAJ
The Hijra in India.

KELLY
The goddess Guanyin in China.

JOSEPH
In Korea, where Pauline was born, the Hwarang were elite archers, male youth who wore long flowing women's gowns and make-up.

PAULINE
I am a transgendered woman.

(*All clap.*)

MOANA
People always ask me where I'm from. They love to guess.

KELLY
The Dominican Republic.

PAULINE
India.

JOSEPH
Hawaii.

RAJ
Mexico.

ZOHRA
Puerto Rico.

PAULINE
Cuba.

JOSEPH
The Philippines.

ZOHRA
I know, you're Navajo!

MOANA
No one ever says:

KELLY
Are you from a small island kingdom in the south pacific called Tonga?

(All clap ten times. Blackout.)

ALL
1763.

KELLY
Louisiana territory.

JOSEPH
Filipino sailors seeking to escape brutal Spanish masters jump ship and make a permanent settlement in the bayous and marshes of Louisiana. They are the first Asian-Americans.

RAJ/MOANA
1839.

PAULINE
1839.

JOSEPH
Afghanistan.

ZOHRA
The British invade Afghanistan in an effort to add it to their ever expanding
(MORE)

ZOHRA (cont.)
empire. But the Afghans are a stubborn and proud people who will not allow themselves to be colonized. Over the next eighty years they will fight three brutal wars against the British in their fight to maintain their independence.

JOSEPH/KELLY
1869.

PAULINE
1869.

MOANA
May 10, 1869.

ALL
Utah.

KELLY
A commemorative photograph is taken when the Central Pacific Railroad meets the Union Pacific Railroad. Although they represent 90% of the workforce of the Central Pacific, 10,000 Chinese pioneers are excluded from the photograph.

ZOHRA
1882.

RAJ
1882.

MOANA
California.

KELLY
After the railroads are built and Chinese labor is no longer needed, anti-Chinese sentiment rises quickly. The Chinese Exclusion Act becomes the first immigration law to exclude on the basis of race.

MOANA
"Hereafter, no state or federal court of the United States shall admit Chinese to citizenship."

KELLY
The Chinese have become:

ALL
Undesirable Elements.

(*All clap.*)

RAJ/ZOHRA/ JOSEPH
1895.

KELLY
After occupying Taiwan as a province for eight years, China loses the Sino-Japanese war, and cedes Taiwan permanently to Japan. Despite efforts to establish the Taiwan Republic, 12,000 Japanese soldiers quickly crush the independence movement and begin a harsh fifty-year occupation.

PAULINE
1898.

MOANA
1898.

ZOHRA
The Philippines.

JOSEPH
Three hundred years of Spanish rule ends in the Philippines. The United States wins the Spanish-American War, and then buys the Philippines from Spain for twenty million dollars.

RAJ
No one consults the Filipino people, who had already set up their own independent republic, thinking they had American support.

JOSEPH
The Philippines becomes the first American colony.

RAJ/MOANA
1919.

PAULINE
1919.

KELLY
Afghanistan.

ZOHRA
King Amanullah finally shakes off the British for the last time. After years of struggle, modern day Afghanistan is sculpted out of what lands the Afghans reclaim from the British, but much territory is lost.

PAULINE/JOSEPH
1922.

KELLY
1922.

ZOHRA
The country of Tonga.

MOANA
Queen Salote is the beloved Queen of Tonga. She will rule for forty-seven years. Her brother, the Prince Kepa, has a romance with a local girl and a child is born. The child, Sauliloa, will be raised in the royal household and well provided for, but she is not allowed to see her mother, for unmarried mothers are:

ALL
Undesirable Elements.

MOANA
Sauliloa will become my grandmother.

    (All clap.)

RAJ
1941.

ZOHRA
1941.

JOSEPH
1941.

KELLY
1941.

PAULINE
1941.

MOANA
1941.

ZOHRA
World War II.

JOSEPH
The Japanese army occupies the Philippines. Rosario Gardner Orense is detained by Japanese soldiers. Her parents are American, but she was born and raised in the Philippines. She has red hair, green eyes, and pale skin. Although she sounds Filipina, she looks American. The soldiers are going to kill her. She pleads with them:

MOANA
"Please, I'm Filipina, I was born here. My husband is from here. Please, I am with child."

RAJ
One

PAULINE
Two

ZOHRA
Three eternities pass.

JOSEPH
They let her go. If Rosario had not escaped that day, I would not be here now. She will become my grandmother.

(All clap.)

RAJ
1945.

MOANA
1945.

KELLY
In China, civil war continues between the Communists, led by Mao Zedong, and the Nationalists, led by Chiang Kai-Shek. When World War II ends, the United Nations allows Chiang Kai-Shek's troops to:

RAJ
Temporarily occupy Taiwan, on behalf of the Allied forces.

KELLY
Fifty years of Japanese occupation ends. At first, the Taiwanese celebrate, but their joy soon turns to sorrow and anger.

ZOHRA
1947.

JOSEPH
1947.

MOANA
February 28, 1947.

KELLY
After two years of harsh rule, tensions between the local Taiwanese people and the Nationalist government boil over. When an elderly woman is beaten for selling black market cigarettes, riots break out. The Nationalists brutally suppress the uprising, killing tens of thousands of civilians.

RAJ
1949.

ZOHRA
1949.

PAULINE
Shanghai.

KELLY
Wang Lan San, a local politician, and his wife, Zheng Quen, are fleeing Shanghai for Taiwan. They decide to leave their youngest daughter with an auntie, thinking they will soon return. But Wang Jing-Hwa cries and cries until her parents decide to take her with them. If Wang Jing-Hwa had been left behind that day, I would not be here now. She will become my mother.

(All clap.)

MOANA/JOSEPH
1954.

PAULINE
1954.

ZOHRA
Gujarat, India.

RAJ
Keshavlal and Chimanlal have a distant relative in common, who suggests that Keshavlal's daughter, Sudha, and Chimanlal's son, Dayanidhan, would be a good match. To fulfill his wish and honor his name, they arrange for their marriage. Dayanidhan and Sudha are engaged. He is ten and she is four.

JOSEPH
1959.

KELLY
1959.

MOANA
Afghanistan.

ZOHRA
The *purdah* or veil that all women have to wear is made optional. Women begin to enroll in universities.

PAULINE
1959.

RAJ
1959.

KELLY
Tonga.

MOANA
My mother is seventeen years old. She receives a scholarship to study in New Zealand. It is the first time she leaves her island home and her family. She is homesick. However, she is soon courted by the most elite Tongan bachelors there. She is not homesick anymore.

> *(All clap two times.)*

JOSEPH/ZOHRA
1960.

PAULINE
1960.

KELLY
Milwaukee, Wisconsin.

PAULINE
Because she is unable to bear children, Sylvia and her husband Kenneth decide
to adopt. At a time when there are still very few international adoptions,
Kenneth and Sylvia adopt twin boys from Korea. They will become my parents.

    (All clap.)

RAJ
1965.

ALL
1965.

JOSEPH
The Immigration and Nationality Act of 1965.

RAJ
For the first time, United States immigration laws are changed so they no long
favor only Europeans. The act lifts the quotas from two hundred people per
country per year from Asia to 20,000 people per country per year. This will
change the face of America.

    (All clap.)

MOANA/PAULINE
1965.

RAJ
1965.

ZOHRA
Taipei, Taiwan.

KELLY
Tsai Boh Chang is an orphaned Taiwanese farm boy. He is studying English before going to the United States. Wang Jing-Hwa is a city girl from Taipei, whose politician father still dreams of re-taking the mainland from the Communists. Wang Jing-Hwa comes late to every single class. Tsai Boh Chang helps her catch up on what she missed. They will become my parents.

    (All clap.)

MOANA/JOSEPH
1965.

ZOHRA
1965.

RAJ
South Clement Avenue School.

MOANA
The south side of Milwaukee.

PAULINE
It's the first day of kindergarten. All the girls in my class are wearing stretch pants with stirrups. Later, I ask my mother if she'll buy me a pair. She looks at me in absolute shock.

MOANA
"But those are for girls!!"

PAULINE
I decide that wanting to dress like a girl, or wanting to be a girl, is something that I will have to hide. I am five years old.

    (All clap.)

MOANA
1968.

PAULINE
1968.

KELLY
Kareli, a small village in India.

RAJ
After a fourteen year engagement, Dayanidhan and Sudha are married. It is a traditional Gujarati Hindu wedding.

ALL
One

RAJ
The Mendhi party.

MOANA
The bride and her female relatives and friends get together before the wedding. Henna is painted on their hands and feet, while the rest of the family celebrates with songs.

ALL
Two

RAJ
Jaan.

JOSEPH
The groom arrives at the wedding ceremony with his entire family and friends. A band plays at the front of the procession, while the groom rides in on a horse.

ALL
Three

RAJ
Puja.

KELLY
The groom is welcomed by his future mother-in-law with a prayer. She leads him to the *mandap*, where the ceremony takes place.

JOSEPH
The future father-in-law washes the groom's feet with milk.

PAULINE
It is at this time that the sisters-in-law will try to steal the groom's shoes. If his shoes are stolen, he must offer the sisters money in order to get them back.

ALL
Four

RAJ
Pheras.

ZOHRA
The marriage ceremony is performed by a Hindu priest in front of a sacred fire.
The groom's scarf is tied to the bride's sari, symbolizing the union of their two
souls.

KELLY
The bride and groom circle the sacred fire four times. The groom helps the
bride touch seven betel nuts with her right toe, while they recite seven vows.

ALL
Five

RAJ
Vidai.

MOANA
After the wedding, the bride bids farewell to her family and friends. She is
leaving her parents' home to build a life with her husband and his family. There
are tears of joy and sorrow.

RAJ
Dayanidhan and Sudha. Sudha and Dayanidhan. They will become my parents.

    (All clap.)

ALL
1968.

MOANA
Milwaukee.

PAULINE
My parents want us to be proud of where we come from and who we are. But
we have very little access to Korean culture or history in Milwaukee. At home,
we are surrounded by the German-American culture of our mother's family. My
grandmother reads to us from her German Bible, we sing Lutheran hymns at
the piano, and we eat all the typical Milwaukee foods:

ZOHRA/RAJ
Kielbasa:

MOANA/KELLY
Polish sausage.

KELLY/ZOHRA/RAJ
Sauerkraut:

MOANA/KELLY
Cabbage.

ZOHRA/RAJ
Punchki:

MOANA/KELLY
Jelly donuts.

PAULINE
… and everyone's favorite, *lutefisk:*

JOSEPH
A Norwegian delicacy of salted white fish soaked in lye and then …

PAULINE
Actually, you really don't want to know!

    (All clap.)

MOANA/ZOHRA
1968.

JOSEPH
1968.

KELLY
Dabka, India.

RAJ
Shortly after the wedding, Dayanidhan gets his visa to study chemistry in
the United States. Sudha is left behind with her husband's family, where, as the

    (MORE)

RAJ (cont.)
daughter-in-law, she's responsible for taking care of twenty-five members of the
household. Nine months after Dayanidhan leaves, my brother is born. My
father will not meet his first son until he is three years old.

(*All clap.*)

JOSEPH/ZOHRA
1968.

MOANA
1968.

RAJ
Milwaukee.

PAULINE
Once or twice a year, our mother takes us to a restaurant where she once
worked as a waitress. It's called Toy's Chinatown Restaurant and is run by a
first-generation Chinese immigrant and his son. Whenever we come to the
restaurant, they give us presents. Mr. Toy and his son are the only Asian adults
we know.

ZOHRA
1968.

RAJ
1968.

KELLY
Nuku'alofa, Tonga.

MOANA
My father drinks and drinks and spends and spends. With three children to
support, my mother applies for a job at the Mormon Church High School.
While teaching there, she is drawn to the wholesome Mormon family programs,
which disapprove of drinking. She converts to the Mormon faith.

ZOHRA/KELLY/JOSEPH
1970.

RAJ
1970.

JOSEPH
December 7, 1970.

PAULINE
My brother and I are the only non-white children in our school, and in our neighborhood. Most families in our community have relatives who served in World War II, like our father did. Every year I dread Pearl Harbor Day. Every year other children will taunt us, call us names, and throw things at us. The fact that we are Korean, and not Japanese, does not matter.

(All clap.)

MOANA
1972.

RAJ
1972.

PAULINE
The Philippines.

JOSEPH
Ferdinand Marcos comes to power as a nationalist leader. Under the Spanish and the Americans, Tagalog, the main Filipino language, was forbidden and our culture and history were ignored. Marcos encourages people to be proud of their Filipino identity. Unfortunately he soon loses sight of his idealism. He is seduced by power and corruption.

(All clap.)

RAJ/ZOHRA
1973.

MOANA
1973.

KELLY
Tippecanoe Library, Milwaukee.

PAULINE
I am thirteen years old. My brother and I spend every Saturday at the local library. All the librarians know us by name. One day, I find a book called,

(MORE)

PAULINE (cont.)
Transvestites and Transsexuals. When I pick up the book, I feel an almost physical shock of recognition, like I'm reading about myself. I don't want anyone to see it, so I hide it behind another book:

ALL
The Land and People of Korea.

    (All clap.)

MOANA/KELLY
1975.

PAULINE
1975.

RAJ
Jalalabad, Afghanistan

ZOHRA
I am six months old. My father takes me to work with him every day. He carries me strapped to his back. Every afternoon at 5pm, he takes me for a stroll in a blue satin carriage. He buys me imported European toys. This is unusual treatment for a girl. My cousin's wife says:

KELLY
"All this trouble for a girl? She'll just end up in another household. Why pamper another person's goods?"

RAJ/MOANA
1975.

JOSEPH
1975.

PAULINE
There is a new pastor at our church. He preaches hellfire and damnation. He calls homosexuality an abomination. Sitting in the front pew with my mother, like I have my whole life, I feel like he's talking straight at me. I think to myself:

JOSEPH
"Well, either I'm wrong, or he's wrong. We can't both be right."

(All clap two times.)

KELLY/RAJ
1976.

MOANA
1976.

ZOHRA
Manila, Philippines.

JOSEPH
I am five years old. I live in a big old two-story Spanish-style house
with my grandmother, Rosario, and dozens of aunts, uncles and tons of cousins.
I love to sit with my mother and aunts in the shared kitchen. They tell stories
and gossip and sing songs in Tagalog. They tell scary folk tales to show me how
to behave:

PAULINE
Don't lean over the window or the devil will push you out!

ZOHRA
Don't go outside in the dark woods or the *tikbalang*, the giant horse with fiery
eyes, will eat you!

MOANA
Don't walk around at night, or else the *dwende*, the magical gnomes, will kidnap
you!

KELLY
Go to bed or else an *aswang*, a vampire, will carry you off to its lair and eat you!

(All clap.)

RAJ
1978.

PAULINE
1978.

MOANA
My family moves to Hawaii. My parents decide to speak Tongan only to each
other, and insist we speak only English to them. They want to prepare us for
the English-speaking world. They want a better life for us.

ZOHRA/KELLY
1978.

PAULINE
My brother and I are applying to college. I want to go to the University of
Wisconsin-Madison. Our mother thinks this is too far away and too liberal. She
tries to bribe us to stay at home and attend the University of Wisconsin-
Milwaukee. She offers to buy us a car! I say:

JOSEPH
"What about our cousin, Marcia? She went to Madison and didn't come back a
radical, a hippie, or pregnant! She even married a Lutheran Minister!"

PAULINE
In the end, we get full scholarships to Madison, so she agrees to let us go. But
she does make one more request:

KELLY
"Promise me that you'll come home virgins!"

PAULINE
My brother promises. I don't!

    (All clap.)

RAJ
1978.

PAULINE
The first week of college, I find the Gay Center. Ironically, it's in the basement
of a Presbyterian church. I walk around and around trying to get up the
gumption to go in.

KELLY
Once

RAJ
Twice

ZOHRA
Three times

PAULINE
Finally, I get up the nerve and go in. By the end of my first semester of college,
I have come out to my friends, gone to my first gay bar, and had my first lover.
But I don't come out to my mother. I know she won't understand.

(*All clap.*)

JOSEPH
1978.

MOANA
April, 1978.

RAJ
Riyadh, Saudi Arabia.

ZOHRA
We are living in Saudi Arabia. My parents are glued to the television. There has
been a *coup d'etat* in Afghanistan. Daoud Khan, the president, has been
murdered. When my father's sponsor learns of the war and the danger of
returning to Afghanistan, he cuts my father's salary in half. My father decides to
take his family to America to find a better life.

(*All clap ten times.*)

JOSEPH
Tumayo Tayo.

(*MUSIC. All close books, stand up, change seats.*)

JOSEPH
Maupo Tayo.

(*All sit, open books.*)

MOANA
1978.

RAJ
1978.

ALL
1978.

KELLY
When I am born my parents give me the English name me Kelly Zen Yie Tsai.
My Chinese name is Tsai Zen-Yie. Kelly is my sister's idea. It's Gaelic for
"maiden warrior." Later, when I ask my mom what my Chinese name means,
she says:

MOANA
"It means kindness and ... good posture."

KELLY
Good posture?!!

MOANA
"I mean, like poise, it's more like poise!"

KELLY
If I start acting too wild, my mother will always say:

ALL
"Remember your name!"

 (All clap.)

PAULINE
1979.

JOSEPH
Sunnyside, Queens.

RAJ
I'm four years old. My father has been working the night shift at Saint Barnabus
Hospital for years. He's been saving his vacation time so he can take us to India.
He hasn't seen his family in seven years. When he finally asks for his vacation,
the boss tells him he can't take it. My father quits his job on the spot and we
prepare to go to India.

KELLY
1979.

RAJ
Two weeks before we arrive in India, my mother's father dies. She never has a
chance to say goodbye. I never meet my grandfather.

(All clap.)

MOANA/ KELLY
1979.

PAULINE
Manila, Philippines.

JOSEPH
Every day when I walk home from school, I pass a group of church ladies who spend all their time drinking cantaloupe juice and gossiping about their neighbors. As I pass by, they whisper:

KELLY
"There goes that heathen Joseph Legaspi!"

ZOHRA
"His family doesn't go to church!"

JOSEPH
The Catholic Church is a big part of the community in the Philippines. When I ask my mom how come we don't go to church, she says:

MOANA
"There's laundry to be done – God's not going to do my laundry!"

(All clap two times.)

JOSEPH
1980.

MOANA
Queens.

RAJ
My father buys a small candy store in Astoria. From now on, he'll never have a boss deny him his vacation. But, as owner of the store, he'll work so hard, he will never take a day off for over fifteen years.

(All clap.)

JOSEPH
1980.

RAJ
I am five years old. My brother and I have to work in the candy store every Saturday. At 4:00 in the morning my father walks in and says:

JOSEPH
"Ooot! Get up!"

RAJ
We eat our Froot Loops in silence under a buzzing fluorescent light. By 4:45 we are out the door, driving to the store. It is still dark and the streets are deserted. We arrive by 5:00, and then we start the routine:

ALL
One

RAJ
Open the metal gate.

ALL
Two

MOANA
Collect the day's newspapers. Check to make sure none have been stolen. Then put them in the racks.

ALL
Three

JOSEPH
Fill the fridge with sodas.

ALL
Four

KELLY
Restock the chips, the candy, and the cigarettes.

ALL
Five

ZOHRA
Open for business.

RAJ
When everything is done, my dad takes a nap on a cot in the tiny backroom. My brother and I watch the register out front. Soon, the old Greek men in the neighborhood come in for their lotto tickets and cigarettes. They all know us by name.

(*All clap.*)

PAULINE
1980.

KELLY
Sheepshead Bay, Brooklyn.

ZOHRA
In Sheepshead Bay and nearby Brighton Beach there are almost fifty Afghan families. It's a little pocket of home, a long way from home. Because we just came from Saudi Arabia, many of our neighbors think we are rich, but really we're struggling to make ends meet. My parents live for a few months on farina, but they make sure my little brother, Sharif, and I get meat and vegetables.

(*All clap.*)

RAJ/KELLY
1982.

PAULINE
I'm studying in London. There I meet Bernard. He's the perfect English gentleman. He's cultured, well-spoken, he works at the BBC, he even has a harpsichord! Soon, I move in with Bernard. I will live with him for one year.

ZOHRA
1982.

MOANA
I'm four years old. We move to Utah for a better life. I'm in preschool. The other kids don't know what to make of me. Nobody's ever heard of Tonga!

(*All clap.*)

RAJ
1982.

JOSEPH
Most members of my Mestizo family have lighter skin, but a few unfortunate ones have "kayumanggi" or darker skin. My mom always carries an umbrella with her to protect her skin from the sun. We even have a soap that's supposed to make your skin lighter. It's called Porcelana. My mom says:

KELLY
"Don't go playing in the sun. I don't want you to get any darker."

JOSEPH
During siesta, when the sun is at its height, she locks us in our rooms. As one of three lighter-skinned families on our street, we are seen as having higher status. It also helps us get away with not going to church!

(All clap two times.)

MOANA
1982.

PAULINE
Halloween.

ZOHRA
I'm dressed as a gypsy, with a long dress and Afghan tribal jewelry. Just as I'm about to go trick-or-treating, the mailman delivers a very thin yellow letter. I read it while sitting under the dining room table.

RAJ
"You have forty-eight hours to pack and leave the country."

ZOHRA
I read the letter over and over. I'm terrified. We can't go back to Afghanistan, and we can't stay in the United States. Where will we go?

JOSEPH
1982.

ZOHRA
At the last minute, my father's dental firm decides to sponsor him, so we can stay.

(All clap.)

MOANA/RAJ
1982.

JOSEPH
London.

PAULINE
I am twenty-two years old. I begin to go out in public dressed as a woman. It's a completely liberating experience. For the first time, I'm able to present myself as how I see myself. Unfortunately, Bernard does not understand this part of me. He's afraid that I will want to get sex reassignment surgery.

KELLY/ZOHRA
1982.

RAJ
My brother Ami is hanging out with a friend at Woolworth's. There is a bag of candy open. He only takes one piece, but the security guards catch him and call my dad. My dad is livid! He says:

JOSEPH
"You're hanging out with a bad crowd. You have brought shame on the family. We're moving!"

RAJ
We move from the diverse world of Sunnyside, Queens to Valley Stream, Long Island. We are the only Indian family on our street.

ZOHRA
1983.

PAULINE
Manila, Philippines.

ALL
LA-BAN, LA-BAN, LA-KAS NANG BAY-AN!

JOSEPH
I am eleven years old. Every day the streets are full of people protesting against the corrupt Marcos regime. The protestors wear yellow, the color of Aquino, the opposition leader living in exile in the United States. Yellow t-shirts, yellow bandanas. Women walk up to soldiers and put yellow flowers in the barrels of their guns. The movement is called:

ALL
People Power.

RAJ
1984.

KELLY
Queens, New York.

ZOHRA
I'm eight years old. I'm playing with other Afghan children in the yard. Because there are four major ethnic groups in Afghanistan, we all look different. Pashtuns and Tajiks have more green eyes and lighter hair, the Uzbek and Hazara from the North have almond-shaped eyes and straight hair. We argue over who looks more Afghan. We fight and yell until a door opens across the street. Joey, a Queens native, comes out and yells at us:

RAJ
"You stupid Arabs. You camel jockeys. Go back where you came from!"

ZOHRA
Instantly we are united. We might fight amongst ourselves, but as soon as an outsider challenges us, we become one people. And that's the history of Afghanistan!

　　　(All clap two times.)

MOANA
1984.

JOSEPH
The economic situation and civil unrest in the Philippines is getting worse and worse. One by one my relatives have left for America. Now, my family's going too. We're looking for a better life. I'm excited. I know all about America from the shows I watch on TV. I am twelve years old.

　　　(All clap.)

RAJ
1984.

ZOHRA
Los Angeles, California.

JOSEPH
After a sixteen hour plane ride, we arrive in the United States. The airport is decorated with balloons, streamers and flags. I see banners saying:

ALL
"Welcome to America."

JOSEPH
I think that my family are the first immigrants to the United States, and that America has rolled out the red carpet just for us. Only later do I find out that we arrived in the middle of the Los Angeles Olympic Games! My uncle, Buddy, meets us at the airport. Later, he takes me for my first American meal:

ALL
Tacos.

(All clap.)

MOANA
1984.

ZOHRA
Chester W. Nimitz Junior High School.

JOSEPH
It's my first day of school. I walk into the school and the first thing I hear is:

PAULINE
"Pssst, Chino!"

MOANA
"Hey, Chino!"

KELLY
"Yo, Chino!"

JOSEPH
I think to myself:

RAJ
"That's weird, I'm not even Chinese!"

PAULINE
1984.

JOSEPH
We are living in a tiny rented house in a mostly Chicano neighborhood. There are three families sharing two bedrooms. This is not the America I was expecting. On TV all the Americans are tall, blonde, and rich. I keep waiting for Farah Fawcett to show up!

(*All clap.*)

KELLY/RAJ
1984.

MOANA
Chicago.

PAULINE
I'm living in Chicago and I get my first professional job. I go to Milwaukee to visit my mother for the weekend. On Saturday night she calls me to her bedside. She tells me she knows that Bernard was my lover and that they had been secretly corresponding. Without ever using the words "homosexual" or "gay", she indicates that she accepts my sexuality and offers a sort of … maternal benediction.

ZOHRA/ MOANA
1984.

PAULINE
On Sunday, I take the bus back to Chicago. On Monday, my brother and I get the news that our mother has had a massive heart attack. We race up to be with her, but she dies a few days later. I believe the greatest challenge for my mother in her final years was to accept me. She had to go against everything she believed in, but, in the end, she learned to love me unconditionally.

(*All clap.*)

JOSEPH/RAJ
1985.

ZOHRA
Three years have passed, and my father's boss dangles the promise of a green card in front of him to keep him working seven days a week with minimum pay. After years of working without a break he says:

RAJ
"I can't work like this anymore. I need a day off or I'll go crazy."

ZOHRA
Finally he quits. He sleeps straight through a day and a half. Our immigration status is at risk again.

MOANA
1985.

PAULINE
Rolling Meadows, Illinois.

KELLY
I am seven years old. My parents want us to succeed in the US, and they feel that speaking proper English is one of the keys to this. At home, they encourage us to speak only English. On Sundays, my sister and I go to Chinese school to learn Mandarin. I try to learn the language, but I'm terrible at it.

(All clap.)

JOSEPH
1985.

MOANA
Valley Stream, Long Island.

RAJ
I like my nickname Raj better than my given name, Snehal. My brother started calling me Roger because he liked Buck Rogers on TV, and then it got Indianized to Raj. Every year on the first day of school, when the teacher gets to me, it's always:

PAULINE
Snee – hell?

KELLY
Snail?

ZOHRA
Snow-ball?

RAJ
I'm always embarrassed. So, I start blurting out:

JOSEPH
"Just call me Raj."

RAJ
Of course, that just makes it worse. Then all the kids say:

ZOHRA
"Hey JustcallmeRaj!"

MOANA
"What's up JustcallmeRaj?"

KELLY
"How's it going JustcallmeRaj?"

   (All clap.)

JOSEPH
1985.

KELLY
I am seven years old. My parents take me and my sister to see our family in Taiwan. Everything smells different there, like preserved plums and sea salt and even car exhaust. I stick close by my sister's side, since her Mandarin is better than mine, and bug her to translate everything. We meet endless amounts of family: aunties and cousins and cousins of cousins. The food seems different and strange, so I survive on orange juice, and spend the trip craving McDonald's.

PAULINE/RAJ
1985.

JOSEPH
In English class, we are reading SE Hinton's classic novel, *The Outsiders*. In it, I read Robert Frost's "Nothing Gold Can Stay":

ZOHRA
Nature's first green is gold,
Her hardest hue to hold.

MOANA
Her early leaf's a flower;
But only so an hour.

ZOHRA
Then leaf subsides to leaf.
So Eden sank to grief

MOANA
So dawn goes down to day.
Nothing gold can stay.

JOSEPH
I begin writing my own poetry in notebooks and journals. I keep my writing to myself. I don't think my family will understand.

KELLY/RAJ
1986.

ZOHRA
There are two places we can see Afghans in the movies, in Bollywood films and in Hollywood films such as:

MOANA
Rambo III with Sylvester Stallone.

RAJ
Spies Like Us with Dan Akroyd and Chevy Chase.

ZOHRA
Rambo shows Afghans as scrawny men in tents ready to fight the Soviets but ultimately needing the help of John Rambo, the one man army, to save the day. But, in the Bollywood films such as *Khuda Gawa*, the Afghan hero is a noble warrior true to his word and honorable in his deeds. Amitabh Bachan plays the Afghan. He is tall and fearless, but with a gentle heart.

MOANA
1986.

RAJ
Rolling Meadows, Illinois.

KELLY
I am eight years old. I follow my big sister's example and start writing at an early age. I write stories and poems, often illustrating them with my own drawings. I win my first poetry contest and read my poem out loud for an audience of senior citizens. The poem is called:

ALL
"What it means to be old."

(All clap.)

PAULINE/ JOSEPH
1987.

RAJ
About once every three months, on a Saturday night when the store is closed, my parents invite everyone they know over to our house. It's the only time I see my dad relax. My mom spends all day cooking vegetarian food. After the meal is served, the adults start singing and my dad plays the tabla. The men and women compete at singing Bollywood songs. Eventually, the kids get bored and wander off to watch "Saturday Night Live." To us, they are just singing the same old songs over and over, but to them, it's a piece of home away from home.

(All clap two times.)

MOANA
1987.

KELLY
I'm nine years old. I'm on the bus on my way home from school. I'm horsing around with another kid. We're yelling. Jimmy Jelenick looks at me in surprise and annoyance. He says:

JOSEPH
"I thought you people were supposed to be quiet!"

ZOHRA/ MOANA
1988.

PAULINE
People often assume that I was raised in Korea or in a Korean-American household. Often when I meet people for the first time they say:

RAJ
"Oh you speak really good English. How long have you lived in America?"

PAULINE
It's hard to explain that I was raised in Milwaukee in a white Lutheran German-American family and that I don't speak Korean. I end up feeling like a "fake" Korean. I'm not Korean enough for Koreans and not American enough for Americans.

(All clap.)

JOSEPH
1989.

RAJ
Orem, Utah.

MOANA
My older sister Fui tells me:

ZOHRA
"I was dating a white guy at Brigham Young University. I used to starve myself and work out constantly so he would think I was beautiful. We were supposed to go meet his family in the south, but after he talked to his father about me, he backed out of it. That was the end of that relationship."

MOANA
I don't want to go through what my sister went through. I make a promise to myself:

KELLY
"I will never date a white guy!"

MOANA
I am eleven years old.

(All clap.)

RAJ
1989.

PAULINE
Bellflower, CA

JOSEPH
I'm a senior in high school. My counselor encourages me to go to Princeton or
Berkeley. My mother wants me to attend a school nearby and live at home like
my sisters did. But I feel stifled at home. I will explode if I don't leave. So, I
make a deal with her:

RAJ
"If you let me move out, I'll only apply to schools within a 45 minute drive."

JOSEPH
She finally agrees. I get a full scholarship to Loyola Marymount University, a
wealthy, private college in Los Angeles.

MOANA/ PAULINE
1990.

RAJ
I am fifteen years old. My dad is out of the house by 4:00 am and when he
comes home at 7:30, he's so exhausted that he just eats his dinner without
talking and goes to bed. I feel like he hardly notices me. To get his attention, I
try to excel at absolutely everything. At school I join every club, play every
sport:

KELLY
Soccer.

JOSEPH
Basketball.

KELLY
Tennis.

JOSEPH
Baseball.

KELLY
Mathletes.

JOSEPH
Honor society.

KELLY
Band.

JOSEPH
Orchestra.

KELLY
Marching band.

ALL
… and Peace Club.

RAJ
I always ask my father to come to my games, my concerts, my assemblies. But he'll never take the day off. He just says:

JOSEPH
"If I come to your game, who's going to run the store?"

(All clap.)

ZOHRA/ PAULINE
1990.

JOSEPH
I arrive at college. It's much more diverse than my high school, but it is also more elite. All those rich, white, blonde people I was looking for when I first arrived in the US? Well, they're all at Loyola. During orientation, we're asked what we did over the summer:

PAULINE
"I summered in the Swiss Alps."

KELLY
"I interned at my father's investment firm."

MOANA
"Joseph, like, what did you do?"

JOSEPH
"Well, I, like, summered in Compton, you know, South Central LA, *Boyz in the Hood*? Oh, and I saw my first Woody Allen film!"

(All clap.)

PAULINE
1990.

JOSEPH
The boys in my dormitory have no sense of their own privilege. They move
through the world as if they own it. They've never struggled. I'm amazed at
their ease. I feel like I'm from a totally different planet. For the first time I'm
becoming aware of being Asian in a white world; for the first time I am lonely.

MOANA
1990.

JOSEPH
Loyola has a peer counseling program for new Asian-American students. My
counselor, Anna Gonzalez, is also Filipina-American. We talk about issues of
identity, how Asians are perceived in American society. It's the first time I have
a sense of a larger Asian-American community, and an Asian-American
consciousness.

(All clap two times.)

KELLY/ ZOHRA
1992.

RAJ
Orem, Utah.

MOANA
I'm attending a school which is predominantly white. I tell my dad I want to go
to a school with more Tongans students. I switch to Provo High School, but I
don't speak much Tongan so my Tongan classmates make fun of me. My
siblings and I start pressuring our parents to speak Tongan to us again.

JOSEPH
1992.

RAJ
I'm a straight-A student, top of my class. I could probably get a scholarship to
any college, but I know I'm going to Hofstra, just like my brother did. I have to
stay at home and work at the store.

KELLY
1992.

ZOHRA
The Mormon Mission.

MOANA
Every Mormon is expected to go on a two year mission to recruit new converts.
My sister Loa is sent to Arkansas, Mississippi, and Tennessee .She writes a 'zine
critical of her mission and its leader. When it's discovered, Loa is suspended
from her mission. My mother begs the church to forgive her. The church
fathers refuse to talk to my mother because she is a woman. They refuse to
pardon Loa. My mother, sisters and I leave the Mormon Church; my father and
brother remain.

   (*All clap.*)

PAULINE
1993.

JOSEPH
I take a poetry workshop with a poet named Gail Wronsky. She assigns books
from living breathing poets. Before, I just assumed all poetry was written by
dead white men about urns and nightingales. The first time I read a poem by
Sharon Olds I'm blown away. I think:

RAJ
"You can write about this? You can write about real life? You can write about a
diaphragm?"

   (*All clap.*)

ZOHRA/RAJ
1994.

MOANA
Palatine, Illinois.

KELLY
My high school English teacher, Mr. Sampson, takes us into Chicago to see
poets perform. We're all underage, but he sneaks us into the Green Mill
Cocktail Lounge, the birthplace of the poetry slam movement. It's one of Al
Capone's old speakeasies, full of dark wood and stained glass. I start performing
my own poetry at local open mic nights and cafes.

MOANA
1994.

RAJ
My father comes home from the store. He is pounding on the door. He says:

JOSEPH
"I feel like I have an elephant on my chest!"

RAJ
I drive him to the hospital. He's having a massive heart attack. The doctors say he needs a quadruple bypass.

ZOHRA
1994.

RAJ
While my father recovers from his heart surgery. I run the store. I get up at five am and go to sleep at ten pm. I'm too tired to see my friends. I'm too tired to do anything. I finally understand why my father never came to my games and concerts. I finally understand how hard he was working for all of us.

(All clap two times.)

MOANA
1995.

JOSEPH
I'm going to graduate school for my MFA in creative writing. I still haven't told my mother that I write poetry. Instead, I tell her I'm going for a Master's degree in journalism. When I tell her I'm moving all the way to New York City she says:

KELLY
"It's too far away."

PAULINE
"It's dangerous."

KELLY
"You're going to get mugged!"

PAULINE
"It's cold there!"

KELLY
"You'll get buried alive by the snow."

(All clap two times.)

RAJ
1996.

ZOHRA
Orem, Utah.

MOANA
I'm tired of being "Other." I'm tired of censoring myself around people who can only embrace a white, Mormon point of view. I'm accepted to a summer art program at Pratt Institute in Brooklyn. Even though I don't have the money to go, I go anyway. I will explode if I don't leave.

JOSEPH
1996.

MOANA
When I arrive at LaGuardia airport I have $1.76 in my pocket. I realize I can't afford a taxi or the shuttle bus. I take a local bus to the "A" train to Brooklyn, which leaves me with twenty-six cents. At the token booth I explain to the attendant that I really need to get to Pratt Institute but that I don't have any money. She says:

PAULINE
"Oh, I'll give you a token. But, how are you going to come back?"

MOANA
"I'm not coming back, I'll be staying at Pratt."

PAULINE
"Oh! This is where your life begins. Good luck!"

MOANA
Before I left Utah, My friend Alicia said to me:

KELLY
"Don't talk to anybody, don't make eye contact, don't trust anybody in New York!"

MOANA
I get off at the wrong stop. I'm 17 blocks from Pratt, lugging a heavy suitcase. I'm exhausted. I meet an African-American man in his thirties.

JOSEPH
"Do you need some help?"

MOANA
"No thanks, that's okay."

JOSEPH
"Are you sure? It looks like a really heavy suitcase."

KELLY
"Don't talk to anybody, don't make eye contact, don't trust anybody in New York!"

JOSEPH
"You look really tired. I just want to help a sister out. You can trust me."

MOANA
I accept. He picks up the suitcase.

JOSEPH
"You know Pratt is still a ways from here. Why don't you take a bus?"

MOANA
He runs to a corner store and comes back with change for the bus. When the bus comes, he says to the driver:

JOSEPH
"Hey, brother, this sister needs to get to Pratt. Can you make sure she gets there?"

RAJ
"Sure thing."

JOSEPH
"All right sister, this bus will take you to Pratt. This is where your life begins. I know you'll make it."

MOANA
I break out in tears. When we arrive at Pratt the driver says:

RAJ
"Good luck. This is where your life begins."

(All clap ten times.)

MOANA
Fakka 'ofa, 'ofa 'ofa 'ofa
lahi atu, lahi atu
Fakka 'ofa, 'ofa 'ofa 'ofa
lahi atu, lahi atu
Cha-hoo!

(MOANA dances.)

ALL
Fakka 'ofa, 'ofa 'ofa 'ofa
lahi atu, lahi atu
Cha-hoo!
Fakka 'ofa, 'ofa 'ofa 'ofa
lahi atu, lahi atu
Fakka 'ofa, 'ofa 'ofa 'ofa
lahi atu, lahi atu.

MOANA
What do people think of when they hear the word Tonga?

RAJ
A Japanese monster movie?

KELLY
A country in Africa?

JOSEPH
It's a form of Roman dress.

PAULINE
Don't they wear grass skirts?

ZOHRA
Is it part of Polynesia?

ALL
I have no idea.

KELLY
Moana, what do you think of when you hear the word Tonga?

MOANA
Pure happiness, strength, and abundance.
A people who are generous and strong.
My Grandfather, Siasosi, and his home, surrounded by mango, tamarind and
mai trees always swaying in the ocean breeze.
A language of vowels, vowels and vowels.
Food – mussels, octopus, pineapples, mangos, manioke, pigs – It ain't Tongan
if there ain't any food!
I think of my grandmother's four-hour long prayers, and her big phone bill
because she is the one that knows all the news in all the villages. I think of my
family, our traditions and our culture we kept in America.

ZOHRA
What do people think of when they think of Afghanistan?

PAULINE
The Taliban

KELLY
Burqas

JOSEPH
Poppy fields

MOANA
Osama Bin Laden

ALL
War! War! War!

RAJ
Zohra?

ZOHRA
Yes, Raj?

RAJ
What do you think of when you think of Afghanistan?

ZOHRA
Pine nuts and dried apricots, served with black tea perfumed with cardamom.
When I'm lonely for the company of gossip-sharers, Afghanistan is the side of
the courtyard filled with women. Afghanistan is their whispering and giggling. I
imagine an old aunt or grandmother reading tea leaves, a row of overturned
cups waiting to be read. Yellow dust and more yellow dust - yellow dust that
covers everything: streets, courtyards, buildings, people. The Hindu Kush
mountain range, which my father says is the trailing skirts of the Himalayas.

PAULINE
Joseph?

JOSEPH
Yes, Pauline?

PAULINE
What do you think of when you think of the Philippines?

JOSEPH
The *palenke*, the open-air market my mother used to take me to. My brother
and me buying warm pan de sal at dawn for the family for breakfast. My
summers in the province running through cornfields with my cousins. The pigs
I fed, the chickens I plucked, the bats I killed. I think of monsoons. The open
sewers, the poverty and the corruption. I think of midnight mass during
Christmas time, then sticky purple rice cakes after. I think of my father at the
race track, my aunts doing laundry side by side, gossiping, and my mother
washing her hair by a river.

MOANA
Kelly, what do you think of when you think of Taiwan?

KELLY
My grandmother's tiny feet shrunken by foot binding.
Goldfish gliding in the pond outside of my auntie's house in
Tainan. My uncle who swims every morning in Taipei and looks like a bullfrog.
My auntie on New Year's Day, dressed in red, smoothing her jacket against her
stomach before she stuffs an entire suitcase full of steamed bread to send to my

(MORE)

KELLY (cont.)
mother. I think of mah jongg tiles clattering beneath my aunties fingers. I think
of my grandfather's feet, his hands curled around the arms of a sitting chair. I
think of orange juice and mayonnaise and octopus, my brown skin hiding
behind my sister's arm.

ZOHRA
Raj, what do you think of when you think of India?

RAJ
My Mom's amazing cooking and the smell of spices in the air. Very colorful
clothes for festive events and a very particular burning smell that I only smell in
India. The noise and chaos of Vadodara, and the quiet and tranquility of the
countryside. The sounds of a sitar and tabla. The cows and other animals that
can wander the streets freely because they are sacred. I think of how much
clearer Gujarati can express a feeling or experience than English can. I think of
my relatives eating pan, drinking chai and laughing.

KELLY
Pauline, what do you think of when you think of Korea?

PAULINE
I think of the Korean birth family that I never knew. I wonder if any of them
are still alive. I think of a land I have no memory of, and I wonder when I might
have the opportunity to go "back" to visit.

RAJ
What do you think of when you think of Milwaukee?

PAULINE
Beer, bratwurst & bowling! The racially segregated public schools of my
childhood. I think of my grandmother who embodied the German-American
culture of Milwaukee: the city of my childhood and youth. The biggest small
town in the United States.

    (*All clap ten times.*)

MOANA
Kataki mou me'a hake.

    (*MUSIC. All close books, stand up, change seats.*)

MOANA
Kataki mou me'a hifo ki lalo.

(*All sit, open books.*)

JOSEPH
1996.

RAJ
1996.

ALL
1996.

ZOHRA
I join Asian-American Writers Workshop as an intern. One of the other interns asks me:

KELLY
"Why would you be considered Asian-American if you are from Afghanistan?"

ZOHRA
I gently explain to her that Afghanistan is part of the land mass known as Central Asia, so why wouldn't I be considered Asian-American?

(*All clap.*)

RAJ
1996.

PAULINE
When I move to New York, I meet some other adult Korean adoptees for the first time. I gradually realize that I have a distinct identity as a Korean adoptee that is different from an ethnic Korean identity or Korean-American identity. I don't feel like a fake Korean anymore. After all, I am the real me!

(*All clap two times.*)

JOSEPH/MOANA
1997.

RAJ
In my family, like in so many Indian immigrant families, the expectation is that
(*MORE*)

RAJ (cont.)
the second generation will become doctors, lawyers, or engineers. One day, my mom steps on a needle and has to go to the emergency room. Of course, my dad won't leave the store, so I drive her to the hospital. The doctors begin to stitch up her foot. As soon as I see the blood, I feel sick. I say:

JOSEPH
"I think I have to sit down."

RAJ
Next thing I know, I wake up on the floor, my mother is standing on one foot leaning over me and screaming:

PAULINE
"My son! My son!"

RAJ
It looks like I won't be a doctor after all.

(All clap two times.)

KELLY/ZOHRA
1997.

PAULINE
I knew that I was transgendered when I was five years old. I have always wanted to live as a woman. Now is the right time. I have moved, I have gone through a career change, and I am ready to transition.

MOANA
1997.

PAULINE
There are many ways one can transition from male to female. I decide I don't need hormones or sex reassignment surgery to live as a woman. This is somewhat unusual within the trans-gender community, but I'm comfortable with who I am.

RAJ
1997.

PAULINE
I must choose a new name for my new identity. At first, I think about using my Korean birth name, but any Korean would immediately recognize it as a male name. So, I decide to use my Korean family name, Park, and Pauline, which is a feminine version of my adopted name, Paul. I practice my new signature over and over again.

KELLY
Pauline Park

ZOHRA
Pauline Park

JOSEPH
Pauline Park

MOANA
Pauline Park

RAJ
Pauline Park.

PAULINE
The act of naming oneself is one of the most powerful acts of self-construction and self-empowerment in which one can engage.

(All clap two times.)

JOSEPH/ZOHRA/KELLY
1997.

RAJ
I get my first job out of college working at a high-end financial management firm in Manhattan.

MOANA
Meaning taking care of rich people's money.

RAJ
Most of the other workers are just going through the motions. When I start asking for extra responsibilities, the other workers look at me like I'm crazy. They say:

KELLY
"Why do you try so hard? Just punch the clock, shut up and work."

MOANA
1997.

ZOHRA
I give a poetry reading at my college. The audience is primarily older white female professors. Afterwards they compliment my poetry, then say in a sympathetic voice:

PAULINE
"You must be so proud to be going to college. Are you the first Afghan woman in college?"

ZOHRA
I'm really shocked. When I tell them that Afghan women are quite educated, and involved in politics, they brush it off as still rare.

    (All clap.)

KELLY
1997.

PAULINE
I become more involved with activism. There's a need for more understanding and acceptance of transgendered people. I co-found Queens Pride House, a center for lesbian, gay, bisexual, and transgendered people in Queens, and Iban/Queer Koreans of New York.

ZOHRA/JOSEPH
1998.

MOANA
I'm an art student at New York University. My art professor says:

KELLY
"Why do you always need to bring up race? You are so angry. Why do you have to be so angry? Your anger is trendy."

MOANA
Later my friend Leona makes me a t-shirt that reads:

ALL
"My anger is trendy!"

(*All clap two times.*)

RAJ
1998.

PAULINE
Transsexual, transgendered, and gender-variant people are not covered by discrimination and hate crimes laws in New York. With a group of colleagues I found NYAGRA, the New York Association for Gender Rights Advocacy. We are fighting for full equality under law.

MOANA
1998.

KELLY
Vermont.

JOSEPH
I'm visiting a friend at an artist colony. There I have the opportunity to meet a very prestigious Japanese-American poet. I have read his work and look up to him. When my friend introduces us he says:

RAJ
"Legaspi, isn't that a Filipino name?"

JOSEPH
"Yes, it is."

RAJ
"So, tell me ... have you ever eaten dog?"

JOSEPH
I'm totally shocked. Did I hear him wrong? But then he says:

RAJ
"Yeah, I heard that different colored dogs taste different!"

JOSEPH
I'm so disappointed. I thought he would know better.

(*All clap two times.*)

ZOHRA
1999.

PAULINE
July 4, 1999:

MOANA
Over Independence Day weekend a white supremacist named Benjamin Smith rages through Illinois and Indiana, targeting African-Americans, Jews and Asians in the name of racial hatred. He kills two people and wounds nine others.

KELLY
I join together with some friends from the poetry scene to perform at anti-hate rallies across the community. We come together as black, brown, and yellow women, representing our voices against racial violence. Almost without knowing it, we form a group, which becomes known as Sirens.

ZOHRA
1999.

RAJ
I'm twenty-four years old. I'm living at home, working eighty hours a week at a technology startup. My dad still wants me to work weekends at the store. It's too much. I need to tell him I can't work at the store anymore, that it's time for me to move out. When I break the news to my father he says:

JOSEPH
"Fine. I don't need you. Move out next weekend. You and your brother don't care for your family!"

RAJ
One week later, he has his second heart attack.

   (All clap.)

MOANA/ZOHRA
1999.

RAJ
My brother and I try to convince our father to give up the store. We say:

KELLY
"Dad, you've had two heart attacks in five years. We don't want to lose you."

JOSEPH
"I'd rather die working in my store then give it up."

RAJ
Finally, after much arguing, we convince him to sell the store and the house and retire in Florida. But he says he'll never forgive us for it!

(All clap.)

ZOHRA
1999.

MOANA
My grandfather is ill. He comes to the United States for treatment. For the first time, I'm really able to get to know him. I tell him that I'm struggling with what it means to be Tongan, that I'm sick of living in the United States and I want to go to Tonga or New Zealand to be with other Pacific Youth. He tells me:

RAJ
"Always be proud of who you are. You are Tongan and Tongan can be whatever you want it to be."

(All clap.)

PAULINE
2000.

KELLY
I graduate from college and move to Chicago to work for a not-for-profit called Urban Options which teaches youth entrepreneurship. I teach eight-year-olds how to start Mother's Day card businesses. I teach high school students how to read supply and demand graphs. I teach older women how to make business plans. At twenty-two, I don't know how to do these things either, but I'm learning along with them. I'd like to make more room in my life for the poetry, but I'm not sure that it can accomplish the same concrete changes as my community-based work.

ZOHRA/MOANA
2000.

RAJ
I help save the start-up company I work for from bankruptcy. After the CEO cries to me in gratitude, he offers to pay half of my tuition for my MBA. Midway through the program, even though business is booming, he revokes his offer. I have to go into debt to finish the program. I feel deeply betrayed.

JOSEPH/KELLY
2000.

MOANA
My friends Angie, Maura and Erica and I are always asking:

ZOHRA
"How do we fit into the New York arts community?"

KELLY
"Who is doing work that represents us?"

MOANA
We decide to form a collective that speaks for us, as women of color, where we can make our own theater, music and poetry. We decide to call our collective "Mahina Movement," after the Tongan word for Moon and playing off of *imaginesa* the Spanish word for imagination.

    (All clap.)

PAULINE
2001.

KELLY
When I leave Urban Options, my student Sheila says:

MOANA
"Well, before you started working here, I thought there were only black people and white people, but now I know there are black people, white people and Chinese people!"

    (All clap.)

JOSEPH/PAULINE
2001.

MOANA
Washington, DC:

PAULINE
I attend the first international gathering of the first generation of adult Korean adoptees. There are over one hundred thousand Korean adoptees in the United States and over two thousand at the conference. During a break from a discussion session, one of the men in my group says to me:

RAJ
"Umm, you know, some people in our group don't know if you're a man or a woman."

PAULINE
I decide to come out as transgendered to the whole group. Eventually everyone in the group comes to accept me, even those who were raised in Evangelical Christian homes like I was. As Korean adoptees we all have something very powerful in common.

(All clap.)

ZOHRA
2001

KELLY
2001

MOANA
2001

JOSEPH
2001

PAULINE
2001

RAJ
2001

MOANA
September 11, 2001.

KELLY
I'm in New York City for a training workshop with some colleagues. I'm braiding my hair in a hotel on the edge of Chinatown, getting ready to leave, when CNN starts showing footage of planes going into the Twin Towers. We call the office and they tell us to come downtown anyway.

ZOHRA
2001:

KELLY
We get on the train and start heading closer to downtown. Almost immediately, the train stops. We realize we have made a very bad decision. There is smoke seeping in. People are starting to panic. I'm sitting next to an older gentleman, and he is calm as day. He turns to me and says:

JOSEPH
"You know what I love about New York? The summertime. All the festivals in the parks. All my kids moved away from New York, but not me. They could drop an atomic bomb on this place, and I would still come crawling back."

KELLY
We're stuck underground for forty-five minutes. The train finally pulls up to the platform, and we walk up the staircase. I've never been so happy to see sunshine in my life.

(All clap.)

PAULINE
2001.

RAJ
After September 11, everyone looks at me differently. I can feel eyes on me everywhere. I suddenly know what it feels like to go from model minority to feared minority. In the weeks after 9/11, people yell at me on the street:

ZOHRA
"You terrorist, why don't you go back where you came from."

RAJ
For two years, I don't grow any facial hair. Still, every time I travel, I'm stopped at security and customs. Every time I get on a plane, people look at me with fear.

(All clap.)

MOANA
2001.

ZOHRA
In the aftermath of 9/11, during the rise of fear and hostility towards Afghans, Arabs, South Asians and whomever else might be viewed as a potential terrorist, a professor at Brooklyn College, where I'm teaching, begins walking back and forth very slowly outside my Medieval Literature lecture, eavesdropping. One day, he stops me and a colleague in the hallway and says:

RAJ
"You better be careful going home tonight."

ZOHRA
He looks at me very closely. Sweat is pouring down his face.

RAJ
"I hear the Moslems are going to bomb something tonight!"

(All clap two times.)

RAJ/MOANA
2002.

KELLY
New York City.

JOSEPH
Although there are resources for Asian-American writers, there is nothing specifically for poets. My friend Sarah and I decide to create a literary group committed to Asian-American poets. We call it, "Kundiman," after a form of love song which disguised a protest song during the Spanish occupation of the Philippines.

RAJ
2002.

MOANA
After years of work by NYAGRA and other organizations, the New York City Council passes a bill amending city human rights law to prohibit discrimination based on gender identity or expression.

PAULINE
Mayor Bloomberg signs the bill into law. I participate in the signing ceremony.
The new law is a huge victory for the transgender community, but there is still
much, much more work to do.

(*All clap.*)

MOANA
2002.

RAJ
I'm tired of the corporate politics and corporate ethics. I just want to do
something for a good cause, something where I can use my business skills. I
find Explore Charter School, founded by Morty Ballen, a man with integrity and
passion for equality in education. His school educates underprivileged and at-
risk kindergarten through third grade children. I take a job with Explore. I also
take a huge pay cut.

PAULINE
2003

MOANA
Chicago.

KELLY
Between my community work and performing across the country,
I don't see my friends or family for months at a time. I have my professional
life, my poetry, and my personal life, but I only have time for two of the three.
Something's got to give. I apply for a month-long writing residency in
Minnesota. I tell myself:

ZOHRA
"If I get the residency – that will be my time to go."

JOSEPH
2003.

MOANA
I'm going back to Tonga for the first time since I was a baby. I arrive on a warm
night, under a full moon. My family meets me at the airport, aunts and uncles
and cousins. We are all weeping. The second I arrive in Tonga, I feel absolute
comfort and familiarity. I have returned to my *Hoku Fonua Totonu*:

JOSEPH
Inang Bayan

RAJ
Des

KELLY
Jia Shang

ZOHRA
Watan

ALL
Homeland.

(*All clap two times.*)

PAULINE/ MOANA
2003

ZOHRA
The Philippines.

KELLY
I'm in Manila for a conference of women playwrights. I meet Debbie from Uganda and Maria from East Timor. We talk about our art and our political work. I am amazed that from so far away, we have so much in common. Maria introduces me to JoJo, her friend from East Timor. He and I spend the next four days together pouring our lives out to each other. Before I leave, JoJo says:

JOSEPH
"Kelly I want you to go home, and change your life. I want you to take care of yourself."

(*All clap ten times. Blackout. MUSIC.*)

MOANA
E fafine Tonga, ko e ngaahi 'ofefine kitautolu mo e
fanga tokotua 'o e lanu melomelo.
Ko e lanu melomelo 'oku 'ikai ma'u ia 'I ha po momoko
'E hoku fanga tokoua, ko e tapuaki 'e tau fakataha mo
'etau lava me'a fakatautefito 'oku ha'aha'a 'a natula.
Ko e lanu melomelo ko e kelekele ia ke tau tu'u ma'u

(*MORE*)

MOANA (cont.)
ai, ma'u ai pe, 'o fakatupulekina ai 'a ho tau ngaahi
tapuaki ne tapuekina 'aki tautolu tukufakaholo.

RAJ
A thirty-two year journey has led me here.
Lots of good times and bad, which I think are ultimately good.
The one who said the eye cannot see itself
Was never brave enough to look in the mirror.
Throughout my journey, battles with abandonment, betrayal and words like
"not good enough" have been overcome.

I have forgiven myself for believing harsh words and
Not realizing how others project their own battles unknowingly.
I thank my brother for being my father figure and
For supporting me throughout my life.
I thank all of my loved ones, who know who they are
For listening and being there whenever I needed.
I continue my journey and healing through laughter, music, self-awareness and
Relentless support to everyone who needs it and is ready to accept it, in any way
that I can.

ZOHRA
Ajab mautam sarra dunya
oulum payauni yugh bilsam
saanam bu sarraiga maghroor bulma
hargiz waafa kilmass
ulumni uoylagan adam bu dunyaga nazar saulmass.

PAULINE
Have you been back? they ask
As if it's been a year or two
Instead of half a century that separates
The country of my birth
From the eight-month-old
Who never called that country home

Have you been back? they ask
A lifetime of experience
Encompassed in the answer
I should give but don't
No time for that; too complicated

(MORE)

PAULINE (cont.)
I've not been back, not yet, I smile

You could have asked, have you been back
To Madison, to London or Chicago?
Champaign-Urbana, Brussels, Paris, Regensburg, Berlin?
I have memories of these
But not of that ancestral land
That you imagine home for me

Have you been back? they ask
As if it were the first time someone asked me
And not the thousandth;
I want to scream; of course I don't
That wouldn't be polite
That wouldn't be Korean, either

Have you been back? they ask
I've not been back
Oh, that's too bad, they say
You really should, you know

I hope to go; I will, one day
But not this year and not today.

JOSEPH
Up on a tree across the yard, a raven thrashes,
showering the ground with pine needle rain.
You jolt in delight, speak
your baby-gurgle, point your pale
caterpillar finger at that dark commotion
not unlike a feathery stirring of memories.
In my nesting arms, I carry you as my father perhaps
once carried me and how I've seen
your father hold you, blood
of my blood, my sister's daughter
                        I have been gone too long,
traveled distances I myself sometimes cannot bear,
but the sweetness of the first words
and raven sounds which roll from your tongue
has made me remember what I left behind:
somewhere in a timeless place
a boy rides a horse through rice puddles

(MORE)

JOSEPH (cont.)
a boy feeds on the ivory meat of coconuts
a boy suckles on the udders of a carabao
and under a tropical twilight dome fireflies scatter like stars
onto a field where that same boy falls into a deep, silent slumber.
Now, you sleep, little blackbird.
I will chase away the cat, destroyer
of the moth of dreams,
and when you awaken
you will again restore my sight to the threads that bind.

KELLY
The illustrations look the same
I remember:
Lao shi hao
Teacher how are you?
Zan qi lai
Stand up
Ju gong
Bow down
Zuo xia
Sit down

These were the first things
they taught us to say in Chinese school
and we would repeat:
Lao shi hao
Zan qi lai
Ju gong
Zuo xia
Acting each motion out like good obedient children, taking cues from the kids
in the books, which opened from the opposite direction.
Lao Shi Hao
The kids were always in school uniforms
with rosy red cheeks and bright white skin jet black hair, braided or bobbed
books carried enthusiastically under one arm.
Zan Qi Lai
So of course, I would recognize them
even fifteen years after failing to learn Chinese beaming at me from a book
opened Western-style screaming:
"I love to brush my teeth!"
"I love to study hard every day!"

(MORE)

KELLY (cont.)
"I love to read my little red book!"
"Long live Mao!"
"Long live Mao!"
"Long live Mao!"
I can tell I have made a mistake
by coming into the revolutionary bookstore.
Surrounded by the enormous heads of Mao and Lenin, I am confused, and start
playing "choose your own adventure" with what I see before me.
Delete Chinese children here.
Insert white, brown, black, red children here.
Delete Mao.
Leave all other text the same.
Insert Saddam.
Insert W.
Insert Paris Hilton.
Insert whoever the fuck you want to.
Ju gong
Is it as funny when the indoctrinated look like you?
Is it as cool, as kitschy, as righteous?
Is it as easy to scream, "Revolution now!"
if you knew you'd have to give up some of your shit?
Is Mao as much of a genius when he tells you that your *bougie* urban intellectual
ass needs to stop reading books and go out into the fields to work?
Did you know that communism is not theoretical for everyone?
Zuo xia
My friend signs off all of his e-mails:
"Siempre luchando, paz y revolucion,"
As if the two were possible: peace and revolution, As if bloodless wars didn't
still tear psyches apart.
Change hurts.
Living it is hard.
We've got to be ready if we decide to ...
Zan qi lai
Stand up
Zan qi lai
Zan qi lai.

PAULINE
You can choose anything in the world you want my child, but you can never
choose your heritage.

    (All clap ten times.)

ALL
2003

JOSEPH
Tonga.

MOANA
For the whole summer, I soak everything up. I see my family everyday. I spend time with my grandmother, and hear stories of my grandfather. Although he is gone, I connect with him through the stories, and through the people who knew him. After a summer in Tonga, I no longer have to fight for my Tongan identity. Still one thing does surprise me. Often when I meet people in Tonga, they will ask:

PAULINE
"Are you Samoan?"

RAJ
"Maori?"

ZOHRA
"Hawaiian?"

JOSEPH
"I know, you're American!"

      (All clap.)

ALL
2003.

KELLY
I'm auditioning for Def Poetry on HBO. At the audition taping, there's a crew of poets on stage called Poetree Chicago – they're friends of mine. I've performed with them a bunch of times. We're all part of the same performance scene. Suddenly I hear some of the rhymes they're dropping:

MOANA
"Yo check it,
I'm going to be like Connie Chung –
ching chung
ching chung
ching chung ching."

KELLY
Before I kick my piece, I ask them and the audience:

ZOHRA
"Where is the respect? Do we stand for what we believe in for all people, or just the ones that look like us? It hurts my heart, because I saw us as brothers and sisters."

　　　　(All clap two times.)

ALL
2004.

KELLY
Suddenly, everything is starting to fall into place. All within one week, I do my first artist residency in New York, find out I am accepted to the writing residency in Minnesota, and learn and that my poem got picked up for Season Four of "Def Poetry." I feel like the whole universe is saying:

MOANA
"Are you ready? C'mon, let's go!"

　　　　(All clap.)

ALL
2004.

ZOHRA
In the years after September 11 and the US invasion of Afghanistan, everyone suddenly wants to understand Afghanistan. People constantly ask me to participate in events and fundraisers. But more often than not, they are looking for a refugee story, a victim story.

ALL
2004.

ZOHRA
I'm participating in a panel at Asia Society. The topic is, "Afghan Women in Film and Television." The first question is:

PAULINE
"So how do you feel about letting go of the *burqa*?"

(All clap two times.)

ALL
2004.

MOANA
Mahina Movement performs at a lot of colleges and universities. Almost every school has Asian-American student groups, but they are always separate. East Asian students with East Asians, South Asians with South Asians. I wonder:

ZOHRA
Where is the community in our community?

ALL
2004.

KELLY
I used to question why my parents insisted on speaking English at home. Now it's about my choices. If I want to learn Mandarin, there is something I can do about it. For the 7th time in my life, I go to Taiwan, with the intention of visiting family and doing an intensive Mandarin language program for three months.

ALL
2004.

KELLY
When I arrive in Taipei, the Level I course has already started, so I decide to try the Level II. On the first day of class the teacher asks each student in Mandarin:

PAULINE
"What is your name, where are you from?"

KELLY
When it is my turn, I panic, I freeze.

PAULINE
"What is your name, where you are from?"

ZOHRA
"I ... I ... I don't know."

KELLY
The other students laugh. I run out of the room in tears. I think to myself:

ZOHRA
"I'm so stupid, what did I think I was doing by coming here? What did I think I would achieve?"

ALL
2004.

MOANA
Three months later:

KELLY
I'm at dinner with my Auntie Dai-yi. My uncle Da-Aie Fu is talking. Midway through a sentence he stops and slaps the table with both hands. He yells out in his Shandong accented Mandarin:

JOSEPH
"You understand what we're saying! This is great, three months ago, she didn't understand anything, now she understands!"

KELLY
I feel truly at home, truly with both sides of my family. They have always shown me unconditional love whenever I visit, but for the first time I feel like I am communicating with them on my own terms as an adult. Learning this language is not a big melodramatic thing, it's a process. It's about the gap between me and my heritage. If I commit the time, I can make that gap smaller one character at a time.

   (All clap.)

ALL
2005

JOSEPH
New York City.

RAJ
One of the great things about New York is all the South Asian culture available. I go to tabla and sitar performances, or go hear an Indian-American author read. I attend performances by SALAAM and Desipina, and go see South Asian comedians. I wish I could read and write Gujarati. I wish I knew my culture and my history better and this is a way to connect. I'm both Indian and American, but I don't know enough about either culture. Sometimes I feel like I am the typical ABCD:

ALL
American Born Confused Desi.

(All clap.)

ALL
2005.

PAULINE
I'm invited to be grand marshal of the New York City Pride March, the oldest and largest pride parade in the country. I'm the first openly transgendered person to be grand marshal. It is a huge honor. It feels like the culmination of my many years of activism.

ALL
2005.

PAULINE
The day of the parade is hot as hell. I'm wearing a new gown, riding in a Rolls-Royce, leading off a parade in front of more than two million people. They are all screaming my name.

JOSEPH
"Pauline, Pauline, wave over here."

MOANA
"Pauline, Pauline, smile for the camera."

PAULINE
It's a heady moment, let me tell you. But I decide I'm not going to let it go to my head.

(All clap.)

ALL
2005.

RAJ
My doctor says:

KELLY
"If you don't cut down your cholesterol and start exercising, you're going to end up having a heart attack just like your dad."

RAJ
Still the overachiever, I decide not just to exercise, but to train for the New York City Marathon. I ask my dad to come up from Florida to cheer me on. He says:

JOSEPH
"Why would you want to do such a thing? Twenty-six miles? What are you, crazy?"

RAJ
But he agrees to come.

ALL
2006.

KELLY
Sometimes it's hard to explain what I do. I say I'm a full time spoken word artist/essayist/playwright/choreographer. So basically, I tour the country all year round and spit poetry. Hands down – the best job in the world. My mom says:

MOANA
"You know it's not just Chinese people who don't know what you do. American people don't know either."

    (All clap.)

ALL
2006.

ZOHRA
I'm writing my dissertation on Afghan-American literature. I used to feel like an imposter when people asked me to represent the Afghan experience. Now, I can speak as an expert.

    (All clap.)

ALL
2006.

RAJ
After four years with Explore Charter School, I have done all that I can do.

                                                 (MORE)

RAJ (cont.)
The school has more than doubled in student population, tripled in staff size
and doubled in annual budget. In my time with Explore, I feel like I've found
my voice at last. I'm ready for a new challenge. I decide to start my own
company, Charter School Business Management, to help charter schools with
their finance and operations needs.

ALL
2006.

PAULINE
As part of a documentary being made about my life and work, I go back to my
childhood home in Milwaukee for the first time in twenty-six years. I visit the
graves of my parents and grandparents, Tippecanoe Library and all the schools I
went to. I even meet with some friends from high school. I haven't seen any of
them since 1978. They're all enthusiastic about re-connecting, even if they
occasionally slip up and call me Paul instead of Pauline.

(All clap.)

ALL
2006

ZOHRA
New York City

ALL
The Marathon.

PAULINE
Five miles

KELLY
Ten miles

JOSEPH
Fifteen miles

MOANA
Twenty miles

ZOHRA
Twenty-five miles.

RAJ
I have a mile to go and I'm struggling to finish. Finally I see my family, they're all jumping up and down screaming my name. My dad has his camera out, he's taking my picture as I run by. I finally know he's proud of me. It's one of the happiest moments of my life.

(All clap two times.)

ALL
2007.

KELLY
I get a call from a booker who wants me for a poetry show with an "international focus." He emphasizes the diversity of the poets performing, and then asks me:

JOSEPH
"Do you think you could do some poems in Chinese? That would be really great for our international flavor."

KELLY
Why do people assume that if I have some Mandarin in a poem that it's "so Chinese"? For me, it's very Asian/Pacific Islander-American or Chinese-American or Taiwanese-American. Are people so unused to seeing a hybrid identity and perspective that could only be formed in the United States, that they can only see the Chinese part?

(All clap.)

ALL
2007.

MOANA
I have kept the promise I made to myself when I was eleven:

KELLY
I will never date a white guy.

MOANA
But then I meet Neil. We get to know each other as friends first. I'm planning a trip to South Africa to teach art to AIDS orphans, and he has done a lot of

(MORE)

MOANA (cont.)
work there. He is a huge help as I plan my trip. As we talk and get to know each other, we connect on a deep level about making a difference in the world. Later, when I tell my friend that I'm dating a white guy she says:

ZOHRA
"What? Why!? I can't believe this!"

MOANA
And I realize how stupid it is. We are all activists, working on building communities and coming together. And we still can't see beyond color?

(All clap.)

ALL
2007.

RAJ
My business is starting to take off. I'm working with twenty-five of the fifty-eight charter schools in NYC and planning to expand into New Orleans soon. But it's a lot of work. Sometimes, I feel like I'm becoming my Dad working so hard to follow this dream, but I'm also making sure to live my life. I even took a vacation this year.

(All clap.)

ALL
2007.

JOSEPH
My first book of poetry is going to be published this year. I decide it's finally time to tell my mother that I'm a poet. I call her up:

RAJ
"Mom, great news, I'm having a book of poetry published."

PAULINE
"That's wonderful! I'm so proud of you."

RAJ
"But, aren't you surprised? You didn't really know I was a poet did you?"

PAULINE
"Of course I knew. Your sister and I just Googled you last week!"

(All clap.)

ALL
2007.

KELLY
My mother told me last year about this Chinese saying: sleep on wood, lick something bitter.

MOANA
There was once a warrior who always slept on wood and licked something bitter before he ate. So, no matter where he was, he would never be too comfortable to leave.

KELLY
After two years of splitting myself between Chicago and New York and touring constantly, I realized that I live somewhere, that I need to live somewhere. For the last 10 years, I've been that warrior, never too comfortable to leave. At first, I thought I would just be in New York for six weeks, but six weeks turned into three months, then into one year, then into two years, and now after three years, I can say that I live in Brooklyn, New York. It's home.

(All clap.)

ALL
2007.

MOANA
I don't always like to be identified as Asian-American or Pacific Islander. I prefer identifying as Tongan-American, even though it requires a commitment to explaining what that means. I'm always the first Tongan anyone has ever met! I used to see that as a burden, now I see it as an opportunity. I can be whomever I want. Whatever I do, it will automatically be Tongan, because I am Tongan.

(All clap.)

ALL
2007.

JOSEPH
I'm planning a trip to the Philippines later this year. I haven't returned since I immigrated to America, almost twenty-three years ago. Even though I was born there, I never left the island of Luzon, so I want to see more of the country and spend time with relatives I haven't seen since I was a child. It will be a big trip, but I don't want to have any expectations. I just want to be open and take it as it comes.

(All clap.)

ALL
2007.

PAULINE
The visit to my childhood home shows me how far I have come since I lived in that little white house on the south side of Milwaukee. Since then, I have consciously reconstructed my identity, first coming out as a gay man, then as a transgendered woman, forming an identity as a Korean adoptee, and becoming an activist and public figure. I have lived all over the world. Now, I am proud to call New York my home. It is where I feel most fully myself.

(All clap.)

ALL
2007.

ZOHRA
I come home from teaching and I share my day with my father and my brother over dinner. I unburden all of my frustrations and share my successes. By expressing the day's challenges and gains in Farsi or Uzbek, I step away and look at them from a new perspective. The family dinner is a tradition, and regardless of where we are, we have rarely missed our dinner ritual. I appreciate this time because it keeps my perspective fresh on both worlds I live in.

(All clap ten times. MUSIC.)

PAULINE
My name is Pauline Park. I was born in Miryang, Korea in October 1960. I have an older twin brother. It was chusok – the harvest season. Moana?

(Close book, stand up.)

MOANA
My name is Vaimoana Litia Makakaufaki Niumeitolu. I was born in Nuku'alofa, Tonga on June 17, 1978 at noon. My name Vaimoana means "deep blue ocean". I was born with a full head of hair. It was a sunny day in paradise. Raj?

(Close book, stand up.)

RAJ
My name is Snehal Dayanidhan Thakkar , but everyone knows me as Raj. I was born on February 14, 1975 in Flushing, Queens during a blizzard. It was Valentines Day. Kelly?

(Close book, stand up.)

KELLY
My name is Kelly Zen-Yie Tsai. I was born in Arlington Heights, Illinois, U.S.A. on July 30, 1978. I was born at 1:30 in the afternoon. It was a hot sunny summer day! Joseph?

(Close book, stand up.)

JOSEPH
My name is Joseph Josel Orense Legaspi. I was born on November 26, 1971 in Manila, Philippines. I was the first born son. It was winter. Zohra?

(Close book, stand up.)

ZOHRA
My name is Zohra Saed. I was born on March 11, 1975 on a rooftop in Jalalabad, Afghanistan at dawn. When I was born, the first word whispered in my ear was the name of God. My name "Zohra" means "morning star." It was Spring.

(Close book, stand up. Lights and MUSIC fade out slowly.)

END OF PLAY

Left to Right: Joseph O. Legaspi, Kelly Zen-Yie Tsai, Pauline Park, Raj Thakkar, Zohra Saed, Vaimoana Niumeitolu

Interviews

Among those answering the call for essay pitches for the 2008 edition was playwright Tommy Smith, who sent me a couple of videos by this guy named Reggie Watts. The videos just blew me away. Watching Reggie perform is like being slammed into some kind of dream logic with a stand-up comedian from another universe who is involuntarily channeling random torrents of pop culture outtakes and detritus – it makes sense while you're there (kind of), but later ... well, you can't really explain it. I can't, anyway. And, although we ultimately went with one of Tommy's plays instead of an essay, I did ask if he would take a few moments to talk with Reggie about his work (or theirs, actually, as Tommy is a frequent collaborator) – and Reggie's uniquely cheerful brand of apocalyptic dystopia.

Unstuck: Reggie Watts
and Situationist Doomsday Theater
An Interview
by Tommy Smith

*T**here's not much Reggie Watts doesn't do.*

A seasoned veteran in the music community, Watts has served as frontman for the bands Soulive and Maktub, and has collaborated on projects with Brian Eno, Fatboy Slim, Prince Paul and countless others. Switching suddenly to comedy upon his arrival to New York in 2006, Watts stormed the scene and won the prestigious Andy Kaufmann Award for absurdist performance. He's an active participant in and commentator on emerging computer technologies. He scores dance performances. He's a rampant underground videographer. And his first foray into the theater world recently played at The Public Theater's Under The Radar Festival – the multidisciplinary multimedia extravaganza Disinformation.

Often billed as an "experimental comedian," Watts fuels his live act with a non-stop barrage of language and sound, an aural collage of impersonated media blips, half-missing narrative tangents, absurdist jokes with no punchlines, high-energy dance bits and soaring improvised beat-box songs. By all accounts, it shouldn't work. It's important to remember that almost everything Watts does on stage is improvised. Some of the language has a loose structure, but Watts literally doesn't know what he's going to do until he steps out under the lights. Armed with only a microphone and a Line 6 vocal sampler, he bares the detritus of his rampant imagination to people who may or may not be prepared to see something so aggressively – and honestly – unprepared.

But this nervous energy only feeds the live act. Leaning on his edgy rapport with the audience, Watts often seems to be channeling some higher voice, or rather, flipping through the stations of our collective memory. A heartfelt story about killing his grandfather might be interrupted for a commercial break about an absurd product that does not and could not exist. A joke about choosing to turn gay veers into a frightening incantation to The Dark Lord. A diatribe against materialist tendencies in human beings transforms itself into a hardcore hip-hop number.

While the thrill of this schizophrenic performance technique is certainly superficial ("He's making all this up on the spot?!") those attuned to the subtext of his banter will start to recognize recurring tropes emerging in the sea of seemingly random sentences. I recently had the chance to sit down with Watts at his Brooklyn Heights apartment to chat about the countless influences and techniques that comprise the formation of his art.

***

TOMMY SMITH: I wanted to ask you about Situationist philosophy. When did you get into that?

REGGIE WATTS: It would have been four and a half years ago. I was researching philosophies – anarchy, Marxism – and that led me to Situationism. So I looked that up and learned about Guy Debord and the movement in the '60s. I just resonated with the ideas. The basic tenants from it, and the actions they performed, those resonate really strong with me. I love some of the pranks they pulled, these *heavy* pranks, like posing as a bishop and performing a mass at Notre Dame and being discovered halfway through it and getting the shit kicked out of them, or like, inciting a riot at the Sorbonne. *My* definition of Situationism is "to provoke to the edge of violence," which is to provoke just before that point where it could turn violent, and you just leave. You just drop it. And it gets people to that point, but it doesn't happen, and then there's nothing to rebel against. So people are just left falling, in their emotions and their hormones. And when people realize that it's just someone manipulating them, then its kind of like testing people's firewall. Like, "What's your security? What's your level of security?"

TS: And how does this factor into your stage work?

RW: When *I'm* on stage I want to be confused, but I like to be pushing the confusion. I love building something up and then immediately switching to a different texture, but being committed to that next texture as if it had been going on the whole time. If I'm really on, it's very effective. I feel more like a prankster, a little bit of a gremlin, a social gremlin. Just annoy people, push them a little bit, but then give them enough of a clue that it was manipulation. And the audience feels intelligent, because they are intelligent, you've given them the opportunity to know they're intelligent people, and you're not trying to fuck with them.

TS: So where do you see this type of performance living?

RW: Well, as a performer I'm not really placed in any place. But I want to hit all the "demos." I want to do the contemporary performance scene, I want to do the theater scene, experimental theater, playing rock shows, doing comedy at rock shows, doing corporate events, doing big time stadium concerts, arena shit, doing people's living rooms, doing webcasts and blogs and web videos and releasing albums and posters and pens: All of these things. For me, that's

generating a type of world. And that world is something that other people can build and be involved with. So by everyone working on their independent worlds – really branching out and building and *thinking* in an entrepreneurial way – it allows for relationships to occur that create a type of unity that is undeniable. It's a movement.

TS: And how do you utilize this "world" in your work?

RW: They become a part of it. Like in *Disinformation*, it's a theater show but at times we bring on people from different disciplines to take over for my banter. I just hand it off to someone else. But there's no explanation as to why they're brought on at all. They just show up. I start talking about something and this woman suddenly just jumps in to further explain the point or sing a song, and I just go sit down. Or someone will start dancing. Or a video will come on. It's a modular experience. It's almost in the style of *Cirque*, where they'll just have a beautiful performance of something. But they mildly try to relate it to the theme of the night – like if it's *Dreams*, they might be in pajamas and perform this brilliant piece. But you didn't really need the pajamas, you could have just come out in your regular shit and rocked it. That's what we do.

TS: So there's no relation between the performance elements and the content of the show, necessarily.

RW: Not necessarily, no. It's for the audience to put together. It's essentially me throwing in an ingredient and the audience going, "Well he obviously knows what he's doing, this has got to mean something."

TS: But you do it earnestly.

RW: Yes, this seriousness, this focus, is what melds it all together. You could put anything in there, as long as the sentiment is the same. This cat-like seriousness, like the ultimate poker face. Cats have probably one of the best poker faces in the animal kingdom. Because they're capable of more expressions, but they only stick with the one usually.

TS: And that's what you want the tone of the show to be?

RW: Yeah, very dryly presenting information. "Here's a thing I'd like to show you." And then I show them the thing, and it might just be weird or crazy or all over the place. And then come back and say, "*That* was very necessary to illustrate my point."

TS: "That kung fu dance you saw obviously illustrates what I just said."

RW: Yeah, exactly. The fact that two women are shadowfucking behind me while I'm singing a song about hip-hop *illustrates* exactly what needs to be illustrated about the end of the world.

TS: This idea – the world ending – it plays a large role in Disinformation.

RW: Yeah, but I'm not really saying "It's the end of the world, follow me." It's mostly about "It's just going to happen, and I'm here to tell you that it's *definitely* going to happen." I'm assuming that everybody knows that as well. That's the tact when I'm talking to the audience. But I just think it's ridiculous. When I'm on stage, I just think it's funny to talk about such a dire subject in such a mundane way. I love that I'm talking about it matter-of-factly, but then I'm talking about things that have *nothing* to do with it at all. I switch topics. I bring up examples. Cite people, cite an example through sonic means. And then explaining that it's a natural part of life: the end of the world and the beginning of a new one will occur simultaneously. And there will be a *shift*. And those people that want to be involved in the shift: fuck yeah. And those people that don't, you know, they just get regenerated. So it's not a bad deal for anybody, really. But there's definitely going to be a lot of destruction. By an alien force.

TS: What's so interesting about the end of the world?

RW: I like that people are afraid of it. And I like to pretend it's not something to be afraid of. And in that pretending, hopefully I start to believe it's not that big of a deal. And if I believe that way then potentially, theoretically, one could live through a very large shift, and continue. Continue on, in some form. I don't really know what that means – if it's physical or not. But it's an exciting thing because it could metaphysically be something more fantastic, in our lifetime, that we get to experience. So I wouldn't be surprised if someday some weird shift occurred that maybe didn't change things right away, but we just started noticing that boundaries aren't boundaries anymore. And that slowly the world starts to deconstruct into this new thing. But I'm not totally married to it. Who knows? It could just not happen, it could just be a spiritual Y2K, a false alarm.

TS: 2012.

RW: Specifically, yeah. The new slogan I've been getting into is "The Beginning is Near." So a shift seems good around this time period. The world seems to be very stuck.

***

A frequent collaborator with Reggie Watts, Tommy Smith co-created and directed Disinformation. *Upcoming projects with Reggie include a co-conceived radio play and a new stage work,* Transition.

Media coverage of NYC alt-theater is evolving so rapidly it is difficult to even try to keep up with any sustained degree of success, not to mention tracking the changes in any viable paradigm shifts, movements or even trends. As the City's print coverage of theater continues its apparently inexorable descent into absolute irrelevance – with the New York Times *reduced to scribbling consumer guides to the gazillioneth revival of* South Pacific *or* Gypsy *(or both) for Aunt Ida and Uncle Bud's next visit from Akron, and the* Village Voice *seemingly content to be the status quo it once railed against, it has fallen to an increasingly perceptive, prevalent and – yes, prominent* ad hoc *network of guerrilla pundits, critics and social observers to fill the yawning abyss left by the decline of the NYC print media. The tool of choice for this millennial brigade is overwhelmingly the internet; the form is the blog, a term that didn't even exist when I arrived here just six years ago. Over the span of several months in late 2007, I got with six of my fave blogsters – or at least the ones I read regularly and have come to depend upon to keep me abreast of what is* really *going on out there – and tossed around some questions that had been on my mind. The voluminous result – squeezed into less than twenty pages here – is an insightful, entertaining and, yes, educational read in addition to providing a document for* The Way We Really Live Now *south of 14th Street.*

Lost in the Theatrosphere:
Finding Our Way in a Post-Print World
An Interview with Six NYC Theater Bloggers

JOHNNA ADAMS
(aka blindsquirrel)
blindsquirrels.blogspot.com

NYTR: You moved to NYC from Southern California in 2007. How have the realities of your discoveries and experiences since making the move compared to whatever preconceptions you might have had about "New York City" and "New York City theater"? I was very surprised at the smallness, i.e., the interconnectedness of the whole scene here. I somehow assumed NYC to be so big that it would be made up primarily of strangers, but no – I have found theater, the alt-theater scene here, at least, to be very much like a small town, with all that incorporates and implies.

JOHNNA ADAMS: I was surprised to discover how much the web really helps define the NYC theater culture. It doesn't work that way in other parts of the country. In Southern California, the theater scene is still categorized and shaped almost entirely by print media. There are a few blog/reviewer sites but they are very fragmented and have little power. There the community looks to the print media to list, evaluate, reward, and comment on theater almost exclusively.

It took me a long time to realize that the web proliferation is a matter of necessity for the NYC theater community. There simply are no print outlets recording the Off-Off and Off-Broadway shows comprehensively. At first I thought it was just a cultural thing, where the New York theater community just preferred to blog and market shows online. It hit me as sort of an epiphany a few months after moving here that everything is online because there isn't really any other choice. I am extremely grateful to have come to New York at a time when the internet is flourishing. I honestly can't imagine what the theater scene was like before the proliferation of blogs and internet-based websites that review all the fabulous low-budget shows that are ignored by the print press.

One of the things that surprised me most was how accessible I found the community here. It took me about seven months to find a theater to audition for when I first moved to Southern California that would cast me (this was probably, 1998 or so). I had to search through countless editions of *Backstage West*, the *Orange County Register*, and *Los Angeles Times*, just to find audition notices. It was almost two years before I joined a writers' group and got a theater to produce a full-length play. Seven months after moving to New York, Flux Theatre Ensemble has asked to produce an unfinished trilogy of mine, I am in two writers' groups and possibly starting up a third, I acted in a short movie with folks from Partial Comfort Productions, and a couple of times when I have introduced myself to people here, they have said, "Oh, yeah, I read your blog." It is a night and day difference in ease of assimilation. And I attribute most of the connections I have made here to the internet. Also, I kept in good touch with playwrights Adam Szymkowicz and Chad Beckim after meeting them at Pataphysics workshops at The Flea Theater before I moved here and they really took me under their wing wherever possible and introduced me to people. But, again, I was only able to keep in touch with them through the internet.

NYTR: So you had some connections back here before making the move.

JA: I didn't expect to feel like a part of the theater community within the first year or possibly two years of living here. I thought there would be a longer, lonelier shut-out period of watching other people's productions, awkwardly introducing myself at intermissions, stalking favored theater companies, and trying to fit in somewhere. The internet really opened a lot of doors for me. I mean, you still have to leave your house and meet people. It doesn't replace that. But the internet really tells you where you should be headed when you leave the house and helps you meet people before you get there. I think of the theater community here as being very large, but broken down into tribes of particular interest. I am becoming very familiar with the small tribe of "we develop new works." There are many other tribes I don't know very well at all, but I have built a little nest where I am comfortable and am constantly amazed at how interconnected and familial it feels.

NYTR: How has the NYC environment influenced you as a playwright? As compared to previous areas of residence – e.g., Southern California, Chicago, Texas, etc.

JA: I find that I can't write easily about a place until a few years after I have lived there. I am only just now starting to write about Los Angeles in my plays. And during college, it was hard for me to write about Texas because I had lived there so recently. Something about distance from a place gives me the perspective, panging nostalgia, and desire to recreate it in my plays. So, while I don't find New York creeping into my plays yet as a setting, the environment has been very inspiring. I have written four full-length plays since I moved here, compared to one and a half plays the previous year. I think that being able to see so many amazing shows is what has kept me continually inspired to write. I don't fear writer's block as much living here as I did in the other places I lived. Writer's block is like a nightmare creature that stalks and preys on your dreams, and he follows you everywhere, but I don't feel his breath on my shoulders so much here.

NYTR: Is there a downside?

JA: The downside is that I know anything I write and premiere in NYC will not get a second chance. Anywhere else you produce a play, you have the hope that it might one day go to New York. Now, I am writing at the end of the line. No safety net and no obscurity. Sometimes it is very freeing to know that not many people are going to come see your play in a garage in Orange County, CA. You can write anything you want very fearlessly. Recreating that faith in yourself and that sense of freedom when everyone is watching is a challenge. And New York can be a big drain on my energy. What it gives, it also takes. There is so much to do that you find yourself doing too much. And there is always a show you wish you had seen and you miss. Always the sense that there is more you could be taking advantage of but aren't.

There is also a healthy surreal sense to everything. That feeling sometimes of being in a movie or in a foreign country. There is a very specific East Coast and New York culture and I am a complete outsider in many ways. The theater community feels very much like home, the City feels like I am on an extended vacation here that is often unpleasant, occasionally wondrous. I can't imagine living any other place after living here, because as a playwright there is no where I would rather be. But, I also can't imagine living here always. So, I find that I have put any future plans on hold and am just living to see what happens next. That is very exciting and a little scary.

JASON GROTE
(aka Jason Grote)
www.jasongrote.com

NYTR: This 2008 edition is an experiment in expanding the horizons of the anthology outside of NYC whilst keeping its focus here in town. Along that line, I'm interested to hear your comparisons of the development and production of the same play – 1001 – in two different environments – the big LORT Rocky Mountain high of DCTC and our own, scrappy "downtown" P73.

I'm especially interested to know your experiences in this process, Denver and NYC, the contrasts and the similarities. Some questions that come to mind are what is often said about producing theater in NYC – the expense, the harsh and brutal critical environment, the purported savviness of NYC audiences compared to the "hinterlands;" the supposed "homogenizing" tendencies of LORT play development practices, etc. Insights?

JASON GROTE: There are a number of assumptions here that I'd like to debunk, which I suspect is one of your reasons for asking me this question. First and foremost is the perception that NYC is in any way more sophisticated than any other part of the country. I found audiences in Denver and West Virginia (where *1001* received its second production, at the Contemporary American Theater Festival) to be every bit as sophisticated as any New York audience (this is based more on my years of experience attending New York theater than my experience with *1001* per se). In fact, I would say that the collective artistic infrastructure of New York – the arts institutions, the media and critical establishment, and to some degree, the audience – is on the whole far more backwards than many other places, not for lack of education, but mostly due to arrogance and complacency.

NYTR: Go. Expound.

JG: This is a huge generalization, of course, as there are multiple groups, individuals, and institutions operating in NYC at any given moment, but taken as a whole, capitalistic values seem to predominate here, and there is something of a herd mentality that takes hold. It's the worst kind of stupidity because it's borne of power, and of the conviction that one has nothing left to learn. It's especially endemic to New York, but one sees it in other (usually East Coast) cities as well. It's precisely this belief that one is more sophisticated than some imagined "other" that cuts one off from experiencing anything new, and reinforces a dull, middlebrow sensibility that lacks intellectual rigor but still manages to be elitist.

NYTR: While out there ... ?

JG: By contrast, the people I encountered in both Denver and Shepherdstown were excited to see something new; they were also interested in the arts and humanities generally, not just theater. In New York, there is a tendency to dismiss anything beyond the immediate frame of reference of the *New York Times*, the *New Yorker*, and NPR as somehow naive or illegitimate. It's as if everyone is possessed by such an overwhelming fear of seeming dumb that they are unable to acknowledge anything unfamiliar or new. I don't want to undersell it, though; clearly there are great New York theaters, and regional theaters who deserve their reputations for being craven and reactionary and dumb – in fact, I'm on the advisory board of Soho Rep, and I've just been fucked over by a regional theater. But institutional cowardice doesn't end at the Hudson River, nor does it obey distinctions of "uptown" or "downtown." Some of the worst theaters in terms of programming and respect for artists exist below 14th Street, and some of the best reside above 42nd, or in the hinterlands. I should also add that *1001* isn't the kind of play that a conservative regional theater would even bother to try and mess with – it's way too odd to begin with. All of the more staid regional theaters just passed on it.

NYTR: What was it like working at Denver Center?

JG: They never once interfered with the play in any way at all – not during the New Play Summit in 2006 (where it was developed), not at the O'Neill, where DCTC Artistic Director Kent Thompson directed it, and not during the production process. The only conflict we had was when they wanted to hire Ethan McSweeny for the project, and I naïvely thought that I could get a major regional theater to premiere the play with its original director, Liesl Tommy (new directors working on new plays being something that almost never happens at that level of production). After Ethan and I began our process, they left us entirely to our own devices, while providing us with fairly enormous resources – it was kind of heavenly. A lot of it involved being in the right place at the right time – almost every theater (except maybe places like Lincoln Center or DC Shakespeare) likes to call itself "edgy" or "risk-taking," but that isn't always the case – often it's just marketing-speak. In Denver's case, though, it was true. Kent Thompson and Bruce Sevy had come from Alabama Shakespeare, where they did some great work supporting new plays, but the work they could do was very circumscribed.

NYTR: How so?

JG: Interestingly, many of the plays that came out of their Southern Writers Project were more frank and interesting in terms of race than much of what you'd see in NYC or LA, but religion and sexuality were pretty much taboo. The city of Denver was simultaneously undergoing a sea change; it was a very conservative place for much of its history, due in part to the presence of the Christian right and the defense industry, but at some point around the turn of the 21st century its economy collapsed, due in large part to Enron, and what arose after the meltdown was a very different, more progressive place. Suddenly a huge, very well-funded regional theater that did mostly classics wanted to be an Actors' Theatre of Louisville-style new home for new plays, and so they picked the most ambitious play they could find, which happened to be *1001*. I should also add that the P73 production wasn't all that scrappy, either. It was their biggest production to date, and it was done with enhancement money and on an Off-Broadway contract. We rented very well-made and expensive costumes and props from Denver at a deep discount, and Ethan McSweeny and the set designer, Rachel Hauck, came with the play. People had to take a pay cut, but in terms of production value, very little was different; in certain aspects, like the lighting (by Tyler Micleau), I would venture to say the production looked better. Interestingly, Rachel actually made the

Baruch Performing Arts Center, which is a very nice space, look more low-rent than it is.

NYTR: *Differences?*

JG: The obvious differences in the respective productions just had to do with how fucking hard it is to produce theater in New York, and the various differences between large institutions and smaller producers generally. DCTC isn't exactly the only game in town (among other companies, Denver has the very well-regarded Curious Theater), but they're the Lincoln Center of the city and as such have a great relationship with the media, an enormous and very intelligent marketing machine, and a subscriber base who anchored the audience. They were very savvy about audience outreach – we hired a DJ for the show, Sara Thurston, who was also a very active music and club promoter, and she was enormously effective at getting younger audiences in. In New York, by contrast, we were up against almost a dozen major openings, both uptown and downtown, as well as the general problem of competing with all of the other things happening on any given night in NYC. Additionally, we had a great press person for the NYC production, but we didn't have much in the way of a marketing plan or budget, and though Baruch is a beautiful space, it's out of the way, so unlike Denver, it took almost half of the run for word-of-mouth and reviews to have any effect. People like to criticize subscriber audiences, and surely they're different in every city, but they're the people who *want* to see our work; I think inflating production costs, a lack of arts funding, and careerist arts administrators deserve much more of the blame. Houses were small in the beginning of the NYC run, but by the time it closed we were turning away anywhere from ten to thirty people a night.

GARRETT EISLER
(aka Playgoer)
playgoer.blogspot.com

NYTR: *As Playgoer covers the full range of NYC theater, I thought this question might be particularly apt for you. Late last year, you wrote of the potential of a Jon Robin Baitz-inspired newspaper that might rise to the challenge of a critical reprise here in the City. What do you think of the chances of a prevalent critical presence that "aggressively supports the endeavor of theater, on all levels" evolving out of the present NYC blogosphere to rival if not supersede the print medium as the primary source of critical credence in matters theater?*

GARRETT EISLER: I'll start by trying to explain why the *New York Times* continues to maintain at least the image of dominant theater coverage and influence. We have to remember the average blog reader is under forty and makes under $40,000 a year. These people may be passionate theater-goers and makers. But as an audience they don't matter a whit to the most prominent theatrical producers and institutions in this town. The *Times* will continue to dominate as long as the most prized audience is their readership – over fifty years old and well over $50,000 a year. (And by the way, these are generally people who are either never going to get into the daily habit of blog reading or are just lucky to be technically adept enough to get onto their email.) This demographic is not just the profile of someone who forks over for three-figure Broadway orchestra seats, but also that's who actually gives a donation to Manhattan Theatre Club, Lincoln Center, etc. This targeting of the "patron class" is the main difference between *Times* theater coverage and blog coverage.

NYTR: What might this mean for the blogs?

GE: What I conclude from this is that blogs will probably not make a dent in the coverage or dialogue about Broadway and large non-profit theater for a very long time (if ever.) Not until the internet generation hits fifty, probably, and you start having "patron" people who are hip to the web, and who gave up reading newspapers when they got BlackBerries.

Where blogs can make a difference now, and will only become increasingly important, is in framing a new coverage of downtown and Off-Off theater. Take what Martin Denton has been able to do with *nytheatre.com* – publishing plays, getting reviews of almost each and every new opening on a website for all to read – these are important achievements that may be off the radar of *Times* readers, but have made a big difference to downtown theater practitioners. Look at the Innovative Theatre Awards or the use of the web by theater activists like John Clancy, Jason Grote, and Isaac Butler. Again, you won't see it covered in the *Times*, but ask struggling theater artists and they'll tell you the web has changed the conversation since ten years ago. Community building is now much more prevalent, successful, and desired.

NYTR: How do you see the blogosphere evolving in the area of community building?

GE: I can indeed envision a kind of "web publication" that could really take off, if it were geared to this alternative "market." It would have to involve extensive reviews and event calendars (maybe with a built-in link to something like SmartTix to facilitate tickets and discounts), but also open comments sections, perhaps bulletin boards, for artists to share about their processes, seek collaborators, and, of course, gripe.

Such a site would be cool and I would visit it. But I also don't think that's a substitute for the kind of blogging going on now. The appeal of blogs is usually the blogger's individual voice, and the bigger the "publication" the more drowned out any voice gets. So I also believe web-readers will continue to congregate around their favorite blogs, whomever they feel either speaks for them, or speaks so against them they want to log on every day and argue!

T. NIKKI CESARE & STEVE LUBER
(aka sharkskin girl & Tweed)
Obscene Jester
obscenejester.typepad.com

NYTR: Such a wide and fascinating range of performance & media the Jester covers. I am going to try to take advantage of that without losing the larger thread of all this and ask you about theater and performance rather than "just" theater and, within that – specifically, multimedia performance.

My first question asks for a bit of soothsaying on your part, but here goes – as media, especially electronic media, continues to become more embedded in our daily lives, and as this media seems to become not only more embedded but more essentially so with each successive generation, do you see its integration into live theater and performance as something that will become permanently integrated as, for example, artificial lighting in the theater reflected a technologically advancing society of the past? Or do you feel that the essential appeal of live theater and live performance – through the very fact that they are indeed "live," will always remain largely the domain of human interaction, both performer/performer and performer/audience, and that the "media" or "multimedia" components will always be subsidiary to the medium's message?

T. NIKKI CESARE: I think technological mediation has always been, to greater and lesser degrees, an integral part of the experience of live performance. While Wagner's mid-nineteenth-century notion of the *Gesamptkunstwerk*, or total art work, is, in many ways, exemplar of the integration of technology in theatrical (and, in this case, musical) performance, one can also look to Alexander Skryabin's conceptual color organ from his unfinished experiment in synaesthia, *Mysterium*, from the early twentieth century, as epitomizing the potential of technological intervention to result in an entirely new type of theatrical production. Though never realized in the form Skryabin intended, *Mysterium* was to have taken place over seven days and nights in India, and to ultimately breakdown the barrier between performer and audience. And of course, one should look much farther back to the use of masks in classical Greek theater, which might be the earliest imagining of technology onstage.

It's the breaking down of the fourth wall, if you will, in Skryabin that I think works as a productive point at which to engage how technology informs and re-forms contemporary theater. Theorist Hans-Thies Lehmann writes of theater as "real virtuality," and discusses the potential for performance that incorporates technology in explicit form (or what he describes as media that is constitutive of rather than inspiration for theater) to "defy reproduction through film or television" – i.e., the Wooster Group's use of video or the new genre of hyperopera. That is, to watch something like the Wooster Group's recent *Hamlet*, which is so dependent upon manipulated video, in any form but live performance collapses the distinction between the "live" and "mediated" bodies – eliminating the very condition of possibility of the performance's success. So, while theorists such as Philip Auslander have long argued against the privileging of the live, there's actually something to be said for technology to enhance and in fact augment the live experience over a sort of televised or filmic reproduction: the document is not always performative.

NYTR: How does this render my question, then? Completely irrelevant?

TNC: I think it's less that "the 'media' or 'multimedia' components will always be subsidiary to the medium's message," or that media will become permanent or essential (as, really, it already is), than that we might be moving away from an internal hierarchy between the live and mediated. Technology certainly informs the way we engage the live – as Auslander points out – both formally and conceptually, but I think even a fully mediated performance, if engaged in the context of what has traditionally been understood as a "live event" – as opposed to the somewhat stickier contexts of installation, visual art, and sound art – will still be considered live.

NYTR: Tweed?

STEVE LUBER: I really like sharkskin's point about the collapsing of the hierarchy. The idea that all aesthetic components are created equal is spot-on. But I'd like to push the bill even further. Embedded in this question is what I refer to as "Platonic anxiety": that is, the impulse that compels we short-sighted humans to reinforce the live-mediated binary; if we don't (or – imagine! – can't), then our very subjectivity is at stake and, well, that is just too much for us to noodle whilst simultaneously watching the newest episode of *America's Next Top Model* on the TV, downloading porn off the internet and nuking our frozen organic dinner. My point is that we *are* mediated beings, constantly extending our bodies and perceptions to a theoretical and – what most people can't deal with – practical destruction of Cartesian worldviews.

So when you ask whether I feel performance "will always remain largely the domain of human interaction," it just goes to show that human interaction has to be two warm bodies occupying the same proximal space, when the idea of "human interaction," to me, has reached far beyond this: one only needs to look to Friendster or MySpace, craigslist, online dating, Rock Band, or Second Life, not to mention e-mail, mobile phones, and digital photography and film, to see that human interaction has been dominated by this electronic connection, which is still a human interaction (posthuman?) .

If we can recalibrate our biases, we can see that sharkskin girl is right about stage technologies going back to masks (and further yet!). The *deus ex machina* is mediation; the curtain is mediation; gas lighting is mediation; sound effects are mediation. Why do we have to be so self-congratulatory with what most call "new media" as some type of seismic paradigm shift? It's not. That's why I disagree so strongly with Lehmann: the "post-dramatic" performance that is constitutive of technology is redundant, a desperate attempt to stroke his coinages. What I'm looking for is performance that utilizes the necessity of technology well. They don't need to be giant, baroque spectacles. We've framed some of these genres for their exemplary uses of technology: *Gesamptkunstwerk* burlesques, the New Stagecraft, the Theatre of Images; but they're all pups from the same litter.

NYTR: Might there come a time in the not-too-distant future when an actor simply speaking to an audience will become both too simple (only one thing happening at a time) and too complex (requiring a level of sustained concentration measured in hours rather than minutes or even seconds)? Trends, movements, speculation, disintegration of order as we now know it — any thoughts you would care to share in this direction?

TNC: For me, this is where performance art was already intervening into the notion of conventional performance over a half century ago. And the audience's reaction to, say, the premiere of John Cage's *4'33"* or the riot that broke out in the Milan performance of his *Empty Words (Parte III)* is indicative of a general resistance to the type of concentration, and in the case of the former, self-realization, these pieces demand. The very fact that performance art, and experimental performance of almost any discipline, operates within a much more depressed economy than Broadway shows, in all their spectacularization and commodification, suggests that audiences are not as open to performance that requests a work on their part rather than handing them what they are supposed to feel in a pat form. So there's a sort of contradiction going on in your question – or in my response to it! I think an actor simply speaking to an audience, as Spalding Gray did in his lifetime, is already too much for some audiences – just think about the mass walk-out on Mike Daisey's *Invincible Summer* last April; but that type of performance exists outside the brackets of commercial success and yet isn't going away. In fact, I think it demonstrates that even as the use of technology in performance becomes more sophisticated and developed so as to point theater in a new, always already mediated direction, there will always also be these moments of an "actor simply speaking to an audience" to challenge and subvert conventional ideas of what theater comprises.

NYTR: Tweed, your thoughts.

SL: All this judgment is making me sneeze! Let's go back to the festival of Dionysus: in its heyday, the final day was all comedies because the audiences were incredibly hung over from the celebratory night before. The groundlings in Elizabethan theater were nothing short of a collection of assholes, throwing fruit, yelling back if they were displeased with the action on stage. Then there's opera: read an Edith Wharton novel! All I'm attempting to say here is that theater as a pure aesthetic form is a fairly new construct, especially no thanks to high modernism, and I feel it's counterproductive to judge the length of these performances or the language or the form, but why we're producing these forms and why they are or are not in demand. I think we could learn a lot more if we could step away for a moment and get off our critical high-art-horse.

That being said, I agree with sharkskin's appraisal of Spalding and Mike, both tremendous performers, who created their own incredibly fruitful theatrical *oeuvre* from very little. But then the flip side of the coin is the field day of stage trickery, from Richard Foreman to Bob Wilson to the Blue Man Group, who, in their own ways, create a challenge to the viewer. Their compositions, juxtapositions, and intricacies force the spectators to deal with their own subjectivities, perceptions, and attention spans; all of these can give us some sort of insight not only into performance movements, but what's required of/desired by the audiences. What can we discuss in the distinction between the more commercial, MTV-ready, ninety-minute Blue Man performance-franchise and the excruciatingly lengthy (in a good way!), opaque opera staged by Wilson at Lincoln Center?

NICK FRACARO
(aka RatSass)
ratconference.com/blog

NYTR: My first question for you has to do with what seems to me to be the rather fragile nature of the NYC blogosphere when it comes to differing viewpoints. In tracking a number of NYC theater blogs over the past few years, it seems as though as long as the local blogosphere has an easy common target to lob missives at, be it George Bush, Satan, Charles Isherwood, whomever – all is pretty much chummy and united. But once someone breaks with what seems to be the current progressive/liberal party line rhetoric, the fur quickly begins to fly. What surprises me most about this is that there seems to be a profound intolerance lurking right below the surface of a purported base of shared ideology, i.e., the inclusiveness of progressive thought.

Would you agree with my perception that the tolerance for opinions and viewpoints among NYC bloggers outside what seems often to be — rather ironically — knee-jerk reactions to the progressive/liberal "party line" is rather low? And, further, that there seems to be very little capacity for argument and debate that doesn't rapidly devolve into some high-school-level name-calling? Or do you think I am being overly selective in drawing this conclusion about the overall NYC blogosphere?

NICK FRACARO: What you say seems essentially true, but I think of it as a condition that existed in conversation and dialogue long before the advent of the blogosphere. Dissent from the politically correct response has always been a disruptive act at dinner parties and such. The blogosphere has more than just provided a written public forum for these once semi-private arguments; it has also established a "speak-your-mind" protocol over the "bite-your-tongue" etiquette of normal face-to-face social intercourse among theater acquaintances.

This "speak-your-mind" modus operandi of blogging does not serve all writers well. Any hysterical reaction is now instantly transformed into the historical reaction. For instance, the theater editors of *Back Stage* and *Time Out New York*, David Cote and Leonard Jacobs, are probably not thrilled about having their hysterical devolution into mutual "high-school-level name-calling" now part of their permanent record in the blogosphere. Both these writers have since retreated from the wild and woolly arena of "speak-your-mind" blogging back into the filtered and edited realm of "bite-your-tongue" more befitting the editors of "serious" and "objective" chronicles and critiques of theater.

Although often bolstered as such, objective journalism is not an ethic in behavior or a tenet in philosophy, but merely a genre of writing. Subject to its own conventions, clichés and protocols, "objectivity" is uniquely different from other genres of storytelling, but it has no moral superiority over any of them.

NYTR: Expand. Please.

NF: Most writers don't realize that objective journalism was instituted as a way of limiting liability for publishers. Beyond these libel concerns, journalistic writing was also defanged within the guidelines of objectivity for another reason: so that the greatest numbers of readers would feel comfortable with it. So this genre of news chronicling developed into the system it is today not in the service of truth-telling as it is usually portrayed, but in the service of the development of a bottom-line product for publishers.

With the advent of internet publishing, especially the blogosphere, the notion that only journalists employed by media outlets are professional is no longer valid. In art journalism, specifically in the theater talk we're examining, the theatrosphere is perhaps now in its high school or adolescent phase (your thesis). But if so, I think the only hope of it growing into adulthood, or "gain credibility as a critical/chronicle source of the local theater scene," is for the theatrosphere to disavow the moribund models inherited from print publication, and create its own creative modes of storytelling and debate.

Some of the most insidious and deceptive notions at work in the theatrosphere arise from the belief that there exists some correct or "professional" way to engage peers with our theater writing. Professional behavior is relative to many different specifics of time and place. The blogosphere is challenging the conventions of our peer relationships in theater on many fronts, but most obviously in the realm of writing. Although now still in its early stages, theater bloggers (including playwrights, directors, actors, and other artists) have usurped much of "the writing about theater" from the once exclusive domain of critics, reviewers, dramaturgs and publicists.

NYTR: Can you cite an example?

NF: Leonard Jacobs seemed to perceive a certain critical mass in the relationship of theater PR to the blogosphere when he went on his September rampage against George Hunka. Was George acting in his role of blogger or artist or critic when he attended the preview production of *100 Saints* (he left at intermission and gave it a bad review)? No matter to Leonard, who felt he could apply journalistic standards of behavior on George's blogging. I was not surprised but still bothered that no one in the New York theatrosphere felt up to the task of arguing this point with the *Back Stage* editor. George himself skulked away with only the briefest of protest of this most fundamental challenge to independent writing.

The old rules had the critic in control of how our art was represented to the non-audience-member public and to history. The review or documentation of "our story" never really belonged to us but to others. The mainstream press needs to cover stories and review plays that will interest the most number of readers. Our publicist helps spin our story to make it as easy as possible for the journalist to sell the story to his editor. Hopefully the journalist, or better yet, the editor is a friend or artistic peer in this quest to bring "our story" into this genre of objective journalism.

The internet, the web, and now the blogosphere have placed the onus of our story into our own hands. The artist as blogger puts up a representation of who, what, where, when, and why his art is, each time he posts. This artist as blogger engages other artists as bloggers also involved in the active representation of who they are. This collective representation is piecing together a new mode of interactive journalism.

There are many modes of talk between "bite your tongue" and "speak your mind," between objectivity and subjectivity. The theatrosphere's exchange of stories and representations among peers will spawn a new form of journalism.

NYTR: Any predictions?

NF: The blogosphere is ushering in a new generation of not just writing, but also behavior in theater. Back stage intrigues or backroom Machiavellian political maneuverings that once would have died as gossip among a few now might surface as news for the many. Many of the big blog brouhahas are rejected by the *Back Stage* editor as unsuitable to be "our story" in print, but followed closely if not generated by this same *Back Stage* editor in the blogosphere. The artist and critic will stand up together as one person in an indelible act of truth-telling. The story will never be the same again. If an artist has a practice, he has an aesthetic stake to defend or explain or propagandize. His criticism of others' work will necessarily have both the bias and the integrity of this practice as its foundation. The artist/critic is able to speak from this specific base of aesthetic knowledge – to define and delineate borders between his practice and others'. This kind of criticism creates a venue and an ethic for an exchange of ideas outside the market, a discourse about the art form itself.

NYTR: OK – group question time now. What do you consider the most positive and the most negative aspects in NYC theater and performance over the past year, and what would you like to see happen in the coming year? Let's start with the positives.

T. NIKKI CESARE: Strangely, I've been noticing that performance derided some fifty years ago as "anti-theatrical" has become indicative of the most interesting work recently. Perhaps this is overly informed by my predilection toward performance art, but two of the most satisfying performances I've seen in the past year were critically antithetical to the definition of the genre from which they emerged. André Lepecki's recuration of Allan Kaprow's *18 Happenings in 6 Parts*, from 1959, and Jérôme Bel's *pichet klunchun and myself*, originally from 2005, both part of this year's "Performa" biennial, challenged notions of theater and dance, respectively, and in doing so – much like how Michael Fried's 1967 objection to Minimalist art provided perhaps the best definition of the genre – offers some of the best examples of the elasticity of these art forms. It happens as well at the macrostructure – PS122's recent embrace of experimental music, for instance (though my bias is even more pronounced there as I've worked with some of the ensembles they've produced). It would seem that as performance art becomes more institutionalized itself, adopting more of the tenets of conventional theater, theater in turn is adopting much of the interdisciplinarity and experimentation of performance art. That sort of reinvention of categorical classification is really exciting to experience.

JASON GROTE: It's been a great year for theater, scripted or otherwise. I've probably seen more excellent plays in 2007 than any other year in recent memory; plays that come to mind are Thomas Bradshaw's *Purity*, Nature Theater of Oklahoma's *No Dice* and *Romeo & Juliet*; Stew and Annie Dorsen's *Passing Strange*, Radiohole's *Fluke*, Yehuda Duenyas' *One Million Forgotten Moments*, Jordan Harrison's *Doris to Darlene*, Young Jean Lee's *Church*, Lucy Thurber's *Scarcity*, Jenny Schwartz' *God's Ear*, Theatre of a Two-Headed Calf's *Drum of the Waves of Horikawa*, Classical Theater of Harlem's *King Lear*, Peter Morgan's *Frost/Nixon*, and Tracy Letts' *August: Osage County*. That gives me hope.

JOHNNA ADAMS: I loved the work in this year's Fringe Fest. Chad Beckim's *Lights Rise on Grace*, Mac Rogers' *Hail Satan*, and Gus Schulenburg's *Riding the Bull* were all shows I wouldn't have gotten to see without the Fringe and they were all touchstone productions for me that I loved and can't stop thinking about. The Peculiar Works East Village tour was everything I'd ever hoped New York would be – exciting, rich with Off-Off Broadway history, legends and stories, beautifully done, featured the City as a character, and made me proud to be a playwright here. Those are my highlights.

STEVE LUBER: This was a year of solid returns and developments: Radiohole's *Fluke*, Theatre of a Two-Headed Calf's *Drum of the Waves of Horikawa*, and the Wooster Group's *Hamlet* were all marvelous pieces by groups that, to varying degrees, have strong footholds in the experimental scene. Stillpoint Productions' *TransFigures* was as close to perfect as anything I saw last year. Lear deBessonet's direction coupled with T. Ryder Smith and Juliana Francis sharing the same stage made me almost as ecstatic as someone with Jerusalem Syndrome. Last, but certainly not least, this is the first year I got excited about musicals, two in particular: Cynthia Hopkins's *Must Don't Whip 'Um* at St. Ann's Warehouse and Stew's *Passing Strange* at the Public. Never before have I checked Amazon.com to see if a musical soundtrack was being recorded, but the brilliant, quirky, and subversive stylings of both these artists created two of the most mind-blowing pieces I've seen.

GARRETT EISLER: I've been encouraged by the increased commitment of bigger, established nonprofit theaters to new writers – playwrights who may not be super-young but basically "early career," "emerging," or never on Broadway. Sarah Ruhl is practically a celeb now, but someone had to go first with her. Both Manhattan Theatre Club and Playwrights Horizons took on Adam Bock after the downtown success of *The Thugs* (not a particularly commercial play). And Playwrights basically devoted its whole season to writers similarly unknown in the larger media. So that, in principle, is a good thing.

GE: The downside has been little visible sign of anything else changing at these other than the programming. For instance, they're interested in taking on these young writers – but not young audiences. I would have loved to have actually seen Bock's *The Receptionist*, but MTC's idea of a "discount" was $45 for a Wednesday matinee. (Wednesday – like, when I'm working!) Plus, you pay all that money to probably sit next to the same old MTC subscribers who are laughing their way through Jane Houdyshell's performance as if it's a sitcom, not realizing they themselves are the targets.

The other night I was at the Brick in Williamsburg. I looked around and realized that everyone in the audience was under forty, and on stage. The space is tiny, the production values super-minimal. But the writing and the acting were as good as – or at least not any worse than – any new play done at the Roundabout or Playwrights lately. It reminded me of what downtown theater in Manhattan was like ten to fifteen years ago – when artists could still afford to rent space there. So the good news is, the talent is out there, and they're still working hard. It'll be up to the blogs, though, to shout from the rooftops about it so the right people come.

JA: I felt that the shows that I saw playwrights self-producing with their own theater groups were, in general, much better than productions I saw playwrights get at large theaters this year. I had hoped that the trend where playwrights are turning themselves into theater artistic directors was more of a fad than a necessity. But, I think it has resulted in much better work. In a reversal of what I expected, I left most big theaters scratching my head wondering, "why would they waste their time and my time on this awful, not-ready script?" more often than I left self-produced shows feeling that way. It's not what I expected and it makes me sad. I think we are seeing the fruits of the over-development reading/workshop/reading/workshop cycle large theaters force plays into. And they are ugly fruits.

TNC: I was disappointed with theater's capacity to maintain any sort of political impetus when it had the opportunity to do so. After all the hullabaloo over the New York Theatre Workshop's canceling of *My Name is Rachel Corrie* last year, and the benefits of the "brawl," in Garrett Eisler's terms, that happened in the press, I'm not sure that theater – on either side of the stage lights – has realized its potential for, if not social change, then at least social shift. However, Culture Project's *A Question of Impeachment* series, following the run of Dan Hoyle's highly successful and incredibly virtuosic critique of Nigerian oil politics in *Tings Dey Happen* (and the many post-show talkbacks that accompanied it), does offer some hope that art with political aspirations will not be overwhelmed by purely aesthetic critique.

SL: I'm going to diverge from sharky on this one: I think *Rachel Corrie* proved precisely the opposite. For the first time in years, I was pleased as punch to see that performance still can really piss people off and, in turn, create a public dialogue. This isn't to say that I thought the circus-like atmosphere and vapid rhetoric were pleasing, but you can't blame "the theater" for this. There are stupid people in this world, and tragically fewer smart ones, and you just have to hope that the smarter ones will make themselves known and heard. This also gets into the trickery terrain that I think is a double-bind among performance critics and scholars that performance must be somehow "effective": *"Hey, everyone! This play is right! My eyes are now open! Let's go get the proletariat and rise up against the machinations of capitalism/racism/the administration, etc. etc. etc."* That's not how the game works really. I'm a big believer in performance effecting action, but not in this strange October Revolution way; the spectrum goes all the way from thinking, seeing the world from a different perspective to out and out activism, like *Corrie*. *Tings Dey Happen* is another great example of this. Sadly, the lack of controversy hasn't brought it the attention it deserves. It's ass-backwards, no?

JG: I think that in the next few decades we'll be revisiting the legacies of the Giuliani and Bloomberg years and seeing how truly disastrous they've been for the cultural life of the City. The more expensive it is to live here, and the less money available to make art, the worse the art gets, and I'm not just talking about schmaltz like *Wicked* – I'm also referring to more middlebrow stuff; as Peter Brook said, theater as "a middle-class weapon to keep the children good." I might just be exhausted, but I'm starting to ask myself what the theater world is willing to do to keep me in the game, rather than vice-versa. Every day the idea of theater as we know it seems less appealing to me, and I'm wondering if the fabulous invalid shouldn't just die already. I'll probably still continue to do some kind of performance art no matter what, and I'll probably try to get more film and TV work, but I'm not so sure if the idea of "plays" is still a viable one. I have at least three more plays in me, because I'm under contract, but that might be it for me. We'll see.

NICK FRACARO: The 365 Days/365 Plays Festival simultaneously represented both the most positive and negative aspects of theater in NYC and the rest of the country. The positive aspects of the project were obvious, utilizing the "largest shared world premiere in the history of the Theater to reveal community where it already exists – a thriving, world-wide theater community – in theaters both grand and modest, in schoolrooms, storefronts, nursing homes and alleyways." The festival probably achieved much of what its PR claimed. However, as what happens often in the competitive world of hype and celebrity, the book is judged by its cover, not by what's inside. The theaters, directors, and other artists who produced the 365 Days/365 Plays Festival never actually read the scripts they were all agreeing to produce. Celebrating such a cavalier and dilettante attitude toward producing theater becomes problematic when placed next to demands that the culture or mainstream press take the "theater festival" genre of production seriously. The Havel Festival (opening at the same time as the Suzan-Lori Parks project) included "one world premiere, five English language premieres and five other new translations, sixteen fully-staged productions in Manhattan and Brooklyn, as well as readings, panels, talkbacks, and a variety of other events." This festival, even with the attendance of the playwright and his concurrent residency at Columbia University, could not compete in the realm of Celebrity Culture into which the 365 Days/365 Plays Festival had positioned itself. Havel was virtually ignored by the mainstream press and the broader theater audience. The synergy created by the theater festival approach to producing is undeniable. I am looking forward to theaters and artistic curators using this medium in more inventive ways than cultivating ambition towards celebrity.

DROP EVERYTHING!!!

for the
2nd-ever

New York

Theater

Review

Fundraiser
Benefit

p.s. 122
150 1st ave.
east village
nyc usa

October 22
2007
8-11 p.m.

NYTR'S 2007 FUNDRAISER

*Above, **The Rising Fallen** (or is that just **Banana, Bag & Bodice**?) burning down the house (or is that just their toast?) The New York Theater Review 2008 edition fundraiser at Performance Space 122 – October 22, 2007*

Singer-composer **Beth Collins** *gets things started*

NYTR's **Jody Christopherson** with Seattle's **Marya Sea Kaminski**

It really is all about the book. Really. No, really.

*Playwright **Adam Szymkowicz** introduces the first round of Tiny Plays*

THE TINY PLAYS
"0 to 366 in 3 Minutes"

You couldn't have been in New York City in 2007 – or various other parts of the country as well – and missed the Suzan-Lori Parks' *365 Days/365 Plays* year-long extravaganza. Not even if you wanted to. We couldn't help but wonder ... OK, so Ms. Parks covered 365 days straight, but ... what about the day before she began this marathon? The day after? What might it have been like right in the middle?

We invited six young downtown theater troupes to imagine the possibilities ... in three minutes or less.

DIRECT ARTS: *Day Zero*

... HER THOUGHTS
But there's nothing in the refrigerator but a rotting tomato and we haven't paid
the electric bill yet and we really need a break from the city and wow, sex this
morning was so great and the situation in the Middle East is so horrible and
isn't heliotropism amazing ...

WRITER
STOP!

> *(WRITER. HER THOUGHTS. The Blank Page. HER THOUGHTS*
> *opens a door and REAL LIFE intrudes. He is a large, coarse man, who is*
> *rather dirty, but strangely compelling.)*

WRITER
Oh, no, not him again!

L to R: **Willie Mullins, Amy Staats, Elizabeth Ruf-Maldonado**

WRITER
STOP!

      (Rest.)

WRITER
I'll write tomorrow ...

BLUEBOX PRODUCTIONS: *The Leaplings Guild, 2008*

... *(ALI and EVE cheer.)*

DAVE
At this time it is my honor to introduce our guest of honor, born on February 29th, 1960 is motivational speaker and fellow leapling, Tony Robbins!
    (hears a voice from off)
What's that? He's not –
    (nods, understanding, back to the crowd)
He's not here yet folks, but I have it on good authority that he'll be here real soon. Uh. Let me tell you about some of the other illustrious personalities born on day 366. Simon Gagne of the Philadelphia Flyers, Richard Ramirez, celebrated serial killer ...

... ALI
You could sing.

DAVE
I'm not gonna sing.

EVE
I even tried JDate. Is there something wrong with me? Am I unpleasant in some way?

ALI
Unpleasant?

DAVE
I'll just level with 'em. He'll be here, right? I mean, he'll be here ...

(DAVE rushes back to the stage.)

L to R: **Ali Ayala, Eve Udesky, David Marcus**

NEW YORK NEO-FUTURISTS
Some Days, Days in May, Are Slightly Better Than Others
(Day 182.5)

L to R: ***Justin Tolley, Rob Neill, Eevin Hartsough***

... RN
I am feelin ya

JT
You feeling me?

EH
And me? You feelin me ... ?

... RN
Fucks them up to the point of / I was riding a bus the other day and I saw all of
this green grass.

EH
      (sings)
green grass green green grass

RN
and corn sweet corn, baby/and I had a vision of the Armageddon/cars stacked
upon cars

EH
      (sings)
cars upon cars/ cars n cars cars

RN
upon the corpses of elephants/and none was there to see it

*Playwright **Anne Washburn** introduces the second wave of Tinyness*

FLUX THEATRE ENSEMBLE: *The Alpha and the Suzan*

*L to R: **Felicia Hudson, Isaiah Tannenbaum, Tiffany Clementi, Cotton Wright, Marnie Schulenburg***

... (Lights up to reveal SUZAN-LORI PARKS, IMP and GOD.)

SUZAN
Where am I? It looks like ...
        (SUZAN sees GOD.)
Oh my God.

IMP
Yes, exactly.

GOD
        (singing for about five to eight seconds in intricate three-part harmony).
Welcome
Suzan-Lori Parks
Amen

SUZAN
You're ... that's ...

GOD
Yes, the Alpha, and the Omega, even the Gamma.

SUZAN
Who are you? ...

.. IMP
The Lord saw you, making a new play every day, and because the Lord could not understand really what was happening in your plays – I mean, the Lord got it, it's not that the Deity doesn't get the *avant-garde*, The Lord made the *avant-garde* –

GOD
(three-part fugue harmony again)
Foreman Pollock Cunningham

IMP
But that God realized the essential mystery was there, in your words, and that maybe you, mortal playwright Suzan-Lori Parks, could take up the reins of daily creation.

SUZAN
I don't think I've got a pen that big.

IMP
No pen. You sing the world ...

THE SHALIMAR: *A Prayer Before Bed*

... S
Flannel Pajamas?

SE
Bow and Arrow?

S –
Sawed off Shotgun?

BOTH
Bible? ...

... SE
Take the seat.

S
You take it. I'll sleep down here.

SE
I'll watch over you.

S
Sounds good to me ...

L to R: **Kim Gainer, Jen Taher**

HOI POLLOI: *The Sound of Whales*

L to R: *Alec Duffy, Nikaury Rodriguez, Amy Laird Webb, Jessica Jelliffe, Marshall York, Arthur Aulisi*

... Nearby I hear them,
Soaking up the sea,
That's how they breathe
(That's how they breathe)
In harmony.

Oooooo, the sound of whales,
Oooooo, the sound of whales.

I find, I find,
Everywhere I turn is a lie, is a lie,
I turn a faucet on and I fail to remember.
I recall a pen in my hand,
Or the power of a keyboard under my fingertips,
But all the ships out in the water,
What blessings they receive
From the sound of whales.

Oooooo, the sound of whales,
Oooooo, the sound of whales.

END OF PLAY

*Playwright **Tommy Smith** introduces co-conspirator **Reggie Watts** (facing)*

Performance Space 122   *October 22 2007*

Contributors

JOHNNA ADAMS (Interviews) – recently relocated to New York from Los Angeles. Her *Angel Eaters Trilogy* will be produced by Flux Theatre Ensemble in Manhattan in November of 2008. Johnna's play, *Sans Merci* was a 2006 finalist for the Princess Grace Award, the Reva Shiner Award, and the Abingdon Theater Company's Christopher Brian Wolk Award. This play was also a semifinalist for the O'Neil and Playlabs Festivals. She has twice won the *OC Weekly*'s Best New Play Award (2006: *The Sacred Geometry of S&M Porn*; 2002: *Cockfighters*). *Cockfighters* and *Sacred Geometry* are published by Original Works Publishing (www.originalworksonline.com). Johnna has a BFA in Acting from the DePaul University Theatre School. **blindsquirrels.blogspot.com**.

SHEILA CALLAGHAN (Cover Design) – is a Brooklyn-based playwright who does design on the side to feed herself, including work for the playwrights' collective 13P, the Flea Theater, The Lark Play Development Center, and various other theater and playwright websites. She spent most of her formative childhood years eating pickles in a sports bar on Route 9 in Jersey. She is very particular about food and is currently addicted to Wheatabix and organic blueberries. She wishes her carbon footprint was smaller. She loves you very much. **www.savagecandy.com**. **www.sheilacallaghan.com**.

T. NIKKI CESARE (Interviews) – aka "sharkskin girl," is currently Adjunct Instructor of Drama at Tisch School of the Arts/NYU and co-founder of *Obscene Jester*, the performance art blog. She has written for *TDR*, *Performance Research*, *Theatre Journal*, *Journal of American Abstract Artists*, *Artforum*, and the *Village Voice*, and has dramaturged experimental music-theater productions in New York City, Chicago, and Morelia, Mexico. She recently wrote the catalogue essay for photographer Frank Dituri's internationally exhibited show, "Zolle," and is finishing her dissertation, entitled "The Aestheticization of Reality: Postmodern Music, Art, and Performance," toward her Ph.D. in Performance Studies at Tisch. **obscenejester.typepad.com**

PING CHONG (Plays) – is an internationally-acclaimed theater director, playwright, choreographer and video and installation artist, and a seminal figure in the Asian-American arts arena. Since 1972, he has created over fifty multidisciplinary theater works, which have been presented around the world. These include *Kind Ness*, *Nosferatu*, *Angels of Swedenborg*, *Deshima*, *Chinoiserie*, *After Sorrow*, *Pojagi* and the puppet theater works, *Obon*, *Kwaidan*, and *Cathay*. Upcoming in 2008, is *Three Vampires: A Parable of the Philippines*, in collaboration with acclaimed author Jessica Hagedorn. He is the recipient of numerous honors and awards, including two OBIES, two Bessies, and a USA Artists Fellowship. **www.pingchong.org**.

JODY CHRISTOPHERSON (Event Producer) – is an actress who likes to throw parties. Most recently, she has appeared on the cover of the *New York Theater Review 2008*, in *The Seagull* (with Dianne Wiest and Alan Cumming) at Classic Stage Company, The Under The Radar Festival (with Young Jean Lee) and *365 Days/365 Plays* (with Bluebox Productions), both at the Public Theatre; *The Necropolis Plays* at The Brick Theater and was featured in a Conair Ceramic Silk Straightening Iron Hair Commercial. She also teaches yoga at East West Yoga in Union Square. **www.myspace.com/redheadjody**.

GARRET EISLER (Interviews) – has been writing the theater blog, *Playgoer* since May, 2005. He has also been contributing reviews and feature articles as of late to the *Village Voice* and *Time Out New York* and an essay in *New York Theater Review 2007*. His essay on the Off-Off Broadway season will appear in the forthcoming *Best Plays of 2006-2007* and he has published academic articles in the *Journal of American Drama & Theatre*, *Studies in Musical Theatre*, *Theater Survey* and *Theatre Journal*. He is currently completing a Ph.D. in theater history at the Graduate Center of the City University of New York and has taught at NYU, Boston University, and Syracuse University. **playgoer.blogspot.com**.

DAVID FLETCHER (Event Photographer) – is the owner of Washington's Best Musicians, Photo & Video. He currently resides in Manhattan with his wife, Stephanie Wickouski. David was formerly the Director of Bands and Choruses at Georgetown University. In Spring, 2008 he served as music director of the Off- Broadway production of *The Deciders* at the Triad. **www.washbest.com**.

NICK FRACARO (Interviews) – co-founded and became artistic director of the cross-disciplinary Thieves Theatre, for which he directed Peter Weiss' *Marat/Sade* at Toronto's Theatre Centre, Heiner Müller's *Despoiled Shore Medeamaterial Landscape with Argonauts* and the world premiere of Fassbinder's *Trash, the City and Death* in New York, among other projects. He was co-founder of RAT, an international coalition of theaters, for which he organized conferences in New York, Philadelphia and Rosario, Argentina. As dramaturg at Dallas' Undermain Theater in 1999, he published possibly the first "theater blog," which he continues today at RatSass (ratconference.com/blog). He is presently resident dramaturg at International Culture Lab. **ratconference.com/blog**

JASON GROTE (Interviews) – has lived in Brooklyn since 1997. His plays include *1001, This Storm is What We Call Progress, Hamilton Township, Maria/Stuart,* and *Box Americana.* Honors include an Ovation Award from The *Denver Post;* the P73 Fellowship; nominations for the Pushcart Prize, the Kesselring Prize, and the Weissberger Award; an NEA Grant via Soho Rep; a NYSCA Grant via

Clubbed Thumb; a Sloan Commission from Ensemble Studio Theatre; and "Best New Play" (for *1001*) from Denver's alternative weekly, *Westword*. He teaches playwriting and screenwriting at Rutgers University, is a member of PEN and New Dramatists, and is a contributor to Comedy Central's "Indecision 2008" blog. Upcoming: productions at Boston Court (LA), Salvage Vanguard (Austin), and Rorschach (DC). **www.jasongrote.com**.

MARYA SEA KAMINSKI (Essays) – was named an "Artist of the Year" by *Seattle Magazine* in 2007, awarded "Best Performing Artist" in 2006 by the readers of the Seattle *Weekly* and honored twice on the Theatre Short List for *The Stranger*'s Genius Awards. Most recently she has performed at On the Boards in Seattle as Hedda Gabler in Washington Ensemble Theatre's new adaptation of Ibsen's classic, titled *blahblahblahBANG!* and in the title role of *My Name is Rachel Corrie* at the Seattle Repertory Theatre. She has created over twenty solo shows and has performed her original work at On the Boards, PS 122 in New York, and the Edinburgh Fringe Festival in Scotland. She is a Founding Co-Artistic Director of the Washington Ensemble Theatre in Seattle. **www.washingtonensemble.org**.

VICTORIA LINCHONG (Essays) – began working Off-Off Broadway in the mid-1980s as a teen actress in the street theater company of Theater for the New City, where she became acquainted with many people who were part of the Caffe Cino. Her screenplays have made it to the final rounds of the Sundance Screenwriters Lab, the Slamdance Screenplay Contest and the Berlin Film Festival Talent Campus. Her plays have been produced by Theater for the New City and Nuyorican Poets Café. She is currently the Artistic Director of Direct Arts, dedicated to producing and promoting plays and films that explore the intersection between different cultures. Visit Direct Arts at: www.directarts.org. **www.directarts.org**.

STEVE LUBER (Interviews) – aka Tweed, is – in addition to general jesterdom, a doctoral candidate in theater at the Graduate Center, CUNY, and a teaching fellow at Brooklyn College. He has published in *PAJ* and *TDR: The Drama Review* and has recently written about the mediated body, George Bernard Shaw, TV, orgasms, and megachurches. He has authored and performed two solo pieces, *Steve Sells Out* (2005) and *Rock Star* (2002), both of which have been described as "interesting," "confounding," and "utterly narcissistic." He has also collaborated with The Builders Association, David Byrne, Mabou Mines Suite, and the Drama Dept. Tweed enjoys doing things "the hard way." **obscenejester.typepad.com**

CRAIG LUCAS (Plays) – is a playwright, screenwriter and director; his works include *Blue Window, Reckless, Prelude to a Kiss, The Dying Gaul, The Light in the Piazza, Longtime Companion* and *The Secret Lives of Dentists.* He recently directed *Birds of America,* starring Matthew Perry, Hilary Swank, Ben Foster, Ginnifer Goodwin and Lauren Graham. He received the Steinberg/American Theater Critics Award for Best American Play (*The Singing Forest*), the New York Film Critics Award for Best Screenplay (*The Secret Lives of Dentists*), the Sundance Audience Award (*Longtime Companion*), and the Excellence in Literature Award from the American Academy of Arts and Letters.

TAYLOR MAC (Plays) – is a performer and playwright creating both solo and large ensemble plays. His most recent works are: *The Young Ladies Of* (NY's HERE Arts Center, Stockholm's Sodre Teatern, and London's Battersea Arts Center), *Red Tide Blooming* (Performance Space 122) and *The Be(A)st of Taylor Mac* (The Sydney Opera House, Under the Radar at the Public Theatre, London's Soho Theatre, Dublin's Project Arts Center, Portland's Time Based Arts Festival, Seattle's Bumbershoot Festival, over thirty additional theaters all around the globe and upcoming at The Spoleto Festival). In 2007 the *Village Voice, Time Out New York,* and the *New York Press* all named him one of the New York's best. He is the recipient of The Edinburgh Festival's Herald Angel Award, three Brighton Best of Festival awards, PS 122's Ethyl Eichelberger award, multiple grants and fellowships and is currently a HERE Arts Center Resident Artist and a member of New Dramatists. **www.taylormac.net**.

ZACHARY R. MANNHEIMER (Essays) – is the Founding Artistic Director of the NYC-based Subjective Theatre Company. He is currently purchasing a building in downtown Des Moines to open another branch of the theater. The building will include a European-inspired, locally-produced restaurant and pub called, "The Actress and the Bishop." The restaurant will be the first not-for-profit entity fully funding another not-for-profit entity. This will be The Des Moines Social Club: January, 2009. In addition, Zachary sits on the board of Modest Needs and is the Co-Chairman of Fractured Atlas's Artists Advisory Board. In his spare time, he is a Sommelier and amateur political consultant. Zachary welcomes your comments on his blog. We've got to do this together, for heaven's sake. **www.zmannheimer.blogspot.com**.

NINA MANKIN (Plays) – is a performer, writer and dramaturg. She was dramaturg for Taylor Mac's *Red Tide Blooming* and *The Young Ladies Of,* and she is currently working with Taylor on his developing musical *The Lily's Revenge* (in which she also plays The Bride.) Nina has worked with numerous theater artists and musicians (both as a performer and as a dramaturg) including Anne Bogart, Robert Een, Tony Kushner, Kristin Marting, John Zorn and others. She has also written about theater and performance for *American Theatre*, New York

Newsday, The Boston *Phoenix*, *PAJ.*, and others. Nina holds an MA in Performance Studies from NYU. **www.ninamankin.com**.

ERICA PARISE (Cover Photographer) – is a freelance photographer working in the film, television and theater world of NYC. From still photography on set to theater promotional shots, Erica has worked with many of New York's best independent film and theater producers and production companies. Her portfolio and contact information can be found on her website. **www.cinestillsnyc.com**.

TOMMY SMITH (Plays) – Tommy's plays include *White Hot, Sextet, Air Conditioning, Sunrise, Demon Dreams* and *Caravan Man* (with Gabriel Kahane). His work has been seen at The Flea Theatre, Williamstown Theatre Festival, The Ontological Theatre, 78th Street Theatre, The Huntington Theatre, ACT Theatre, Portland Center Stage, Eugene O'Neill National Playwrights Conference, Soho Rep Writer/Director Lab, among others. He is a two-time winner of the Lecomte du Nouy Prize for emerging writers (2005 and 2006). Recently, he directed/co-conceived Reggie Watts' *Disinformation* at The Public Theatre's Under The Radar Festival. Tommy is also a graduate of The Juilliard School's Playwriting Program, and recipient of the 2008 P73 Playwriting Fellowship. **www.vimeo.com/dumbfilms**.

SARA MICHELLE ZATZ (Plays) – has been affiliated with Ping Chong & Company since 1997, and in 2002 became the project manager for the *Undesirable Elements* series. Since then, Sara has managed the production of over a dozen original works in the series and served as co-author with Ping Chong on six productions. Other arts management experience includes work with the Henson International Festival of Puppet Theater, the composer Tan Dun, Lincoln Center Festival and Reel to Real at Lincoln Center. She holds a Master's degree in Irish Theatre Studies from Trinity College, Dublin, and a BA from Bryn Mawr College. **www.undesirableelements.org**.

Last Word

14th St. A/C   *Manhattan*